THE SIXTH SENSE

THE SIXTH SENSE

STEPHEN McKENNA

WILDSIDE PRESS

BOOK INFORMATION

Published by Wildside Press, LLC
www.wildsidebooks.com

PROLOGUE
LONDON AFTER TWENTY YEARS

"As when a traveller, bound from North to South,
Scouts fur in Russia: what's its use in France?
In France spurns flannel: where's its need in Spain?
In Spain drops cloth, too cumbrous for Algiers!
Linen goes next, and last the skin itself,
A superfluity at Timbuctoo.
When, through his journey was the fool at ease?
I'm at ease now, friend; worldly in this world,
I take and like its way of life; I think
My brothers who administer the means,
Live better for my comfort—that's good too;
And God, if he pronounce upon such life,
Approves my service, which is better still."

—Robert Browning:
"Bishop Blougram's Apology."

I paused, with my foot on the lowest step of the Club, to mark the changes that had overtaken Pall Mall during my twenty years' absence from England.

The old War Office, of course, was gone; some of the shops on the north side were being demolished; and the Automobile Club was new and unassimilated. In my day, too, the Athenæum had not been painted Wedgwood-green. Compared, however, with the Strand or Mall, Piccadilly or Whitehall, marvellously little change had taken place. I made an exception in favour of the character and velocity of the traffic: the bicycle boom was in its infancy when I left England: I returned to find the horse practically extinct, and the streets of London as dangerous as the railway stations of America.

I wondered how long it would take me to get used to the

London of 1913.... Then I wondered if I should find anything to keep me long enough to grow acclimatised. Chance had brought me back to England, chance and the "wandering foot" might as easily bear me away again. It has always been a matter of indifference to me where I live, what I do, whom I meet. If I never seem to get bored, it is perhaps because I am never long enough in one place or at one occupation. There was no reason why England should not keep me amused....

A man crossed the road and sold me a *Westminster Gazette*. I opened it to see what was engaging the England of 1913, remembering as I did so that the *Westminster* was the last paper of importance to be published before I went abroad. As I glanced at the headlines, twenty years seemed to drop out of my life. Another Home Rule Bill was being acclaimed as the herald of the Millennium; Ulster was being told to fight and be right: the Welsh Church was once more being disestablished, while in foreign politics a confederation of Balkan States was spending its blood and treasure in clearing Europe of the Turk, to a faint echoing accompaniment of Gladstone's "bag and baggage" trumpet call. At home and abroad, English politics repeated themselves with curiously dull monotony.

Then I turned to the middle page, and saw I had spoken too hastily. "Suffragette Outrages" seemed to fill three columns of the paper. My return to England had synchronised with a political campaign more ruthless, intransigeant and unyielding than anything since the Fenian outrages of my childhood. I read of unique fifteenth-century houses burnt to the ground, interrupted meetings, assaults on Ministers, sabotage in public buildings, and the demolition of plate-glass windows at the hands of an uncompromising, fearless and diabolically ingenious army of destroyers. On the other side of the account were entered long sentences, hunger-strikes, forcible feeding and something that was called "A Cat and Mouse Act." I was to hear more of that later: it was indeed the political parent of the "New

Militant Campaign" whose life coincided with my own residence in England. I fancy the supporters of the bill like Roden, Rawnsley or Jefferson genuinely believed they had killed hunger-striking—and with it the spirit of militancy—when the Government assumed the power of imprisoning, releasing and re-imprisoning at will. The event proved that they had only driven militancy into a fresh channel....

It is curious to reflect that as I at last mounted the steps and entered the Club, I was wondering where it would be possible to meet the resolute, indomitable women who formed the Council of War to the militant army. It would be a new, alluring experience. I was so occupied with my thoughts that I hardly noticed the hall porter confronting me with the offer of the New Members' Address Book.

"Surely a new porter?" I suggested. At ten guineas a year for twenty years, it was costing me two hundred and ten pounds to enter the Club, and I did not care to have my expensive right challenged.

"Seventeen years, sir," he answered with the gruff, repellent stiffness of the English official.

"I must have been before your time, then," I said.

Of course he disbelieved me, on the score of age if for no other reason; and the page boy who dogged my steps into the Cloak Room, was sent—I have no doubt—to act as custodian of the umbrellas. My age is forty-two, but I have never succeeded in looking more than about eight and twenty: perhaps I have never tried, as I find that a world of personal exertion and trouble is saved by allowing other people to do my trying, thinking, arranging for me ... whatever I am, others have made me.

There was not a single familiar face in the hall, and I passed into the Morning Room, like a ghost ascending from Hades to call on Æneas. Around me in arm-chair groups by the fire, or quarrelsome knots suspended over the day's bill of fare, were sleek, full-bodied creatures of dignified girth and portentous gravity—fathers of families, successes in life. These—I told myself—were my contemporaries; their faces were for the most part unknown, but this was hardly surprising as many of my friends are dead and most of the survivors are to be found at the Bar. A barrister with anything of a practice cannot afford time to lunch in the spacious atmosphere of Pall Mall, and the smaller the practice, the greater his anxiety to conceal his leisure. For a moment I felt painfully insignificant, lonely and unfriended.

I was walking towards the Coffee Room when a heavy hand descended on my shoulder and an incredulous voice gasped out—

"Toby, by Gad!"

No one had called me by that name for fifteen years, and I turned to find a stout, middle-aged man with iron-grey hair and a red face extending a diffident palm.

"I beg your pardon," he added hastily, as he saw my expression of surprise. "I thought for a moment...."

"You were right," I interrupted.

"Toby Merivale," he said with profound deliberation. "I thought you were dead."

The same remark had already been made to me four times that morning.

"That's not original," I objected.

"Do you know who I am?" he asked.

"You used to be Arthur Roden in the old days when I knew you. That was before they made you a Privy Councillor and His Majesty's Attorney-General."

"By Gad, I can hardly believe it!" he exclaimed, shaking my hand a second time and carrying me off to luncheon. "What have you been doing with yourself? Where have you been? Why did you go away?"

"As Dr. Johnson once remarked...." I began.

"'Questioning is not a mode of conversation among gentlemen,'" he interrupted. "I know; but if you drop out of the civilised world for the third of a lifetime...."

"You've not ordered yourself any lunch."

"Oh, hang lunch!"

"But you haven't ordered any for me, either."

My poor story—for what it was worth—started with the plovers' eggs, and finished neck-to-neck with the cheese. I told him how I had gone down to the docks twenty years before to see young Handgrove off to India, and how at the last moment he had cajoled me into accompanying him.... Arthur came with me in spirit from India to the diamond mines of South Africa where I made my money, took part with me in the Jameson Raid, and kept me company during those silent, discreet months when we all lay *perdus* wondering what course the Government was going to pursue towards the Raiders. Then I sketched my share in the war, and made him laugh by saying I had been three times mentioned in despatches. My experience of black-water fever was sandwiched in between the settlement of South Africa, and my departure to the scene of the Russo-Japanese war: last of all came the years of vegetation, during which I had idled round the Moorish fringe of the Desert or sauntered from one Mediterranean port to another.

"What brings you home now?" he asked.

"Home? Oh, to England. I've a young friend stationed out at Malta, and when I was out there three weeks ago I found his wife down with a touch of fever. He wanted her brought to London, couldn't come himself, so suggested I should take charge. *J'y suis....*"

I hesitated.

"Well?"

"I don't know, Arthur. I've no plans. If you have any suggestions to make...."

"Come and spend Whitsun with me in Hampshire."

"Done."

"You're not married?"

"'Sir,'" I said in words Sir James Murray believes Dr. Johnson ought to have used, "'in order to be facetious it is not necessary to be indecent.'"

"And never will be, I suppose."

"I've no plans. You, of course...."

I paused delicately, in part because I was sure he wanted to tell me all about himself, in part because I could not for the life of me remember what had come of the domestic side of his career during my absence abroad. He was married, and the father of a certain number of children before I left England; I had no idea how far the ramifications went.

It appeared that his wife—who was still living—had presented him with Philip, now aged twenty-six, his father's private secretary and member for some Scotch borough; Sylvia, aged twenty-four, and unmarried; Robin, aged twenty-one, and in his last year at Oxford; and Michael, an *enfant terrible* of sixteen still at Winchester. I fancy there were no more; these were certainly all I ever met, either in Cadogan Square or Brandon Court.

In his public life I suppose Arthur Roden would be called a successful man. I remember him during the barren first few years of practice, but soon after my departure from England reports used to reach me showing the increasing volume of his work, until he became one of the busiest juniors on the Common Law side, reading briefs at four in the morning, and sending a clerk out to buy his new clothes. After taking silk at an early age, he had entered the House and been made Attorney-General in 1912.

"I was appointed the same day your brother was raised to the Bench," he told me.

"I should think he makes a pretty bad Judge," I suggested.

"Resolute," said Arthur. "We want firmness."

I knew what that meant. According to unsympathetic papers, Mr. Justice Merivale had conducted a Bloody Assize among the Militants of the Suffrage Army. When Roden prosecuted in person, there was short shrift indeed.

"We've killed militancy between us," he boasted.

"And I understand you're burnt together in effigy."

His face grew suddenly stern.

"They haven't stopped at that. There've been two attempts to fire Brandon Court, and one wing of your brother's house was burnt down a few weeks ago. I expect you found him rather shaken."

"I haven't seen him yet."

Arthur looked surprised.

"Oh, you ought to," he said. "I'm afraid he won't be able to last out the rest of the term without a change. It's got on his nerves. Got on his wife's nerves, too. Your niece is the only one who doesn't seem to care; but then I think girls have very little imagination. It's the same with Sylvia. By the way, I suppose you know you've got a niece?"

We paid our bills, and walked upstairs to the Smoking Room.

"What'll be their next move?" I asked.

"I don't think there will be a next move," he answered slowly. "What can they do?"

I shrugged my shoulders.

"I'm only an onlooker, but d'you believe this Cat and Mouse Act is going to stop them? My knowledge is mere newspaper knowledge, but to be beaten by a device like that—it isn't in keeping with the character of the women who've organised the Militant Campaign so far."

"What *can* they do?" he repeated.

"I don't know."

"They don't either. One or two of the most determined law breakers are in reality spies; they've kept us posted in the successive steps of the campaign up to the present. Now they report that there's no plan for the future. They know it would be futile to start assassination; if they go on burning and breaking, a proportion of them get caught and punished. Hunger striking's been killed by the Cat and Mouse Act. Well, militancy's dead, Toby. If you come down to the House to-night, you'll be present at the funeral."

"What's happening?"

"It's the division on the Suffrage amendment to the Electoral Reform Bill. Hullo! here's Philip. Let me introduce my eldest son."

I made friends with Philip as we crossed the Park and entered the House. He was curiously like the Arthur I had known twenty years before—tall, dark-haired, clean-featured, with an exuberant zest for life tempered to an almost imperceptible degree by the reserve of the responsible public man. The physical and mental vigour of father and son left me silently admiring; as they hurried along at a swinging five miles an hour, I took stock of their powerful, untiring frames, quick movements, and crisp, machine-made speech. They were hard, business-like, unimaginative, with the qualities of those defects and the defects of those qualities; trained, taught, and equipped to play the midwife to any of the bureaucratic social reforms that have been brought into the English political world the last few years, but helpless and impotently perplexed in face of an idea outside their normal ken. They were highly efficient average English politicians. Either or both would reform you the Poor Law, nationalise a railway, or disestablish a Church; but send Philip to India, set Arthur to carry out Cromer's work in Egypt, and you would see English dominion driven from two continents as speedily as North drove it from America. It was one of the paradoxes of English politics that Arthur should have been entrusted with the problem of Suffrage militancy, a paradox of the same order as that whereby Strafford grappled with the problem of a parliamentary system.

"You'll stay a few minutes," Philip urged as I abandoned him to Empire and wandered off to pay my belated respects to my brother.

I glanced round me and shook my head. I would not grow old all at once, and yet—Gladstone was Prime Minister when I left England: his statue now dominated the public lobby. And Salisbury, Harcourt, Chamberlain, Parnell, Labby—their voices were sunk in the great silence. In my day Committee Room Number Fifteen used to be an object of historic interest....

> *"They say the lion and the lizard keep*
> *The Halls where Jamshyd gloried, and drank deep:*
>   *And Bahram, the great hunter, the wild ass*
> *Stamps o'er his head, and he lies fast asleep."*

I quoted the lines to Philip apologetically, reminding him that the Omar Khayyam vogue had not come in when I left England. "I shall see you at Brandon Court," I added.

"What are you going to do till then?" he asked.

"Heaven knows! I never make arrangements. Things just happen to me. I always contrive to be in the thick of whatever's going on. I don't know how long I shall stay in England, or where I shall go to afterwards. But whether it's a railway strike or a coronation, I shall be there. I don't like it, I'm a peaceful man by nature, but I can't help it. I always get dragged into these things."

Philip scratched his chin thoughtfully.

"I don't know that we've got any great sensations at the present time," he said.

"Something will turn up," I answered in the words of one greater than myself, as I waved my hand in farewell and started back in the direction of the Club.

I knew my brother would not leave Court till at least four o'clock, so I had to dispose of an hour before it was time to call round in Pont Street. The Club had emptied since luncheon, and I drew blank in one place after another until fate directed my steps to the Card Room. There were two men playing bézique, one of them poor Tom Wilding whom I had left lame and returned to find half paralysed and three parts blind. The other—who played with a wonderful patience, calling the names of the cards—I recognised as my young friend Lambert Aintree who had parted from me in Morocco five years before. I reminded them both of my identity, and we sat gossiping till an attendant arrived to wheel poor Wilding away for his afternoon drive.

Leaving the card-table, Aintree joined me on the window-seat and subjected my face, clothes and general appearance to a rapid scrutiny. It was the practised, comprehensive glance of an old physician in making diagnosis, and I waited for him to pronounce on my case. Five years ago in Morocco he had exhibited a disconcerting and almost uncanny skill in reading character and observing little forgotten points that every one else missed. The results of his observation were usually shrouded in the densest veils of uncommunicativeness: I sometimes wonder if I have ever met a more silent man. When you could get him to talk, he was usually worth hearing: for the most part, however, talking like every other form of activity seemed too much of an exertion. I understand him now better than I did, but I am not so foolish as to pretend that I understand him completely. I am a man of three dimensions: Aintree, I am convinced, was endowed with the privilege of a fourth.

"Well?" I said invitingly, as he brought his examination to an end and looked out of the window.

His answer was to throw me over a cigarette and light one himself.

"Take an interest in me," I said plaintively. "Say you thought I was dead...."

"Everyone's said that."

"True," I admitted.

"And they've all asked you when you landed, and how long

you were staying, and what brought you to England."

"It would be rather friendly if you did the same."

"You couldn't tell me—any more than you could tell them."

"But I could. It was Sunday morning."

"About then. I knew that. You've been here long enough to get English clothes, and," he gave me another rapid look, "to have them made for you. How long you're here for—you don't know."

"Not to a day," I conceded. "Well, why did I come?"

"You don't know."

"Pardon me." I told him of my visit to Malta and the charitable guardianship of my friend's convalescent wife.

"But that wasn't the real reason."

"It was the only reason."

"The only one you thought of at the time."

I was amazed at the certainty of his tone.

"My dear fellow," I said. "I am a more or less rational creature, a reason comes along and compels me to do a thing. If I were a woman, no doubt I should do a thing and find reasons for it afterwards."

"Don't you ever do a thing on impulse, instinctively? And analyse your motives afterwards to see what prompted you?"

"Oh, possibly. But not on this occasion."

"You're sure?"

"What are you driving at?" I asked.

"You'll find out in time."

"I should like to know now."

Aintree inhaled the smoke of his cigarette and answered with eyes half-closed.

"Most men of your age wake up one morning to find they've turned forty. They feel it would be good to renew their youth, they play with the idea of getting married."

"Is this to my address?" I asked.

"D'you feel it applies to your case?"

"I can solemnly assure you that such an idea never crossed my mind."

"Not consciously."

"Nor unconsciously."

"What do you know of the unconscious ideas in your own mind?"

"Hang it," I said, "what do *you* know of the unconscious ideas in my—or any one else's mind?"

"I'm interested in them," he answered quietly. "Tell me if you ever feel my prophecy coming true."

"You shall be best man," I promised him. "Married! One doesn't marry at my age."

It was a glorious spring afternoon, and I suggested that he should accompany me part of my way to Pont Street.

"Tell me what you've been doing with yourself since you stayed with me five years ago," I said as we stepped into Pall Mall.

He seemed to shiver and retreat into his shell as soon as the conversation became focussed on himself.

"I've done nothing," he answered briefly, and relapsed into one of his wonted spells of silence.

In the blazing afternoon sunlight I returned him the compliment of a careful scrutiny. He had come to Morocco five years before as a boy of one-and-twenty just down from Oxford. A girl to whom he had been engaged had died of consumption a few months before, and he was straying into the Desert, broken, unnerved, and hopeless, to forget her. I must have seemed sympathetic, or he would not have unburdened himself of the whole pitiful little tragedy. At twenty-one you feel these things more keenly perhaps than in after life; there were moments when I feared he was going to follow her....

Five years may have healed the wound, but they left him listless, dispirited, and sore. He was more richly endowed with nerves than any man or woman I know, and all the energy of his being seemed requisitioned to keep them under control. Less through love of mystery than for fear of self-betrayal his face wore the expressionless mask of a sphynx. He was fair, thin, and pale, with large frightened eyes, sapphire blue in colour, and troubled with the vague, tired restlessness that you see in overwrought, sensitive women. The nose and mouth were delicate and almost ineffeminate, with lips tightly closed as though he feared to reveal emotion in opening them. You see women and children with mouths set in that thin, hard line when they know a wickering lip or catch in the breath will give the lie to their brave front. And there were nerves, nerves, nerves everywhere, never so much present as when the voice was lazily drawling, the hands steady, and the eyes dreamily half-closed. I wonder if anything ever escaped those watchful, restless eyes; his entire soul seemed stored up and shining out of them; and I wonder what was the process of deduction in his curious, quick, feminine brain. Before I left England I tried to evolve a formula that would fit him; "a woman's senses and intuition in a man's body" was the best I could devise, and I am prepared at once to admit the inadequacy of the label. For one thing his intuition transcended that of any woman I have ever known.

As he would not talk about himself, I started to wile away the time by telling him of my meeting with the Rodens, and their invitation to Hampshire.

"I was asked too," he told me. "I shan't go."

"But why not?"

"Unsociability, I suppose. I don't go out much."

"It's a bachelor's party, I understand."

"That's the best thing I've heard about it. Did they say who'd be there? If you're not careful you'll have politics to eat, politics to drink, and politics to smoke."

"Come and create a diversion," I suggested.

"I'll think about it. Is Phil going to be there? Oh, then it won't be a bachelor party. I could name one young woman who will be there for certain, only I mustn't make mischief. Did you find Roden much changed?"

I tried to sort out my impressions of Arthur.

"Harder than he used to be. I shouldn't care to be a militant prosecuted by him."

Aintree raised his eyebrows slightly.

"I don't think they mind him; they can look after themselves."

"I've never met one."

"Would you like to?"

"Who is she?"

"Joyce Davenant, the queen bee of the swarm. Dine with me to-night at the Ritz; seven o'clock, I'm afraid, but we are going to a first night."

"Is she a daughter of old Jasper Davenant? I used to shoot with him."

"The younger daughter. Do you know her sister, Mrs. Wylton? She's coming too. You'd better meet her," he went on with a touch of acidity in his tone, "you'll hear her name so much during the next few months that it will be something to say you've seen her in the flesh."

I only remembered Elsie Wylton as a young girl with her hair down her back. Of her husband, Arnold Wylton, I suppose every one has heard; he enjoys the reputation of being a man who literally cannot be flogged past a petticoat. How such a girl came to marry such a man no rational person has ever been able to explain; and it never sweetens the amenities of debate to talk vaguely of marriages being made in heaven. I met Wylton twice, and on both occasions he was living in retirement abroad. I have no wish to meet him a third time.

"How did she ever come to marry a fellow like that?" I asked.

Aintree shrugged his shoulders.

"Her father was dead, or he'd have stopped it. Nobody else felt it their business to interfere, and it wouldn't have made the slightest difference if they had. You know what the Davenants are like—or perhaps you don't. Nothing shakes them when they've made up their minds to do a thing."

"But didn't she know the man's reputation?" I persisted.

"I don't suppose so. Wylton had never been mixed up in any overt scandal, so the women wouldn't know; and it's always a tall order for a man to lay information against another man when a girl's engaged to marry him. She just walked into it with her eyes shut."

"And now she's divorcing him at last?"

"The other way about."

I felt sure I could not have heard him correctly.

"The other way about," he repeated deliberately. "Oh, she'd have got rid of him years ago if he'd given her the chance! Wylton was too clever; he knew the divorce law inside out; he was alive to all its little technicalities. He's sailed close to the wind a number of times, but never close enough to be in danger."

"And what's happening now?" I asked.

"She's forced his hand—gone to some trouble to compromise herself. She couldn't divorce him, it was the only way, she's making him divorce her. Rather a burlesque of justice, isn't it? Elsie Wylton, the respondent in an undefended action! The daughter of Jasper Davenant—one of the finest, cleanest, bravest women I know. And the successful petitioner will be Arnold Wylton, who ought to have been thrashed out of half the houses and clubs in London. Who ought to have been cited as a co-respondent half a dozen times over if he hadn't been so clever in covering up his tracks. I wonder if he's got sufficient humour to appreciate the delicate irony of *his* coming sanctimoniously into court to divorce *her*. It's a sickening business, we won't discuss it—but it will be the one topic of conversation in a few weeks' time."

We walked in silence for a few yards.

"Was the man any one of note?" I asked. "The co-respondent?"

"Fellow in the Indian Army," Aintree answered. "I don't suppose you know him. It was a bogus case; he just lent his name."

I sniffed incredulously.

"The world won't believe *that*," I said.

"Elsie's going to make it."

I shook my head.

"She can't. Would you?"

"Most certainly. So will you when you've met her. You knew the father well? She's her father's own daughter."

The gospel of Jasper Davenant was simple and sound. Never pull a horse, never forge a cheque, never get involved in the meshes of married women. Apart from that, nothing mattered: though to be his true disciple, you must never lose your head, never lose your temper, never be afraid of man or woman, brute or devil. He was the North American Indian of chivalrous romance, transplanted to Cumberland with little loss of essential characteristics.

"I look forward to meeting them both," I said as we parted at Buckingham Gate. "Seven o'clock? I'll try not to be late."

Walking on alone through Sloane Square, something set me thinking of my boast to Philip Roden. Within three hours I was apparently going to meet one woman whose name was mixed up with the most prominent *cause célèbre* of the year, and another who was a *cause célèbre* in herself—the redoubtable Miss Joyce Davenant of the Militant Suffrage Union. That my introduction should come from the peace-loving, nerve-ridden Aintree, was in accordance with the best ironical traditions of life. I was not surprised then: I should have still less reason to be surprised now. In the last six months he has placed me under obligations which I shall never be able to meet: in all probability he expects no repayment; the active side of his unhappy, fatalistic temperament is seen in his passionate desire to make life less barren and melancholy for others. Tom Wilding can testify to this at the bézique table: Elsie and Joyce and I can endorse the testimony in a hundred ways and half a hundred places.

As I turned into Pont Street a private car was drawn up by the kerb opposite my brother's house. I dawdled for a few steps while a pretty, brown-eyed, black-haired girl said good-bye to a friend at the door and drove away. It was no more than a glimpse that I caught, but the smiling, small-featured face attracted me. I wondered who she was, and who was the girl with auburn hair who persisted in standing on my brother's top step long after the car was out of sight, instead of retiring indoors and leaving me an unembarrassed entry.

I pretended not to see her as I mounted the steps, but the pretence was torn away when I heard her addressing me as "Uncle Simon."

"You must be Gladys," I said, wondering if I looked as sheepish as I felt. "How did you recognise me?"

"By your photograph," she said. "You haven't altered a bit."

On the whole I carried it off fairly well, though I was glad Arthur Roden was not present after my implied familiarity with my niece's existence. Of course I knew I had a niece, and that her birthday fell—like the Bastille—on July 14th. Usually I remembered the date and sent her some little trifle, and she would write me a friendly letter of thanks. If I had kept count of the number of birthdays, I should have known she was now nineteen, but then one never does keep count of these things. Frankly, I had imagined her to be about seven or eight, and her handwriting—by becoming steadily more unformed and sporadic the older she grew—did nothing to dispel the illusion. Instead of curious little pieces of jewellery I might easily have sent her a doll....

"Where's the Judge?" I asked as she kissed me and led the way upstairs to her room.

"He's not home yet," she answered to my relief.

"And your mother?"

But my sister-in-law also was out, and I reconciled myself without difficulty to the prospect of taking tea alone with my niece. Possibly as a romantic reaction from her father, possibly with her mother Eve's morbid craving for forbidden fruit, Gladys had elevated me into a Tradition. The whole of her pretty, sun-splashed room seemed hung with absurd curios I had sent her from out-of-the-way parts of the world, while on a table by the window stood a framed photograph of myself in tweeds that only an undergraduate would have worn, and a tie loosely arranged in a vast sailor's knot after the unsightly fashion of the early 'nineties. My hair was unduly long, and at my feet lay a large dog; it must have been a property borrowed for the purpose, as I hate and have always hated dogs.

"A wasted, unsatisfactory life, Gladys," I said as my tour of inspection concluded itself in front of my own portrait. "I wish I'd known about you before. I'd have asked Brian to let me adopt you."

"Would you like to now?"

In the East a complimentary speech is not usually interpreted so literally or promptly.

"I'm afraid it's too late," I answered regretfully.

"Afraid?"

"Your father and mother...."

"Would you if I were left an orphan?"

"Of course I would, but you mustn't say things like that even in joke."

Gladys poured me out a cup of tea and extended a cream jug at a menacing angle.

"Not for worlds if it's China," I exclaimed.

"It is. Uncle Toby...." She seemed to hesitate over the name, but I prefer it to Simon and bowed encouragement, "I'm going to be an orphan in three days' time. At least, it's that or very sea-sick."

I begged for an explanation. It appeared that Pont Street was in domestic convulsion over the health of Mr. Justice Merivale. As Roden had hinted, a succession of militant outrages directed against his person and property, not to mention threatening letters and attempted violence, had seriously shaken his nerve. Under doctor's orders he was leaving England for a short sea cruise as soon as the Courts rose at Whitsun.

"He's only going to Marseilles and back," she explained. "Mother's going with him, and something's got to be done with me. I don't want to make a nuisance of myself, but I should simply die if they tried to take me through the Bay."

"Do you think they'd trust me?" I asked. From an early age my brother has regarded me as the Black Sheep of an otherwise irreproachable family of two.

"They'd jump at it!" Irreverently I tried to visualise Brian jumping. "The Rodens wanted me to go to them, but it wouldn't be fair on Sylvia. She'd be tied to me the whole time."

"I can imagine worse fates."

"For her? or for me?"

"Either or both."

"I'll tell her. Did you see her driving away as you arrived? If you'll adopt me, I'll introduce you."

"I've arranged that already. Whitsuntide will be spent at Brandon Court improving my acquaintance with her."

Gladys regarded me with frank admiration.

"You haven't wasted much time. But if you're going there, you may just as well adopt me. I shall be down there too, and if you're my guardian...."

"It'll save all trouble with the luggage. Well, it's for your parents to decide. You can guess my feelings."

I waited till after six in the hopes of seeing my brother, and was then only allowed to depart on the plea of my engagement with Aintree and a promise to dine and arrange details of my stewardship the following night.

"Write it down!" Gladys implored me as I hastened downstairs. "You'll only forget it if you don't. Eight-fifteen to-morrow. Haven't you got a book?"

I explained that on the fringe of the desert where I had lived of late, social engagements were not too numerous to be carried in the head.

"That won't do for London," she said with much firmness, and I was incontinently burdened with a leather pocket-diary.

Dressing for dinner that night, the little leather diary made me reflective. As a very young man I used to keep a journal: it belonged to a time when I was not too old to give myself unnecessary trouble, nor too disillusioned to appreciate the unimportance of my impressions or the ephemeral character of the names that figured in its pages. For a single moment I played with the idea of recording my experiences in England. Now that the last chapter is closed and the little diary is one of the bare half-dozen memorials of my checkered sojourn in England, I half wish I had not been too lazy to carry my idea into effect. After a lapse of only seven months I find there are many minor points already forgotten. The outline is clear enough in my memory, but the details are blurred, and the dates are in riotous confusion.

It is fruitless to waste regrets over a lost opportunity, but I wish I had started my journal on the day Gladys presented me with my now shabby little note-book. I should have written "Prologue" against this date—to commemorate my meetings with Roden and Joyce Davenant, Aintree and Mrs. Wylton, Gladys and Philip. To commemorate, too, my first glimpse of Sylvia....

Yes, I should have written "Prologue" against this date: and then natural indolence would have tempted me to pack my bag and wander abroad once more, if I could have foreseen for one moment the turmoil and excitement of the following six months.

I can only add that I am extremely glad I did no such thing.

CHAPTER I
WAR À OUTRANCE

"RIDGEON: I have a curious aching; I dont know where; I
cant localise it. Sometimes I think it's my heart; sometimes I suspect my spine. It doesn't exactly hurt me,
but it unsettles me completely. I feel that something is
going to happen....

SIR PATRICK: You are sure there are no voices?

RIDGEON: Quite sure.

SIR PATRICK: Then it's only foolishness.

RIDGEON: Have you ever met anything like it before in
your practice?

SIR PATRICK: Oh yes. Often. It's very common between
the ages of seventeen and twenty-two. It sometimes
comes on again at forty or thereabouts. You're a bachelor, you see. It's not serious—if you're careful.

RIDGEON: About my food?

SIR PATRICK: No; about your behaviour.... Youre not going
to die; but you may be going to make a fool of yourself."

—Bernard Shaw
"The Doctor's Dilemma."

I was a few minutes late for dinner, as a guest should be.
Aintree had quite properly arrived before me, and was standing
in the lounge of the Ritz talking to two slim, fair-haired women,
with very white skin and very blue eyes. I have spent so much
of my time in the East and South that this light colouring has
almost faded from my memory. I associated it exclusively with
England, and in time began to fancy it must be an imagination
of my boyhood. The English blondes you meet returning from
India by P & O are usually so bleached and dried by the sun that
you find yourself doubting whether the truly golden hair and
forget-me-not eyes of your dreams are ever discoverable in real

life. But the fascination endures even when you suspect you are cherishing an illusion.

I had been wondering, as I drove down, whether any trace survived of the two dare-devil, fearless, riotous children I had seen by flashlight glimpses, when an invitation from old Jasper Davenant brought me to participate in one of his amazing Cumberland shoots. I was twenty or twenty-one at the time; Elsie must have been seven, and Joyce five. Mrs. Davenant was alive in those days, and Dick still unborn. My memory of the two children is a misty confusion of cut hands, broken knees, torn clothes, and daily whippings. Jasper wanted to make fine animals of his children, and set them to swim as soon as they could walk, and to hunt as soon as their fingers were large enough to hold a rein.

When I was climbing with him in Trans-Caucasia, I asked how the young draft was shaping. That was ten years later, and I gathered that Elsie was beginning to be afraid of being described as a tomboy. On such a subject Joyce was quite indifferent. She attended her first hunt ball at twelve, against orders and under threat of castigation; half the hunt broke their backs in bending down to dance with her, as soon as they had got over the surprise of seeing a short-frocked, golden-haired fairy marching into the ball-room and defying her father to send her home. "You know the consequences?" he had said with pathetic endeavour to preserve parental authority. "I think it's worth it," was her answer. That night the Master interceded with old Jasper to save Joyce her whipping, and the next morning saw an attempt to establish order without recourse to the civil hand. "I'll let you off this time," Jasper had said, "if you'll promise not to disobey me again." "Not good enough," was Joyce's comment with grave deliberate shake of the head. "Then I shall have to flog you." "I think you'd better. You said you would, and you'd make me feel mean if you didn't. I've had my fun."

The words might be taken for the Davenant motto, in substitution of the present "Vita brevis." Gay and gallant, half savage, half moss-rider, lawless and light-hearted, they would stick at nothing to compass the whim of the moment, and come up for judgment with uncomplaining faces on the day of inevitable retribution. Joyce had run away from two schools because the Christmas term clashed with the hunting. I never heard the reason why she was expelled from a third; but I have no doubt it was adequate. She would ride anything that had a back, drive anything that had a bit or steering-wheel, thrash a poacher with her own hand, and take or offer a bet at any hour of the day or night. That was the character her father gave her. I had seen and heard little of the family since his death, Elsie's marriage and Joyce's abrupt, marauding descent on Oxford, where she worked twelve hours a day for three years, secured two firsts, and brought her name before the public as a writer of political pamphlets, and a pioneer in the suffrage agitation.

"We really oughtn't to need introduction," said Mrs. Wylton, as Aintree brought me up to be presented. "I remember you quite well. I shouldn't think you've altered a bit. How long is it?"

"Twenty years," I said. "You have—grown, rather."

She had grown staider and sadder, as well as older; but the bright golden hair, white skin, and blue eyes were the same as I remembered in Cumberland. A black dress clung closely to her slim, tall figure, and a rope of pearls was her only adornment.

I turned and shook hands with Joyce, marvelling at the likeness between the two sisters. There was no rope of pearls, only a thin band of black velvet round the neck. Joyce was dressed in white silk, and wore malmaisons at her waist. Those, you would say, were the only differences—until time granted you a closer scrutiny, and you saw that Elsie was a Joyce who had passed through the fire. Something of her courage had been scorched and withered in the ordeal; my pity went out to her as we met. Joyce demanded another quality than pity. I hardly know what to call it—homage, allegiance, devotion. She impressed me, as not half a dozen people have impressed me in this life—Rhodes, Chamberlain, and one or two more—with the feeling that I was under the dominion of one who had always had her way, and would always have it; one who came armed with a plan and a purpose among straying sheep who awaited her lead.... And with it all she was twenty-eight, and looked less; smiling, soft and childlike; so slim and fragile that you might snap her across your knee like a lath rod.

Aintree and Mrs. Wylton led the way into the dining-room.

"I can't honestly say I remember you," Joyce remarked as we prepared to follow. "I was too young when you went away. I suppose we *did* meet?"

"The last time I heard of you...." I began.

"Oh, don't!" she interrupted with a laugh. "You must have heard some pretty bad things. You know, people won't meet me now. I'm a.... Wait a bit—'A disgrace to my family,' 'a traitor to my class,' 'a reproach to my upbringing!' I've 'drilled incendiary lawlessness into a compact, organised force,' I'm 'an example of acute militant hysteria.' Heaven knows what else! D'you still feel equal to dining at the same table? It's brave of you; that boy in front—he's too good for this world—he's the only non-political friend I've got. I'm afraid you'll find me dreadfully changed—that is, if we ever did meet."

"As I was saying...."

"Yes, and I interrupted! I'm so sorry. You drop into the habit of interrupting if you're a militant. As you were saying, the last time we met...."

"The last time we met, strictly speaking we didn't meet at all. I came to say good-bye, but you'd just discovered that a pony was necessary to your happiness. It was an *idée fixe*, you were a fanatic, you broke half a Crown Derby dinner-service when you couldn't get it. When I came to say good-bye, you were locked in the nursery with an insufficient allowance of bread and water."

Joyce shook her head sadly.

"I was an awful child."

"Was?"

She looked up with reproach in her blue eyes.

"Haven't I improved?"

"You were a wonderfully pretty child."

"Oh, never mind looks!"

"But I do. They're the only things worth having."

"They're not enough."

"Leave that to be said by the women who haven't any."

"In any case they don't last."

"And while they do, you slight them."

"I? They're far too useful!" She paused at the door of the dining-room to survey her reflection in the mirror; then turned to me with a slow, childlike smile. "I think I'm looking rather nice to-night."

"You looked nice twenty years ago. Not content with that, you broke a dinner-service to get a pony."

"Fancy your remembering that all these years!"

"I was reminded of it the moment I saw you. *Plus ça change, plus c'est la même chose.* You are still not content with looking extremely nice, you *must* break a dinner-service now and again."

Joyce raised her eyebrows, and patiently stated a self-evident proposition.

"I must have a thing if I think I've a right to it," she pouted.

"You were condemned to bread and water twenty years ago to convince you of your error."

"I get condemned to that now."

"Dull eating, isn't it?"

"I don't know. I've never tried."

"You did then?"

"I threw it out of the window, plate and all."

We threaded our way through to a table at the far side of the room.

"Indeed you've not changed," I said. "You might still be that wilful child of five that I remember so well."

"You've forgotten one thing about me," she answered.

"What's that?"

"I got the pony," she replied with a mischievous laugh.

How far the others enjoyed that dinner, I cannot say. Aintree was an admirable host, and made a point of seeing that every one had too much to eat and drink; to the conversation he contributed as little as Mrs. Wylton. I did not know then how near the date of the divorce was approaching. Both sat silent and reflective, one overshadowed by the Past, the other by the Future: on the opposite side of the table, living and absorbed in the Present, typifying it and luxuriating in its every moment, was Joyce Davenant. I, too, contrive to live in the present, if by that you mean squeezing the last drop of enjoyment out of each sunny day's pleasure and troubling my head as little about the future as the past....

I made Joyce tell me her version of the suffrage war; it was like dipping into the memoirs of a prescribed Girondist. She had written and spoken, debated and petitioned. When an obdurate Parliament told her there was no real demand for the vote among women themselves, she had organised great peaceful demonstrations and "marches past": when sceptics belittled her processions and said you could persuade any one to sign any petition in favour of anything, she had massed a determined army in Parliament Square, raided the House and broken into the Prime Minister's private room.

The raid was followed by short terms of imprisonment for the ringleaders. Joyce came out of Holloway, blithe and unrepentant, and hurried from a congratulatory luncheon to an afternoon meeting at the Albert Hall, and from that to the first round of the heckling campaign. For six months no Minister could address a meeting without the certainty of persistent interruption, and no sooner had it been decided first to admit only such women as were armed with tickets, and then no women at all, than the country was flung into the throes of a General Election, and the Militants sought out every uncertain Ministerial constituency and threw the weight of their influence into the scale of the Opposition candidate.

Joyce told me of the papers they had founded and the bills they had promoted. The heckling of Ministers at unsuspected moments was reduced to a fine art: the whole sphere of their activities seemed governed by an almost diabolical ingenuity and resourcefulness. I heard of fresh terms of imprisonment, growing longer as the public temper warmed; the institution of the Hunger Strike, the counter move of Forcible Feeding, a short deadlock, and at last the promulgation of the "Cat and Mouse" Bill.

I was not surprised to hear some of the hardest fighting had been against over-zealous, misdirected allies. It cannot be said too often that Joyce herself would stick at nothing—fire, flood or dynamite—to secure what she conceived to be her rights. But if vitriol had to be thrown, she would see that it fell into the eyes of the right, responsible person: in her view it was worse than useless to attempt pressure on A by breaking B's windows. She had stood severely aloof from the latter developments of militancy, and refused to lend her countenance to the idly exasperating policy of injuring treasures of art, interrupting public races, breaking non-combatants' windows and burning down unique, priceless houses.

"Where do you stand now?" I asked as dinner drew to a close. "I renewed my acquaintance with Arthur Roden to-day, and he invited me down to the House to assist at the final obsequies of the Militant movement."

Joyce shook her head dispassionately over the ingrained stupidity of mankind.

"I think it's silly to talk like that before the battle's over.

Don't you?"

"He seemed quite certain of the result."

"Napoleon was so certain that he was going to invade England that he had medals struck to commemorate the capture of London. I've got one at home. I'd rather like to send it him, only it 'ud look flippant."

I reminded her that she had not answered my question.

"Roden says that the 'Cat and Mouse' Act has killed the law-breakers," I told her, "and to-night's division is going to kill the constitutionalists. What are you going to do?"

Joyce turned to me with profound solemnity, sat for a moment with her head on one side, and then allowed a smile to press its way through the serious mask. As I watched the eyes softening and the cheeks breaking into dimples, I appreciated the hopelessness of trying to be serious with a fanatic who only made fun of her enemies.

"What would *you* do?" she asked.

"Give it up," I answered. "Yield to *force majeure*. I've lived long enough in the East to feel the beauty and usefulness of resignation."

"But if we *won't* give it up?"

I shrugged my shoulders.

"What *can* you do?"

"I'm inviting suggestions. You're a man, so I thought you'd be sure to be helpful. Of course we've got our own plan, and when the Amendment's rejected to-night, you'll be able to buy a copy of the first number of a new paper to-morrow morning. It's called the *New Militant*, only a penny, and really worth reading. I've written most of it myself. And then we're going to start a fresh militant campaign, rather ingenious, and directed against the real obstructionists. No more window-breaking or house-burning, but real serious fighting, just where it will hurt them most. Something must come of it," she concluded. "I hope it may not be blood."

Aintree roused himself from his attitude of listless indifference.

"You'll gain nothing by militancy," he pronounced. "I've no axe to grind, you may have the vote or go without it. You may take mine away, or give me two. But your cause has gone back steadily, ever since you adopted militant tactics."

"The Weary Seraph cares for none of these things," Joyce remarked. I requested a moment's silence to ponder the exquisite fitness of the name. Had I thought for a year I could not have found a better description for the shy boy with the alert face and large frightened eyes. "Every one calls him that," Joyce went on. "And he doesn't like it. I should love to be called seraphic, but no one will; I'm too full of original sin. Well, Seraph, you may disapprove of militancy if you like, but you must suggest something to put in its place."

"I don't know that I can."

Joyce turned to her sister.

"These men-things aren't helpful, are they, Elsie?"

"I'm a good destructive critic," I said in self-justification.

"There are so many without you," Joyce answered, laying her hand on my arm. "Listen, Mr. Merivale. You've probably noticed there's very little argument about the suffrage; everything that can be said on either side has already been said a thousand times. You're going to refuse us the vote. Good. I should do the same in your place. There are more of us than there are of you, and we shall swamp you if we all get the vote. You can't give it to some of us and not others, because the brain is not yet born that can think of a perfect partial franchise. Will you give it to property and leave out the factory workers? Will you give it to spinsters and leave out the women who bear children to the nation? Will you give it to married women and leave out the unprotected spinsters? It's all or none: I say all, you say none. You say I'm not fit for a vote, I say I am. We reach an impasse, and might argue till daybreak without getting an inch further forward. We're fighting to swamp you, you're fighting to keep your head above water. We're reduced to a trial of strength."

She leant back in her chair, and I presented her with a dish of salted almonds, partly as a reward, partly because I never eat them myself.

"I admire your summary of the situation," I said. "You've only omitted one point. In a trial of strength between man and woman, man is still the stronger."

"And woman the more resourceful."

"Perhaps."

"She's certainly the more ruthless," Joyce answered, as she finished her coffee and drew on her gloves.

"War *à outrance*," I commented as we left the dining-room. "And what after the war?"

"When we've got the vote...." she began.

"Napoleon and the capture of London," I murmured.

"Oh well, you don't think I go in for a thing unless I'm going to win, do you? When we get the vote, we shall work to secure as large a share of public life as men enjoy, and we shall put women on an equality with men in things like divorce," she added between closed teeth.

"Suppose for the sake of argument you're beaten? I imagine even Joyce Davenant occasionally meets with little checks?"

"Oh yes. When Joyce was seven, she wanted to go skating, and her father said the ice wouldn't bear and she mustn't go. Joyce went, and fell in and nearly got drowned. And when she got home, her father was very angry and whipped her with a crop."

"Well?"

"That's all. Only—he said afterwards that she took it rather well, there was no crying."

I wondered then, as I have always wondered, whether she in any way appreciated the seriousness of the warfare she was waging on society.

"A month in the second division at Holloway is one thing...." I began.

"It'll be seven years' penal servitude if I'm beaten," she interrupted. Her tone was innocent alike of flippancy and bravado.

"Forty votes aren't worth that. I've got three, so I ought to know."

Joyce's eyes turned in the direction of her sister who was coming out of the dining-room with Aintree.

"*She's* worth some sacrifice."

"You couldn't make her lot easier if you had every vote in creation. She's up against the existing divorce law, and that's buttressed by every Church, and every dull married woman in the country. You're starting conversation at the wrong end, Joyce."

Her little arched eyebrows raised themselves at the name.

"Joyce?" she repeated.

"You were Joyce when last we met."

"That was twenty years ago."

"It seems less. I should like to blot out those years."

"And have me back in nursery frocks and long hair?"

"Better than long convict frocks and short hair," I answered with laborious antithesis.

"Then I haven't improved?"

"You're perfect—off duty, in private life."

"I have no private life."

"I've seen a glimpse of it to-night."

"An hour's holiday. I say good-bye to it for good this evening when I say good-bye to you."

"But not for good?"

"You'll not want the burden of my friendship when war's declared. If you like to come in as an ally...?"

"Do you think you could convert me?"

She looked at me closely.

"Yes."

I shook my head.

"What'd you bet?" she challenged me.

"It would be like robbing a child's money-box," I answered. "You're dealing with the laziest man in the northern hemisphere."

"How long will you be in England?"

"I've no idea."

"Six months? In six months I'll make you the Prince Rupert of the militant army. Then when we're sent to prison—Sir Arthur Roden's a friend of yours—you can arrange for our cells to be side by side, and we'll tap on the dividing wall."

I had an idea that our unsociable prison discipline insisted on segregating male and female offenders. It was not the moment, however, for captious criticism.

"If I stay six months," I said, "I'll undertake to divorce you from your militant army."

"The laziest man in the northern hemisphere?"

"I've never found anything worth doing before."

"It's a poor ambition. And the militants want me."

"They haven't the monopoly of that."

Joyce smiled in spite of herself, and under her breath I caught the word "Cheek!"

"I'm pledged to them," she said aloud. "Possession's nine points of the law."

"I don't expect to hear *you* calling the law and the prophets in aid."

"It's a woman's privilege to make the best of both worlds," she answered, as Elsie carried her off to fetch their cloaks.

"There is only one world," I called out as she left me. "This is it. I am going to make the best of it."

"How?"

"By appropriating to myself whatever's worth having in it."

"How?" she repeated.

"I'll tell you in six months' time."

Aintree sauntered up with his coat under his arm as Joyce and her sister vanished from sight.

"Rather wonderful, isn't she?" he remarked.

"Which?" I asked.

"Oh, really!" he exclaimed in disgusted protest.

"They are astonishingly alike," I said *à propos* of nothing.

"They're often mistaken for each other."

"I can well believe it."

"It's a mistake you're not likely to make," he answered significantly.

I took hold of his shoulders, and made him look me in the eyes.

"What do you mean by that, Seraph?" I asked.

"Nothing," he answered. "What did I say? I really forget; I was thinking what a wife Joyce would make for a man who likes having his mind made up for him, and feels that his youth is slipping imperceptibly away."

I made no answer, because I could not see what answer was possible. And, further, I was playing with a day-dream.... The Seraph interrupted with some remark about her effect on a public meeting, and my mind set itself to visualise the scene. I could imagine her easy directness and gay self-confidence capturing the heart of her audience; it mattered little how she spoke or what she ordered them to do; the fascination lay in her happy, untroubled voice, and the graceful movements of her slim, swaying body. Behind the careless front they knew of her resolute, unwhimpering courage; she tossed the laws of England in the air as a juggler tosses glass balls, and when one fell to the ground and shivered in a thousand pieces she was ready to pay the price with a smiling face, and a hand waving gay farewell. It was the lighthearted recklessness of Sydney Carton or Rupert of Hentzau, the one courage that touches the brutal, beef-fed English imagination....

"Why the hell does she do it, Seraph?" I exclaimed.

"Why don't you stop her, if you don't like it?"

"What influence have *I* got over her?"

"Some—not much. You can develop it. I? Good heavens, *I*'ve no control. You've got the seeds.... No, you must just believe me when I say it is so. You wouldn't understand if I told you the reason."

"It seems to me the more I see of you the less I do understand you," I objected.

"Quite likely," he answered. "It isn't even worth trying."

The play which the Seraph was taking us to see was *The Heir-at-Law*, and though we went on the first night, it was running throughout my residence in England, and for anything I know to the contrary may still be playing to crowded houses. It was the biggest dramatic success of recent years, and for technical construction, subtlety of characterization, and brilliance of dialogue, ranks deservedly as a masterpiece. As a young man I used to do a good deal of theatre-going, and attended most of the important first nights. Why, I hardly know; possibly because there was a good deal of difficulty in getting seats, possibly because at that age it amused us to pose as *virtuosi*, and say we liked to form our own opinion of a play before the critics had had time to tell us what to think of it. I remember the acting usually had an appearance of being insufficiently rehearsed, the players were often nervous and inaudible, and most of the plays themselves wanted substantial cutting.

"The last things I saw in England," I told Mrs. Wylton, "were *The Second Mrs. Tanqueray*, and *A Woman of No Importance*."

Dramatic history has developed apace since those days. I recollect we thought Pinero the most daring dramatist since Ibsen; we talked sagely of a revolution in the English theatre. There must have been many revolutions since then! Even the wit of Wilde has grown a little out-moded since '93. As we drove down to the Cornmarket I was given to understand that the dramatic firmament had been many times disturbed in twenty years; Shaw had followed a meteoric path, Barker burned with fitful brilliance, while aloft in splendid isolation shone the inexorable cold light of Galsworthy....

"Who's the new man you're taking us to see?" Joyce asked the Seraph.

"Gordon Tremayne," he answered.

"The man who wrote 'The Child of Misery'? I didn't know he wrote plays."

"I believe this is his first. Do you know his books?"

"Forward and backward and upside down," I answered. "He's one of the coming men."

I am not a great novel reader, and have no idea how I came across Tremayne's first book, "The Marriage of Gretchen," but when once I had read it, I watched the publisher's announcements for other books from the same pen. The second one belonged still to the experimental stage: then the whole literary world was convulsed by the first volume of his "Child of Misery."

I suppose by now it is as well-known as that other strange masterpiece of self-revelation—"Jean Christophe"—which in many ways it so closely resembles. In one respect it shared the same immortality, and "Jean Christophe's" future was not more eagerly watched in France than "Rupert Chevasse's" in England. The hero—for want of a better name—was torn from the pages of the book and invested by his readers with flesh and blood reality. We all wanted to know how the theme would develop, and none of us could guess. The first volume gave you the childhood and upbringing of Rupert—and incidentally revealed to my unimaginative mind what a hell life must be for an oversensitive boy at an English public school. The second opened with his marriage to Kathleen, went on to her death and ended with the appalling mental prostration of Rupert. I suppose every one had a different theory how the third volume would shape....

"What sort of a fellow is this Tremayne?" I asked the Seraph.

"I've never met him," he answered, and closured my next

question by jumping up and helping Mrs. Wylton out of the taxi.

From our box we had an admirable view of both stage and house. One or two critics and a sprinkling of confirmed first-nighters had survived from the audiences I knew twenty years before, but the newcomers were in the ascendant. It was a good house, and I recognised more than one quondam acquaintance. Mrs. Rawnsley, the Prime Minister's wife, was pointed out to me by Joyce: she was there with her daughter, and for a moment I thought I ought to go and speak. When I recollected that we had not met since her marriage, and thought of the voluminous explanations that would be necessitated, I decided to sit on in the box and talk to Joyce. Indeed, I only mention the fact of my seeing mother and daughter there, because it sometimes strikes me as curious that so large a part should have been played in my life by a girl of nineteen with sandy hair and over-freckled face whom I saw on that occasion for the first, last and only time.

The Heir-at-Law went with a fine swing. There were calls at the end of each act, and the lights were kept low after the final curtain while the whole house rang from pit to gallery with a chorus of "Author! Author!" The Seraph began looking for his coat as soon as the curtain fell, but I wanted to see the great Gordon Tremayne.

"He won't appear," I was told when I refused to move.

"How do you know?"

Aintree hesitated, and then pointed to the stage, where the manager had advanced to the footlights and was explaining that the author was not in the house.

We struggled out into the passage and made our way into the hall.

"Where does one sup these times?" I asked the Seraph.

He suggested the Carlton and I handed on the suggestion to Mrs. Wylton, not in any way as a reflection on his admirable dinner, but as a precautionary measure against hunger in the night. Mrs. Wylton in turn consulted her sister, who appeared by common consent to be credited with the dominant mind of the party.

"I should love...." Joyce was beginning when something made her stop short. I followed the direction of her eyes, and caught sight of a wretched newspaper boy approaching with the last edition of an evening paper. Against his legs flapped a flimsy newsbill, and on the bill were four gigantic words:—

DEFEAT OF SUFFRAGE AMENDMENT.

Joyce met my eyes with a determined little smile.

"Not to-night, thanks," she said. "I've a lot of work to do before I go to bed."

"When shall I see you again?" I asked.

She held out a small gloved hand.

"You won't. It's good-bye."

"But why?"

"It's war *à outrance*."

"That's no concern of mine."

"Exactly. Those that are not with me are against me."

I offered a bribe in the form of matches and a cigarette.

"Don't you have an armistice even for tea?" I asked.

She shook her head provokingly.

"Joyce," I said, "when you were five, I had every reason, justification and opportunity for slapping you. I refrained. Now when I think of my wasted chances...."

"You can come to tea any time. Seraph'll give you the address."

"That's a better frame of mind," I said, as I hailed a taxi and put the two women inside it.

"It won't be an armistice," she called back over her shoulder.

"It'll have to be. I bring peace wherever I go."

"I shall convert you."

"If there's any conversion...."

"When are you coming?" she interrupted.

"Not for a day or two," I answered regretfully. "I'm spending Whitsun with the Rodens."

Joyce shook my hand in silence through the window of the taxi, and then abruptly congratulated me.

"What on?" I asked.

"Your week-end party. How perfectly glorious!"

"Why?"

"You're going to be in at the death," she answered, as the taxi jerked itself epileptically away from the kerb.

CHAPTER II

SUPPER WITH A MYSTIC

"I can look into your soul. D'you know what I see...? ... I see your soul."

—John Masefield
"The Tragedy of Nan."

I stood absent-mindedly staring at the back of the taxi till it disappeared down Pall Mall and the Seraph brought me to earth with an invitation to supper.

"...if it won't be too much of an anti-climax to have supper with me alone," I heard him murmuring.

At that moment I wanted to stride away to the Park, tramp up and down by myself, and think—think calmly, think savagely, try every fashion of thinking.

"To be quite candid," I said, as I linked arms and turned in the direction of the Club, "if you nailed me down like a Strasburg goose, I don't believe you could fill me fuller than you've already done at dinner."

"Let me bear you company, then. It'll keep you from thinking. Wait a minute; I want to have this prescription made up."

I followed him into a chemist's shop and waited patiently while a powerful soporific was compounded. I have myself subsisted too many years on heroic remedies to retain the average Englishman's horror of what he calls "drugs." At the same time I do not like to see boys of six and twenty playing with toys as dangerous as the Seraph's little grey-white powders; nor do I like to see them so much as feeling the need.

"Under advice?" I asked, as we came out into the street.

"Originally. I don't need it often, but I'm rather unsettled to-night."

He had been restless throughout the play, and the hand that

paid for the powders had trembled more than was necessary.

"You were all right at dinner," I said.

"That was some time ago," he answered.

"Everything went off admirably; there's been nothing to worry you."

"Reaction," he muttered abruptly, as we mounted the steps of the Club.

Supper was a gloomy meal, as we ate in silence and had the whole huge dining-room to ourselves. I ought not to complain or be surprised, as silence was the Seraph's normal state, and my mind was far too full of other things to discuss the ordinary banalities of the day. With the arrival of the cigars, however, I began to feel unsociable, and told him to talk to me.

"What about?" he asked.

"Anything."

"There's only one thing you're thinking about at the moment."

"Oh?"

"You're thinking of the past three months generally, and the past three hours in particular."

"That doesn't carry me very far," I said.

He switched off the table lights and lay back in his chair with legs crossed.

"Don't you think it strange and—unsettling? Three months ago life was rounded and complete; you were all-sufficient to yourself. One day was just like another, till the morning when you woke up and felt lonely—lonely and wasted, gradually growing old. Till three, four hours ago you tried to define your new hunger.... Now you've forgotten it, now you're wondering why you can't drive out of your mind the vision of a girl you've not seen for twenty years. Shall I go on? You've just had a new thought; you were thinking I was impertinent, that I oughtn't to talk like this, that you ought to be angry.... Then you decided you couldn't be, because I was right." He paused, and then exclaimed quickly, "Now, now there's another new thought!

You're not going to be angry, you know it's true, you're interested, you want to find out how I know it's true, but you want to seem sceptical so as to save your face." He hesitated a second time, and added quietly, "Now you've made up your mind, you're going to say nothing, you think that's non-committal, you're going to wait in the hope that I shall tell you how I know."

I made no answer, and he sat silent for a while, tracing his initials with the end of a match in the little mound of cigar ash on his plate.

"I can't tell you how I know," he said at last. "But it was true, wasn't it?"

"Suppose it was?"

His shoulders gave a slight shrug.

"Oh, I don't know. I just wanted to see if I was right."

I turned up the table lamp again so that I could see his face.

"Just as a matter of personal interest," I said, "do you suggest that I always show the world what I'm thinking about?"

"Not the world."

"You?"

"As a rule. Not more than other people."

"Can you tell what everybody's thinking of?"

"I can with a good many men."

"Not women?"

He shook his head.

"They often don't know themselves. They think in fits and starts—jerkily; it's hard to follow them."

"How do you do it?"

"I don't know. You must watch people's eyes; then you'll find the expression is always changing, never the same for two minutes in succession—you just *see*."

"I'm hanged if I do."

"Your eyes must be quick. Look here, you're walking along in evening dress, and I throw a lump of mud on to your shirt front. In a fraction of a second you hit me over the head with your cane. That's all, isn't it? But you know it isn't all; there are a dozen mental processes between the mud-throwing and the head-hitting. You're horror-stricken at the mess I've made of your shirt, you wonder if you'll have time to go back and change into a clean one, and if so, how late you'll be. You're annoyed that any one should throw mud at you, you're flabbergasted that *I* should be the person. You're impotently angry. Gradually a desire for revenge overcomes every other feeling; you're going to hurt me. A little thought springs up, and you wonder whether I shall summon you for assault; you decide to risk it Another little thought—will you hit me on the body or the head? You decide the head because it'll hurt more. Still another thought—how hard to hit? You don't want to kill me and you don't want to make me blind. You decide to be on the safe side and hit rather gently. Then—then at last you're ready with the cane. Is that right?"

I thought it over very carefully.

"I suppose so. But no one can see those thoughts succeeding each other. There isn't time."

The Seraph shook his head in polite contradiction.

"The same sort of thing was said when instantaneous photography was introduced. You got pictures of horses galloping, and people solemnly assured you it was physically impossible for horses' legs to get into such attitudes."

"How do you account for it?" I asked.

"Don't know. Eyes different from other people's, I suppose."

I could see he preferred to discuss the power in the abstract rather than in relation to himself, but my curiosity was piqued.

"Anything else?" I asked.

He listened for a moment; the Club was sunk in profound silence. Then I heard him imitating a familiar deep voice: "Oh—er—porter, taxi, please."

"Why d'you do that?" I asked, not quite certain of his meaning.

"Don't you know whose voice that was supposed to be?"

"It was Arthur Roden's," I said.

He nodded. "Just leaving the Club."

I jumped up and ran into the hall.

"Is Sir Arthur Roden in the Club?" I asked the porter.

"Just left this moment, sir," he answered.

I came back and sat down opposite the Seraph.

"I want to hear more about this," I said. "I'm beginning to get interested."

He shook his head.

"Why not?" I persisted.

"I don't like talking about it. I don't understand it, there's a lot more that I haven't told you about. I only—"

"Well?"

"I only told you this much because you didn't like to see me taking drugs. I wanted to show you my nerves were rather—abnormal."

"As if I didn't know that! Why don't you do something for them?"

"Such as?"

"Occupy your mind more."

"My mind's about as fully occupied as it will stand," he answered as we left the dining-room and went in search of our coats.

As I was staying at the Savoy and he was living in Adelphi Terrace, our homeward roads were the same. We started in silence, and before we had gone five yards I knew the grey-white powder would be called in aid that night. He was in a state of acute nervous excitement; the arm that linked itself in mine trembled appreciably through two thicknesses of coat, and I could feel him pressing against my side like a frightened woman. Once he begged me not to repeat our recent conversation.

As we entered the Strand, the sight of the theatres gave me a fresh train of thought.

"You ought to write a book, Seraph," I said with the easy abruptness one employs in advancing these general propositions.

"What about?"

"Anything. Novel, play, psychological study. Look here, my young friend, psychology in literature is the power of knowing what's going on in people's minds, and being able to communicate that knowledge to paper. How many writers possess the power? If you look at the rot that gets published, the rot that gets produced at the theatres, my question answers itself. At the present day there aren't six psychologists above the mediocre in all England; barring Henry James there's been no great psychologist since Dostoievski. And this power that other people attain by years of heart-breaking labour and observation, comes to you—by some freak of nature—ready made. You could write a good book, Seraph; why don't you?"

"I might try."

"I know what that means."

"I don't think you do," he answered. "I pay a lot of attention to your advice."

"Thank you," I said with an ironical bow.

"I do. Five years ago, in Morocco, you gave me the same advice."

"I'm still waiting to see the result."

"You've seen it."

"What do you mean?"

"You told me to write a book, I wrote it. You've read it."

"In my sleep?"

"I hope not."

"Name, please? I've never so much as seen the outside of it."

"I didn't write in my own name."

"Name of book and pseudonym?" I persisted.

His lips opened, and then shut in silence.

"I shan't tell you," he murmured after a pause.

"It won't go any further," I promised.

"I don't want even you to know."

"Seraph, we've got no secrets. At least I hope not."

We had come alongside the entrance to the Savoy, but neither of us thought of turning in.

"Name, please?" I repeated after we had walked in silence to the Wellington Street crossing and were waiting for a stream of traffic to pass on towards Waterloo Bridge.

"'The Marriage of Gretchen,'" he answered.

"'The History of David Copperfield,'" I suggested.

"You see, you won't believe me," he complained.

"Try something a little less well—known: get hold of a book that's been published anonymously."

"'Gretchen' was published over a *nom de plume*."

"By 'Gordon Tremayne,'" I said, "whoever he may be."

"You don't know him?"

"Do you? No, I remember as we drove down to the theatre you said you didn't."

"I said I'd never met him," he corrected me.

"A mere quibble," I protested.

"It's an important distinction. Do you know anybody who *has* met him?"

I turned half round to give him the benefit of what was intended for a smile of incredulity. He met my gaze unfalteringly. Suddenly it was borne in upon me that he was speaking the truth.

"Will you kindly explain the whole mystery?" I begged.

"Now you can understand why I was jumpy at the theatre to-night," he answered in parenthesis.

He told me the story as we walked along Fleet Street, and we had reached Ludgate Circus and turned down New Bridge Street before the fantastic tangle was straightened out.

Acting on the advice I had given him when he stayed with

me in Morocco, he had sought mental distraction in the composition of "Gretchen," and had offered it to the publishers under an assumed name through the medium of a solicitor. We three alone were acquainted with the carefully guarded secret. His subsequent books appeared in the same way: even the *Heir-at-Law* I had just witnessed came to a similar cumbrous birth, and was rehearsed and produced without criticism or suggestion from the author.

I could see no reason for a *nom de plume* in the case of "Gretchen" or the other novel of nonage; with the "Child of Misery" it was different. I suspect the first volume of being autobiographical; the second, to my certain knowledge, embodies a slice torn ruthlessly out of the Seraph's own life. An altered setting, the marriage of Rupert and Kathleen, were two out of a dozen variations from the actual; but the touching, idyllic boy and girl romance, with its shattering termination, had taken place a few months—a few weeks, I might say—before our first meeting in Morocco. I imagine it was because I was the only man who had seen him in those dark days, that he broke through his normal reserve and admitted me to his confidence.

"When do you propose to avow your own children?" I asked.

He shook his head without answering. I suppose it is what I ought to have expected, but in the swaggering, self-advertising twentieth century it seemed incredible that I had found a man content for all time to bind his laurels round the brow of a lay figure.

"In time...." I began, but he shook his head again.

"You can stop me with a single sentence. I'm in your hands. 'Gordon Tremayne' dies as soon as his identity's discovered."

Years ago I remember William Sharp using the same threat with "'Fiona Macleod.'"

"You think it's just self-consciousness," he went on in self-defence. "You think after what's passed...."

"It's getting farther away each day, Seraph," I suggested

gently as he hesitated.

"I know. 'Tisn't that—altogether. It's the future."

"What's going to happen?"

"If 'Gordon Tremayne' knew that," he answered, "you wouldn't find him writing plays."

Arm-in-arm we walked the length of the Embankment. As I grew to know the Seraph better, I learnt not to interrupt his long silences. It was trying for the patience, I admit, but his natural shyness even with friends was so great that you could see him balancing an idea for minutes at a time before he found courage to put it into words. I was always reminded of the way a tortoise projects its head cautiously from the shell, looks all round, starts, stops, starts again, before mustering resolution to take a step forward....

"D'you believe in premonitions, Toby?" he asked as we passed Cleopatra's Needle on our second journey eastward.

"Yes," I answered. I should have said it in any case, to draw him out; as a matter of fact, I have the greatest difficulty in knowing what I do or do not believe. On the rare occasions when I do make up my mind on any point I generally have to reconsider my decision.

"I had a curious premonition lately," he went on. "One of these days you may see it in the third volume of 'The Child of Misery.'"....

I cannot give the story in his own words, because I was merely a credulous, polite listener. He believed in his premonition, and the belief gave a vigour and richness to the recital which I cannot hope or attempt to reproduce. Here is a prosaic record of the facts. At the close of the previous winter he had found himself in attendance at a costume ball, muffled to the eyes in the cerements of an Egyptian mummy. The dress was too hot for dancing, and he was wandering through the ball-room inspecting the costumes, when an unreasoning impulse drove him out into the entrance hall. Even as he went, the impulse seemed more than a caprice; in his own words, had his feet been manacled, he would have gone there crawling on his knees.

The hall was almost deserted when he arrived. A tall Crusader in coat armour stood smoking a cigarette and talking to a Savoyard peasant-girl. Their conversation was desultory, but the words spoken by the girl fixed a careless, frank, self-confident voice in his memory. Then the Crusader was despatched on an errand, and the peasant-girl strolled up and down the hall.

In a mirror over the fireplace the Seraph watched her movements. She was slight and of medium height, with small features and fine black hair falling to the waist in two long plaits. The brown eyes, set far apart and deep in their sockets, were never still, and the face wore an expression of restless, rebellious energy.... Once their eyes met, but the mummy wrappings were discouraging. The girl continued her walk, and the Seraph returned to his mirror. Whatever his mission, the Crusader was unduly long away; his partner grew visibly impatient, and once, for no ostensible reason, the expression reflected in the mirror changed from impatience to disquiet; the brown eyes lost their fire and self-confidence, the mouth grew wistful, the whole face lonely and frightened.

It was this expression that came to haunt the Seraph's dreams. In a fantastic succession of visions he found himself talking frankly and intimately with the Savoyard peasant; their conversation was always interrupted, suddenly and brutally, as though she had been snatched away. Gradually—like sunlight breaking waterily through a mist—the outline of her features become visible again, then the eyes wide open with fear, then the mouth with lips imploringly parted.

The Seraph had quickened his pace till we were striding along at almost five miles an hour. Opposite the south end of Middle Temple Lane he dragged his arm abruptly out of mine, planted his elbows on the parapet of the Embankment, and stared out over the muddy waters, with knuckles pressed crushingly to either side of his forehead.

"I don't know what to make of it!" he exclaimed. "What does it mean? Who is she? Why does she keep coming to me like this? I don't know her, I've caught that one glimpse of her. Yet night after night. And it's so real, I often don't know whether I'm awake or asleep. I've never felt so ... so *conscious* of anybody in my life. I saw her for those few minutes, but I'm as sure as I'm sure of death that I shall meet her again—"

"Don't you want to?"

He passed a hand wearily in front of his eyes, and linked an arm once more in mine.

"I don't know," he answered as we turned slowly back and walked up Norfolk Street into the Strand. "Yes, if it's just to satisfy curiosity and find out who she is. But there's something more, there's some big catastrophe brewing. I'd sooner be out of it. At least ... she may want help. I don't know. I honestly don't know."

When we got back to the Savoy I invited him up to my room for a drink. He refused on the score of lateness, though I could see he was reluctant to be left to his own company.

"Don't think me sceptical," I said, "because I can't interpret your dreams. And don't think I imagine it's all fancy if I tell you to change your ideas, change your work, change your surroundings. The Rodens have invited you down to their place, why don't you come?"

He shivered at the abrupt contact with reality.

"I do hate meeting people," he protested.

"Seraph," I said, "I'm an unworthy vessel, but on your own showing I shall be submerged in politics if there isn't some one to create a diversion. Come to oblige me."

He hesitated for several moments, alternately crushing his opera hat and jerking it out straight.

"All right," he said at last.

"You will be my salvation."

"You deserve it, for what it's worth."

"God forbid!" I cried in modest disclaimer.

"You're the only one that isn't quite sure I'm mad," he answered, turning away in the direction of Adelphi Terrace.

For the next two days I had little time to spare for the Seraph's premonitions or Joyce Davenant's conspiracies. My brother sailed from Tilbury on the Friday, I was due the following day at the Rodens, and in the interval there were incredibly numerous formalities to be concluded before Gladys was finally entrusted to my care. The scene of reconciliation between her father and myself was most affecting. In the old days when Brian toiled at his briefs and I sauntered away the careless happy years of my youth, there is little doubt that I was held out as an example not to be followed. We need not go into the question which of us made the better bargain with life, but I know my brother largely supported himself in the early days of struggle by reflecting that a more than ordinarily hideous retribution was in store for me. Do I wrong him in fancying he must have suffered occasional pangs of disappointment?

Perhaps I do; there was really no time for him to be disappointed. Almost before retribution could be expected to have her slings and arrows in readiness, my ramblings in the diamond fields of South Africa had made me richer than he could ever hope to become by playing the Industrious Apprentice at the English Common Law Bar. More charitable than the Psalmist—from whom indeed he differs in all material respects—Brian could not bring himself to believe that any one who flourished like the green bay tree was fundamentally wicked. At our meeting he was almost cordial. Any slight reserve may be attributed to reasonable vexation that he had grown old and scarred in the battle of life while time with me had apparently stood still.

For all our cordiality, Gladys was not given away without substantial good advice. He was glad to see me settling down, home again from my curious ... well, home again from my wanderings; steadying with age. I was face to face with a great responsibility.... I suppose it was inevitable, and I did my best to appear patient, but in common fairness a judge has no more right than a shopwalker to import a trade manner into private life. The homily to which I was subjected should have been reserved for the Bench; there it is expected of a judge; indeed he is paid five thousand a year to live up to the expectation.

When Brian had ended I was turned over to the attention of my sister-in-law. Like a wise woman she did not attempt competition with her husband, and I was dismissed with the statement that Gladys would cause me no trouble, and an inconsistent exhortation that I was not to let her get into mischief. Finally, in case of illness or other mishap, I was to telegraph immediately by means of a code contrived for the occasion. I remember a great many birds figured among the code-words: "Penguin" meant "She has taken a slight chill, but I have had the doctor in, and she is in bed with a hot water-bottle"; "Linnet" meant "Scarlatina"; "Bustard" "Appendicitis, operation successfully performed, going on well." Being neither ornithologist nor physician, I had no idea there were so many possible diseases, or even so that there were enough birds to go round. It is perhaps needless to add that I lost my copy of the code the day after they sailed, and only discovered it by chance a fortnight ago when Brian and his wife had been many months restored to their only child, and I had passed out of the life of all three—presumably for ever.

In case no better opportunity offer, I hasten to put it on record that my sister-in-law spoke no more than the truth in saying her daughter would cause me no trouble. I do not wish for a better ward. During the weeks that I was her foster father, circumstances brought me in contact with some two or three hundred girls of similar age and position. They were all a little more emancipated, rational, and independent than the girls of my boyhood, but of all that I came to know intimately, Gladys was the least abnormal and most tractable.

I grew to be very fond of her before we parted, and my chief present regret is that I see so little likelihood of meeting her again. She was affectionate, obedient, high-spirited—tasting life for the first time, finding the savour wonderfully sweet on her lips, knowing it could not last, determined to drain the last drop of enjoyment before wedlock called her to the responsibilities of the drab, workaday world. She had none of Joyce Davenant's personality, her reckless courage and obstinate, fearless devilry; none of Sylvia Roden's passionate fire, her icy reserve and imperious temper. Side by side with either, Gladys would seem indeterminate, characterless; but she was the only one of the three I would have welcomed as a ward in those thunderous summer days before the storm burst in its fury and scorched Joyce and Sylvia alike. There were giants in those days, but England has only limited accommodation for supermen. Had I my time and choice over again, my handkerchief would still fall on the shoulder of my happy, careless, laughing, slangy, disrespectful niece.

I accompanied Gladys to Tilbury and saw her parents safely on board the *Bessarabia*. On our return to Pont Street I found a letter of instructions to guide us in our forthcoming visit to Hampshire. My niece had half opened it before she noticed the address.

"It was Phil's writing, so I thought it must be for me," was her ingenious explanation.

As I completed the opening and began to read the letter, my mind went abruptly back to some enigmatic words of Seraph's: "Is Phil going to be there?". I remembered him asking. "Oh then it certainly won't be a bachelor party."

CHAPTER III

BRANDON COURT

"I remember waiting for you when the steamer came in. Do you?"

"At the Lily Lock, beyond Hong Kong and Java?"

"Do *you* call it that too?" ...

... "You're the Boy, my Brushwood Boy, and I've known you all my life!"

—Rudyard Kipling
"The Brushwood Boy."

The following morning I took up my new duties in earnest, and conveyed myself and my luggage from the Savoy to Pont Street.

"I'm allowing plenty of time for the train," I told Gladys when she had finished keeping me waiting. "Apparently we've got to meet the rest of the party at Waterloo, and Phil isn't certain if he'll be there."

As we drove down to the station I refreshed my memory with a second reading of his admirably lucid instructions.

"Eleven fifteen is the train," he wrote. "If I'm not there, make the Seraph introduce you: he knows everybody. If he cries off at the last minute (it's just like him), you'll have to manage on your own account, with occasional help from Gladys. She doesn't know Rawnsley or Culling, but she'll point out Gartside if you don't recognize him...."

"Do you *know* him?" Gladys asked me in surprise.

"I used to, many years ago. In fact I did him a small service when he had for the moment forgotten that he was in the East and that the Orient does not always see eye to eye with the West."

Gladys' feminine curiosity was instantly aroused, but I refused to gratify it. After all it was ancient history now,

Gartside was several years younger at the time, and in the parlance of the day, "it was the sort of thing that might have happened to any one." He is now a highly respected member of the House of Lords, occupying an important public position. I should long ago have forgotten the whole episode but for his promise that if ever he had a chance of repaying me he would do so. I have every reason now to remember that the bread I cast on the waters returned to me after not many days.

"What's he like now?" I asked Gladys.

"Oh, a topper!"

I find the rising generation defines with a minimum of words.

"I mean he's a real white man," she proceeded, *per obscurans ad obscurantius*; I was left to find out for myself how much remained of the old Gartside. I found him little changed, and still a magnificent specimen of humanity, six feet four in height, fifteen stone in weight, as strong as a giant, and as gentle as a woman. He was the kindest, most courteous, largest-hearted man I have ever met: slow of speech, slow of thought, slow of perception. I am afraid you might starve at his side without his noticing it; when once he had seen your plight he would give you his last crust and go hungry himself. He was brave and just as few men have the courage to be; you trusted and followed him implicitly; with greater quickness and more imagination he would have been a great man, but with his weak initiative and unready sympathy he might lead you to irreparable disaster. I suppose he was five and thirty at this time, balder than when I last met him, and stouter than in the days when he backed himself to stroke a Leander four half-way over the Putney course against the 'Varsity Eight.

I went on with Philip's letter of explanation.

"Nigel Rawnsley you will find majestic, Olympian, and omniscient. He is tall, sandy-haired, and lantern-jawed like his father; do not comment on the likeness, as he cherishes the belief that the Prime Minister's son is of somewhat greater importance than the Prime Minister. If you hear him speak before you see him, you will recognise him by his exquisite taste in recondite epithets. He will hail you with a Greek quotation, convict you of inaccuracy and ignorance on five different matters of common knowledge in as many minutes, and finally give you up as hopeless. This is just his manner. It is also his manner to wear a conspicuous gold cross to mark his religious enthusiasms, and to travel third as an earnest of democratic instincts. He is not a bad fellow if you don't take him too seriously; he is making a mark in the House."

"Prig," murmured Gladys with conviction, as I came to the end of the Rawnsley dossier. She did not know him, but was giving expression to a very general feeling.

I crossed swords more than once with Nigel Rawnsley in the course of the following few months, and in our duelling caught sight of more than one unamiable side to his character. While my mood is charitable, I may perhaps say a word in his favour. It is just possible that I have met more types of men than Philip Roden; it takes me longer to size them up; perhaps also I see a little deeper than he did. Nigel went through life handicapped by an insatiable ambition and an abnormal self-consciousness. Without charm of manner or strength of personality, he must have been from earliest schooldays one of those who—like the Jews—trample that they be not trampled on. He became overbearing for fear of being insignificant, corrected your facts for fear of being squeezed out of the conversation, and sharpened his tongue to secure your respect if not your love. Some one in the House christened him "Whitaker's Almanack," but in fact his knowledge was not exceptionally wide. He was always right because he had the wisdom to keep silent when out of his depth, and intervene effectively when he was sure of his ground.

I never heard him in Court, but his defect as a statesman must have been apparent as a barrister; he would take no risks, try no bluff, make no attack till horse, foot, and gun were marshalled in readiness. Given time he would win by dogged perseverance, but, as in my own case, he must know to his cost that a slippery opponent will give him no time for his ponderous grappling. Nigel's great natural gifts will carry him to the front when he has learnt a little more humanity; and humanity will come as he loses his dread of ridicule. At present the youngest parliamentary hand can brush aside his weighty facts and figures by a simple ill-natured witticism; and the fact that I am not now languishing in one of His Majesty's gaols is due to my discovery of the weak spot in his armour. Though my heart beat fast, I was still able to laugh at him in my moment of crisis; and so long as I laughed—though he had all the trumps in his hand—he must needs think I had reason for my laughter.

"The last of the party," Philip's letter concluded, "will be Pat Culling. He is an irrepressible Irishman of some thirty summers, with a brogue that becomes unintelligible whenever he remembers to employ it. You will find him thin and short, with a lean, expressionless face, grey eyes, and black hair. He can play any musical instrument from a sackbut to a Jew's harp, and speak any language from Czech to Choctaw. Incidentally he is the idlest and most sociable man in Europe, and gets (and gives) more amusement out of life than any one I know.

"You should look for him first at the front of the train, where he will be bribing the driver to let him travel on the engine; failing that, try the station-master's office, where he will be ordering a special in broken Polish; or the collector's gate, where he will be losing his ticket and discovering it in the inspector's back hair. He is a skilled conjuror, and may produce a bowl of gold fish from your hat at any moment. On second thoughts, you will more probably find him gently baiting the incorruptible Rawnsley, who makes an admirable foil. Don't be lured into playing poker on the way down; Paddy will deal himself five aces with the utmost *sang froid.*"

"Now we know exactly where we are," I remarked replacing

the letter in my pocket, as our taxi mounted the sloping approach to Waterloo.

"And it's all wasted labour," said Gladys as I began to assemble her belongings from different corners of the cab. "Phil's here the whole time."

I reminded myself that I stood *in loco parentis*, shook hands with Philip and plunged incontinently into a sea of introductions.

The journey down was unexpectedly tranquil. Gladys and Philip conversed in a discreet undertone, paying no more attention to my presence than if I had been the other side of the world. Gartside told me how life had treated him since our parting in Asia Minor; while Culling produced a drawing block and embarked on an illustrated history of Rawnsley's early years. It was entitled "L'Avénement de Nigel," and the series began with the first cabinet council hastily summoned to be informed of the birth—I noticed that the ministers were arrayed in the conventional robes of the Magi—it concluded with the first meeting of electors addressed by the budding statesman. For reasons best known to the artist, his victim was throughout deprived of the consolation of clothing, though he seldom appeared without the badge of the C.E.M.S. Rawnsley grew progressively more uncomfortable as the series proceeded, and in the interests of peace I was not sorry when we arrived at Brandon Junction.

We strolled out into the station yard while our luggage was being collected. A car was awaiting us, with a girl in the driving-seat, and from the glimpse gained a few days earlier in Pont Street, I recognized her as Sylvia Roden. I should have liked to enjoy a long rude stare, but my attention was distracted by the changed demeanour of my fellow travellers. Gartside advanced with the air Mark Antony must have assumed in bartering away a world for a smile from Cleopatra; Rawnsley struggled to produce a Sir Walter Raleigh effect without the cloak; even Culling was momentarily sobered.

When I turned from her admirers to Sylvia herself, it was to marvel at the dominion and assurance of an English girl in her beauty and proud youth. She sat in a long white dust-coat, her fingers toying with the ends of a long motor veil. The small oval face, surmounted by rippling black hair, was a singularly perfect setting for two lustrous, soft, unfathomable brown eyes. As she held her court, a smile of challenge hovered round her small, straight mouth, as though she were conscious of the homage paid her, and claimed it as a right; behind the smile there lurked—or so I fancied—a suggestion of weariness as with one whom mere adoration leaves disillusioned. Her manner was a baffling blend of frankness and reserve. The *camaraderie* of her greeting reminded me she was one girl brought up in a circle of brothers; fearless and unaffected, she met us on equal terms and was hailed by her Christian name. But the frankness was skin deep, and I pitied the man who should presume on her manner to attempt unwelcome intimacy. It was a fascinating blend, and she knew its fascination; her friends were distantly addressed as "Mr. Rawnsley," "Lord Gartside," "Mr. Culling."

Gladys and I had lingered behind the others, but at our approach Sylvia jumped down from the car and ran towards us. Her movements were astonishingly light and quick, and when I amused an idle moment in trying to fit her with a formula I decided that her veins must be filled with radium. Possibly the description conveys nothing to other people; it exactly expresses the feeling that her mobile face, quick movements of body and passionate nature inspired in me. Later on I remember the Seraph pointed to the tremendous mental and physical energy of her father and brothers, asking how a slight girl's frame could contain such fire without eruption.

Eruptions there certainly were, devastating and cataclysmic....

"How are you, my child?" she exclaimed, catching Gladys by the hands. "And where's the wicked uncle?"

My niece indicated my presence, and I bowed.

"You?" Sylvia took me in with one rapid glance, and then held out a hand. "But you look hardly older than Phil."

"I feel even younger," I began.

"Face massage," Culling murmured.

"A good conscience," I protested.

"Why did you have to leave England?" he retorted.

It was the first time I had heard it suggested that my exile was other than voluntary. I attempted no explanation as I knew Culling would outbid me. Instead, we gathered silently round the car and watched Philip attempting with much seriousness to allot seats among an excessive population that spent its time criticising and rejecting his arrangements.

"It's the fault of the Roden family!" he exclaimed at last in desperation. "Why did I come down by this train, and why did you come to meet us, Sylvia? We're two too many. Look here, climb in, everybody, and Bob and I'll go in the other car."

"You can't ask a Baron of the United Kingdom to go as luggage," objected Culling who had vetoed twice as many suggestions as any one else.

"Well, you come, Pat," said Phil.

"We Cullings aren't to be put off with something that's not good enough for Lord Gartside," was the dignified rejoinder.

Philip was seized with inspiration.

"Does any one care to walk?" he asked. "Gladys?"

"You're not going to take this child over wet fields in thin shoes," his sister interposed. "She's got a cold as it is."

My eyes strayed casually to the ground and taught me that Sylvia was shod with neat, serviceable brogues.

"I'll walk," I volunteered in an aside to her, "if you'll show me the way."

Within two minutes the car had been despatched on its road, and Sylvia and I set out at an easy, swinging pace through the town and across the four miles of low meadow land that separated us from Brandon Court.

"Rather good, that," I remarked as we got clear of the town.

"What was?" she asked.

"Abana, Pharpar and yet a third river of Damascus flowed near at hand, but it was the sluggish old waters of Jordan that were found worthy."

We were walking single-file along a footpath, and a stile imposed a temporary check. Sylvia mounted it and sat on the top bar, looking down on me.

"Are we going to be friends?" she asked abruptly.

"I sincerely hope so."

"It rests with you. And you must decide now, while there's still time to go back and get a cab at the station."

"We were starting rather well," I pointed out.

"That's just what you weren't doing," she said with a determined shake of the head. "If we're going to be friends, you must promise never to make remarks like that. You don't mean them, and I don't like them. Will you promise?"

"The flesh is weak," I protested.

"Am I worth a little promise like that?"

"Lord! yes," I said. "But I always break my promises."

"You mustn't break this one. It's bad enough with Abana and Pharpar, as you call them. You know you're really—you won't mind my saying it?—you're old enough...."

"Age only makes me more susceptible," I lamented. The statement was perfectly true and I have suffered much mental disquiet on the subject. So far as I can see, my declining years will be one long riot of senile infidelity.

"I don't mind that," said Sylvia with a close-lipped smile; "but I don't want pretty speeches." She jumped down from the stile and stood facing me, with her clear brown eyes looking straight into mine. "You're not in love with me, are you?"

I hesitated for a fraction of time, as any man would; but her foot tapped the ground with impatience.

"Don't be absurd!" she exclaimed, "you know you're not;

you've known me five minutes. Well,"—her voice suddenly lost any asperity it may have contained, and she laid her hand almost humbly on my arm—"please don't behave as if you were. I hate it, and hate it, and hate it, till I can hardly contain myself. But I should like you as a friend. You've knocked about the world, you're seasoned—"

I held out my hand to seal the bargain.

"I was horribly rude just now!" she exclaimed with sudden penitence. "I was afraid you were going to be like all the rest."

"Tell me what's expected of me," I begged.

"Nothing. I just want to be friends. You'll find I'm worth it," she added with a flash of pride.

"I think I saw that the moment we met."

"I wonder."

It was some time before I did full justice to Sylvia, some time before I appreciated the pathetic loneliness of her existence. For twenty years she and Philip had been staunch allies. His triumphs and troubles had been carried home from school to be discussed and shared with his sister; on the first night of every holiday the pair of them had religiously taken themselves out to dinner and a theatre, and Sylvia had been in attendance at every important match in which he was taking part, and every speech day at which he was presented with a prize. The tradition was carried on at Oxford, and had only come to an end when Philip entered public life and won his way into the House of Commons. Their confidences had then grown gradually less frequent, and Sylvia, whose one cry—like Kundry's—had ever been, "Let me serve," found herself without the opportunity of service. The Roden household, when I first entered it, was curiously unsympathetic; she was without an ally; there was much affection and woefully little understanding. Her father never took counsel with the women of his family, Philip had slipped away, and neither Robin nor Michael was old enough to take his place. With her vague, ill-defined craving to be of account in the world, it was small wonder if she felt herself unfriended and her devotional overtures rejected. Had her father been any one else, I am convinced that Sylvia would have joined Joyce Davenant and sought an outlet for her activities in militancy.

"You're remarkably refreshing, Sylvia," I said. She raised her eyebrows at the name. "Oh, well," I went on, "if we're going to be friends.... Besides, it's a very pretty name."

"I hate it!" she exclaimed. "Sylvia Forstead Mornington Roden. I hate them all!"

"Were you called after Lady Forstead?" I asked.

"Yes. Did you know her?"

I shook my head. Of course I had heard of her and the money left by her husband, who had chanced to own the land on which Renton came afterwards to be built. Most of that money, I learned later, was reposing in trust till Sylvia was twenty-five.

"Your taste in godmothers is commendable," I remarked.

"You think so?" she asked without conviction.

It is not good for a young girl to be burdened with great possessions; they distort her outlook on life. I wondered to what extent Sylvia was being troubled in anticipation, but the wonder was idle: nature had troubled her with sufficient good looks to make mercenary admirers superfluous.

"Most people...." I began, but stopped as she came to a sudden standstill.

"I *say*, we forgot all about Mr. Aintree!" she exclaimed.

"He didn't come," I reassured her.

"Oh, Phil said perhaps he mightn't. I gather he usually does accept invitations and not turn up. I hate people who can't be reasonably polite."

"He usually refuses the invitation," I said in the Seraph's defence.

"Why?"

I shrugged my shoulders.

"Shyness, I suppose."

"I hate shy people."

"You must ask him."

"I don't know him. What's he like?"

"Oh, I thought you did. He...." I paused and tried to think how the Seraph should be described; it was not easy. "Medium height," I ventured at last, "fair hair, rather a white face; curious, rather haunting dark eyes. Middle twenties, but usually looks younger. Very nervous and overwrought, frightfully shy...."

"Sounds like a degenerate poet."

"He's had a good deal of trouble," I added. "Be kind to him, Sylvia. Life's a long agony to him when he's with strangers."

"I hate shy people," she repeated. "It's so silly to be awkward."

"He's not awkward. Incidentally, what a number of things you find time to hate!"

"I know. I'm composed entirely of hates and bad tempers. And I hate myself more than anybody else."

"Why?"

"Because I don't understand myself," she answered, "and I can't control myself."

On arriving at the house I was introduced to my hostess. Lady Roden was a colourless woman who had sunk to a secondary position in the household. This was perhaps not surprising in a family that contained Arthur as the nominal head, and Philip, Sylvia, Robin, and Michael as Mayors of the Palace. What she lacked in authority was made up in prestige. On no single day of her life of fifty years did she forget that she was a Rutlandshire Mornington. I fear I have little respect for Morningtons—or any other pre-Conquest families—whether they come from Rutlandshire or any other part of the globe. Such inborn reverence as I in common with all other Englishmen may ever have possessed has been starved by many years absence abroad. At Brandon Court I found the sentiment flourishing hardily: Lady Roden dug for pedigrees as a dog scratches for a bone. "You are a brother of the Judge?" she said when we met. "Then—let me see—your sister-in-law was a Hylton."

I had expected to find the atmosphere oppressive with Front Bench politics, but the influence of Pat Culling was salutary. Discussion quailed before his powers of illustration, and the study of "The Rt. Hon. Sir Arthur Roden Mixing his Metaphors in the Cause of Empire"—it now hangs in the library of Cadogan Square—rescued the conversation from controversial destruction. In lieu of politics we had to arrange for the arrival of our last two guests; Aintree had wired that he was coming by a later train, and Rawnsley's sister Mavis had to be brought over some twenty miles from Hanningfold on the Sussex borders. Sylvia volunteered for the longer journey in her own little runabout, while the Seraph was to be fetched in the car that went nightly to Brandon Junction for Arthur's official, cabinet-minister's despatch case.

"What's come over our Seraph the last few years?" Culling asked me, when the two cars had gone their respective ways and we were smoking a cheroot in the Dutch Garden. "I've known him from a bit of a boy that high, and now—God knows—it's in a decline you'd say he was taken. You can't please him and you can't even anger him. He's like a man has his heart broken."

I did not know what answer to give.

"Just a passing mood," I suggested.

"It's a mood will have him destroyed," said Culling, gloomily.

He was a kind-hearted, pleasant, superficial fellow, one of those feckless, humorous Irishmen who laugh at the absurdities of the world and themselves, and go on laughing till life comes to hold no other business—a splendid engine for work or fighting, but too idle almost to make a start, too little concentrated ever to keep the wheel moving, a man of short cuts and golden roads.... He talked with easy kindness of the Seraph till a horn sounded far away down the drive and the Brandon car swept tortuously through the elm avenue to the house.

"A common drunk and disorderly!" Culling shouted as the

Seraph came towards us with his right arm in a sling. He had that morning shut his thumb in the front door of his flat, and while we dragged the depths of Waterloo for his body, he had been sitting with his doctor, sick and faint, having the wound dressed. His face was whiter than usual, and his manner restless.

"I've kept my promise," he remarked to me.

"I was giving up hope."

"I *had* to come," he answered in vague perplexity, and relapsed into one of his longest silences.

We wandered for an hour through the grand old-world gardens, reverently worshipping their many-coloured spring splendour. Flaming masses of azaleas blazed forth from a background of white and mauve rhododendrons; white, grey, and purple lilac squandered their wealth in riotous display, while the Golden Rain flashed in the evening sun, and a scented breeze spread the grass walks with a yellow carpet. We drew a last luxurious deep breath, and turned to watch the nymphæas closing their eyes for the night.

Beyond the water garden, in an orchard deep with fallen apple-blossom, Rawnsley and Gartside were stretched in wicker chairs watching an old spaniel race across the grass in sheer exhilaration of spirit.

"Come and study the Sixth Sense," Gartside called out as we approached.

"There isn't such a thing, but there's no harm in your studying it," said Rawnsley, in a tone that indicated it mattered little what any of us did to improve or debase our minds.

"Martel!" The dog bounded up at Gartside's call, and he showed us two glazed, sightless eyes. "Good dog!" He patted the animal's neck, and Martel raced away to the far end of the orchard. "That dog's as blind as my boot, but he steers himself as though he'd eyes all over his head. By Jove! I thought he'd brained himself that time!"

Martel had raced at top speed to the foot of a gnarled apple tree. At two yards' distance he swerved as though a whip had struck him, and passed into safety. The same thing happened half a dozen times in as many minutes.

"He *knows* it's there," said Gartside. "He's got a sense of distance. If that isn't a sixth sense, what is it?"

"Intensified smell-sense," Rawnsley pronounced. "If *you* were blind, you'd find your smelling and hearing intensified."

"Not enough," said Gartside.

"It's all you'll get. A sense is the perceptiveness of an organ. You've eyes, ears, a nose, a palate, and a number of sensitive surfaces. If you want a sixth sense, you must have a sixth perceive organ. You haven't. Therefore you must be content with seeing, hearing, smelling, tasting, and touching."

Gartside was not satisfied with the narrow category.

"I know a man who can always tell when there's a cat in the room."

"Before or after seeing it?" Rawnsley inquired politely.

"Oh, before. Genuine case. I tested him by locking a cat in the sideboard once when he was coming to dine with me. He complained the moment he got into the room."

"Acute smell-sense," Rawnsley decided.

"You hear of people who can foretell a change in the weather," Gartside went on.

"Usually wrong," said Rawnsley. "When they're right, and it isn't coincidence, you can trace it to the influence of a changed atmosphere on a sensitive part of their body. An old wound, for instance. Acute touch sense."

I happened to catch sight of the Seraph lying on his face piling the fallen apple-blossoms into little heaps.

"What about a sense of futurity?" I asked.

"Did you ever meet the man could spot a Derby winner?" asked Culling, infected by Rawnsley's scepticism.

"Futurity in respect of yourself," I defined. "What's called 'premonition.'"

Rawnsley demolished me with patient weightiness.

"You come down to breakfast with a headache...."

"Owin' to the unwisdom of mixin' your drinks," Culling interposed.

"...Everything's black. In the course of the day you hear a friend's dead. 'Ah!' you say, 'I knew something was going to happen.' What about all those other mornings...."

"Terribly plentiful!" said Culling.

"...When everything's black and nothing happens? It's pure coincidence."

I defined my meaning yet more narrowly.

"I have in mind the premonition of something quite definite."

"For instance?"

I told him of a phenomenon that has frequently come under my observation in the East—the power possessed by many natives of foretelling the exact hour of their death. Quite recently I came across a case in the Troad where I fell in with a young Greek who had been wasting for months with some permanent, indefinable fever. One morning I found him sitting dressed in his library, the temperature was normal and the pulse regular; he seemed in perfect health. I congratulated him on his recovery, and was informed that he would die punctually at eight that evening.

In the course of the day his will was drawn up and signed, the relatives took their farewells, and a priest administered supreme unction. I called again at seven o'clock. He seemed still in perfect health and full possession of his faculties, but repeated his assertion that he would pass away at eight. I told him not to be morbid. At ten minutes to eight he warned me that his time was at hand; after another three minutes he undressed and lay motionless on his bed. At two minutes past eight the heart had ceased to beat.

"Auto-hypnosis," said Rawnsley when I had done. "A long

debilitating illness in which the mind became more and more abnormal and subject to fancies. An idea—from a dream, perhaps—that death will take place at a certain hour. The mind becomes obsessed by that idea until the body is literally done to death. It's no more premonition than if I say I'm going to dine to-night between eight and nine. I've an idea I shall, I shall do my best to make that idea fruitful, and nothing but an unforeseen eventuality will prevent my premonition coming true. Stick to the five senses and three dimensions, Merivale. And now come and dress, or I may not get my dinner after all."

"I think Rawnsley's disposed of premonitions," said the Seraph from the grass. Possibly I was the only one who detected a note of irony in his voice.

We had been given adjoining rooms, and in the course of dressing I had a visit from him with the request that I should tie his tie.

"Choose the other hand next time," I advised him, when I had done my bad best. "Authors and pianists, you know—it's your livelihood."

"It'll be well enough by the time I've anything to write."

"Is your Miserable Child causing trouble?"

Never at that time having been myself guilty of a line of prose or verse, I could only judge of composition by the light of pure reason. To write an entirely imaginative work would be—as the poet said of love—"the devil." An autobiographical novel, I thought, would be like keeping a diary and chopping it into chapters of approximately equal length.

"Have you ever kept a diary a week in advance?" the Seraph asked when I put this view before him.

"Why not wait a week?" I suggested, again in the light of pure reason.

"You'd lose the psychology of expectation—uncertainty."

"I suppose you would," I assented hazily.

"I want to dispose of my premonition on the Rawnsley lines."

"What form does it take?"

His lips parted, and closed again quickly.

"I'll let you know in a week's time," he answered.

Sylvia had not returned when we assembled in the drawing-room, and after waiting long enough to chill the soup and burn the *entrée*, it was decided to start without her. Nothing of that dinner survives in my memory, from which I infer that cooking and conversation were unrelievedly mediocre. With the appearance of the cigars I moved away from Lady Roden's empty chair to the place vacated by Gladys between Philip and the Seraph.

"Thumb hurting you?" I asked.

He looked so white that I thought he must be in pain.

"I'm all right, thanks," he answered. Immediately to belie his words the sudden opening of the door made him jump almost out of his chair. I saw the footman who was handing round the coffee bend down and whisper something to Arthur.

"Sylvia's turned up at last," we were told.

"Did the car break down?" I asked; but Arthur could only say that she had returned twenty minutes before and was changing her dress.

"Has she brought Mavis?" asked Rawnsley.

"The man only said...."

Arthur left the sentence unfinished and turned his head to find Sylvia framed in the open doorway. She had changed into a white silk dress, and was wearing a string of pearls round her slender throat. Posed with one hand to the necklace and the other still holding the handle of the door, she made a picture I shall not easily forget. A study in black and white it was, with the dark hair and eyes thrown into relief by her pale face and light dress.... I must have stared unceremoniously, but my stare was distracted by a numbing grip on my forearm. I found the Seraph making his fingers almost meet through bone and muscle; he had half risen and was gazing at her with parted lips and shining eyes. Then we all rose to our feet as she came into the room.

"The car went all right," she explained, slipping into an empty chair by her father's side. "Please sit down, all of you, or I shall be sorry I came. I'm only here for a minute. Mavis hasn't come, Mr. Rawnsley. Your mother didn't know why she was staying on in town; she ought to have been down last night or first thing this morning. She hadn't wired or anything, so I waited till the six-forty got in, and as she wasn't on that, I came back alone. No, no dinner, thanks. Mrs. Rawnsley gave me some sandwiches."

"I hope there's nothing wrong," I said in the tone that tries to be sympathetic and only succeeds in arousing general misgiving.

Sylvia turned her eyes in my direction, catching sight of the Seraph as she did so.

"I'm so sorry!" she exclaimed, jumping up and walking round to him with that wonderful flashing smile that I once in poetical mood likened to a white rose bursting into flower. "I didn't see you when I came in. Oh, poor child, what have you done to your hand?"

I watched their faces as the Seraph explained; strong emotion on the one, polite conventional sympathy on the other.

"Move up one place, Phil," she commanded when the explanation was ended. "I want to talk to our invalid."

Sylvia's presence kept us lingering long over our cigars, and when at last we reached the drawing-room, it was to find that Gladys had already been packed off to bed with mustard plasters and black currant tea. Life abruptly ceased to have any interest for Philip. I stood about till my host and hostess were established at the bridge table with Culling and Gartside, and then accepted the Seraph's invitation for a stroll on the terrace.

He executed one of the most masterly silences of my experience. Time and again we paced that terrace till the others had retired to bed and a single light in the library shone like a Polyphemus eye out of the face of the darkened house. I pressed for no confidences, knowing that at the fitting season he would feel the need of a confidant and unburden himself to me. That was the most feminine of the Seraph's many feminine characteristics.

It was a wonderfully still, moonlight evening. You would have said he and I were the two last men in the world, and Brandon Court the only house in England—till you rounded the corner of the terrace and found two detectives from Scotland Yard screened by the angle of the house. Since the beginning of the militant outrages, no cabinet minister had been allowed to stir without a bodyguard; through the mists of thirty years I recalled the dynamiter days of my boyhood. In one form or other the militants, like the poor, were always with us.

It was after one when the Seraph stalked moodily through the open library window on his way to bed. Had he been less pre-occupied, he would have seen something that interested me, though I suppose it would have enlightened neither of us.

On a table by the door stood a photograph of Sylvia. I noticed the frame first, then the face, and finally the dress. She had arrayed herself as a Savoyard peasant with short skirt, bare arms and hair braided in two long plaits. It was not a good likeness, because no portrait could do justice to a face that owed its fascination to the fact of never being seen in repose; but it was good enough for me to judge the effect of such a face on a man of impressionable temperament....

I had an admirable night's rest, as I always do. I awoke once or twice, it is true, but dropped off again immediately—almost before I had time to appreciate that the Seraph was pacing to and fro in the adjoining room.

CHAPTER IV
THE FIRST ROUND

"BRASSBOUND: You are not my guest: you are my prisoner.

SIR HOWARD: Prisoner?

BRASSBOUND: I warned you. You should have taken my warning.

SIR HOWARD: ... Am I to understand, then, that you are a brigand? Is this a matter of ransom?

BRASSBOUND: ... All the wealth of England shall not ransom you.

SIR HOWARD: Then what do you expect to gain by this?

BRASSBOUND: Justice...."

—Bernard Shaw
"Captain Brassbound's Conversion."

But for Pat Culling the library was deserted when I entered it the following morning. I found him with a lighted cigarette jauntily placed behind one ear, at work on an illustrated biography of the Seraph. Loose sheets still wet from his quick, prolific pen lay scattered over chairs, tables and floor, and ranged from "The Budding of the Wing" to "The Chariot of Fire." Fra Angelico, as an irreverent pavement artist, was Culling's artistic parent for the time being.

"Merivale! on my soul!" he exclaimed as he caught sight of me. "Returning from church, washed of all his sins and thinkin' what fun it'll be to start again. We want more paper for this."

As a matter of fact I had not been to church, but Philip had kindly arranged for my coffee to be brought me in bed, and I saw no reason for refusing the offer. It was not as if I had work to neglect, and for some years I have found that other people tend to be somewhat irritating in the early morning. When I breakfast alone, I am not in the least fretful, but I believe it to be physiologically true that the facial muscles grow stiff during sleep, and this makes it difficult for many people to be smiling and conversational for the first few hours after waking. So at least I was informed by a medical student who had spent much time studying the subject in his own person.

"Seraph up yet?" I asked.

"Is ut up?" Culling exclaimed in scorn, and I learnt for the first time that the Seraph habitually lived on berries and cold water, slept in a draught, and mortified his flesh with a hair shirt. He had, further, seen the sun rise, wetted his wings in an icy river and escorted Sylvia to the early service.

"I'm glad one of us was there," I said.

"Be glad it wasn't you," answered Culling darkly. "Seraph's in disgrace over something."

The reason, as I heard some time later, was his unwillingness to enter Sylvia's place of worship. The Seraph has devoted considerable time and money to the study of comparative religion, he will analyse any known faith, and when he has traced its constituent parts back to their magical origin, he feels he has done something really worth doing. Sylvia—like most *dévôtes*—could not believe in the existence of a conscientious free-thinker. Why two attractive young people should have bothered their heads over such matters, passes my comprehension. I have always found the man who demolishes a religion only one degree less tiresome than the man who discovers religion for the first time. Most men seem fated to do one or the other—and to tell me all about it.

"Where's she hiding herself now?" I asked.

"Only gone to bring the rest of the family home."

Almost before the words were out of his mouth, the door burst open and admitted Robin and Michael. The Roden boys were all marked with a strong family likeness, thin, lithe, and active, with black hair and brown eyes. Robin had outgrown the age of eccentricity in dress, but Michael persevered with a succession of elaborate colour-schemes. He was dressed that morning in brown shoes, brown socks, a brown suit and brown Homburg hat; even his shirt had a faint brown line, and his handkerchief a brown border. Of a Sphinx-like family, he was the most enigmatic; his leading characteristics were a surprisingly fluent use of the epithet "bloody," and a condition of permanent insolvency. The first reminded me of the great far-off day when I tested the efficacy of that word in presence of my parents; the second was the basis of our too short friendship. Finding a ten-pound note in my pocket, I tossed Michael whether I should give it to him or keep it myself. I forget who won; he certainly had the note.

A leave-out day from Winchester accounted for Michael's presence. Robin had slipped away from Oxford for the nominal purpose of a few days' rest before his Schools, and with the underlying intention of perfecting certain intricate arrangements for celebrating his last Commemoration.

"You'll come, won't you?" he asked as soon as we had been introduced. "House, Bullingdon and Masonic...."

"Who's paying?" asked Michael.

"Guv'nor, I hope."

"*Je* ne *pense pas*," murmured Michael, as he wandered round the library in search of a chair that would fit in with his colour-scheme.

"You come," Robin went on regardless of the interruption. "I've got six tickets for each. You, and Gladys. Two. Phil, three. Me, four...."

"Only one girl so far," Culling interposed. "D'you and Phil dance together? And who has the beads? Some one's got to wear a bead necklace, you aren't admitted without it even in Russia. University dancing costume, I believe it's called."

"Silly ass!" Robin murmured without heat, but Culling was already depicting two nude gladiators struggling in front of the Town Hall for the possession of an exiguous necklace. The Vice-Chancellor and Hebdomadal Council hurried in horror-stricken file down St. Aldates from Carfax.

"You, Gladys, and Phil," continued Robin dispassionately. "Sylvia...."

"Oh, am I coming?" asked Sylvia who had just entered the room, and was unpinning a motor-veil.

"Oh, *yes*, darling Sylvia!" Robin—I know—was both fond and proud of his sister, but the tone of *ad hoc* blandishment suggested that experience had taught him to persuade rather than coerce. "You'll come, if you love me, and bring Mavis," he added with eyes bashfully averted. "Now another man, and a girl for Mr. Merivale."

"Is mother included?" asked Sylvia.

"Not if Mr. Merivale comes," Robin answered in modest triumph. "Who'd you like?" he asked me.

"Keep a spare ticket up your sleeve," I counselled. "Don't lay on any one specially for me, I've seen my best dancing days. In any case I shouldn't last the course three nights running. You'll find me drifting away for a little bridge if I see you're not getting up to mischief."

Robin sucked his pencil meditatively, waved to the Seraph who had just entered the room, and turned to his sister.

"Well, who's it to be?" he asked.

"I don't yet know if I'm coming," Sylvia answered.

"Rot! You must!" said Robin in a tone of mingled firmness and misgiving that suggested memories of previous unsuccessful efforts to hustle his sister. "Think it over," he added more mildly, "but let me know soon, I want the thing fixed up. Whose car, Phil? It's the driving of Jehu, for he driveth furiously."

Philip closed a Blue Book, removed his feet from the back of Culling's chair and strolled to the window. A long green touring car was racing up the drive, cutting all corners.

"The Old Man, by Jove!" he exclaimed.

"Who?"

"Rawnsley. I wonder what he wants."

Michael, who had at last found a brown leather armchair to accord with the day's colour scheme, took on himself to explain the Prime Minister's sudden appearance.

"He's come to fetch that bloody Nigel away," he volunteered. "Praise God with a loud voice. Or else it's a war with Germany."

"Or the offer of a peerage," I suggested pessimistically.

"I much prefer the war with Germany," answered Michael, with the selfishness of youth. "I've no use for honourables, and he'd only be a viscount. 'Gad, I wonder if old Gillingham's handed in his knife and fork! That means the Chancellorship for the guv'nor, and they'll make him an earl, and you'll be Lady Sylvia, my adored sister. How perfectly bloody! I shall emigrate."

We were soon put out of our suspense. The library was in theory the inviolable sanctuary of the Attorney General, and at Philip's suggestion we began to retreat through the open French windows into the garden. The Seraph and I, however, stood at the end of the file and were caught by Arthur and the Prime Minister before we could escape. Rawnsley had forgotten me during my absence abroad, and we had to be introduced afresh.

"Don't go for a moment," said Arthur, as we made another movement towards the window. "You may be able to help us."

I pulled up a chair and watched Rawnsley fumbling for a spectacle-case. He had aged rather painfully since the day I first met him five-and-twenty years before, as President of the Board of Trade, coming to Oxford to address some political club.

"Sheet of paper? A.B.C., Roden?" he demanded in the quick, staccato voice of a man who is always trying to compress three weeks' work into three days. He had his son's ruthless vigour and wilful assurance without any of Nigel's thin-skinned self-consciousness. "Thanks. Now. My daughter's missing, Mr. Merivale. You may be able to help. Do you know her by sight?"

I mentioned the glimpse I had caught of her at the theatre.

"Quite enough. She left Downing Street yesterday morning at a quarter to ten and was to call at her dressmaker's and come down to Hanningford by the eleven-twenty. We've only two decent trains in the day, and if she missed that she was to lunch in town and come by the four-ten. You left at eleven-fifteen, from platform five. The eleven-twenty goes from platform four. May I ask if you saw anything of her before you left?"

I said I had not, and added that I was so busily engaged in meeting old friends and being introduced to new ones that I had had neither time nor eyes....

"Thank you!" he interrupted, turning to the Seraph. "Mr. Aintree, you know my daughter, and Roden tells me you came down by the four-ten yesterday afternoon. The train slips a coach at Longfield, a few miles beyond Hanningford. Did you by any chance see who was travelling by the slip?"

The Seraph was no more helpful than I had been, and Rawnsley shut the A.B.C. with an impatient slap.

"We must try in other directions, then," he said. "She never left London."

"Have you tried the dressmaker's?" I asked.

"Arrived ten, left ten-forty," said Rawnsley.

"Are any of her friends ill?" I asked. "Is she likely to have been called away suddenly?"

"Oh, I know why she's disappeared," Rawnsley answered. "This letter makes that quite plain. I want to find where it took place—with a view to tracing her."

He threw me over a typewritten letter, with the words, "Received by first delivery to-day, posted in the late fee box of the South-Western District Office at Victoria."

The letter, so far as I remember it, ran as follows:

"DEAR SIR,
    "This is to inform you that your daughter is well and in safe keeping, but that she is being held as a hostage pending the satisfactory settlement of the Suffrage Question. As you

are aware, Sir George Marklake has secured second place in the ballot for Private Member's Bills. Your daughter will be permitted to communicate with you by post, subject to reasonable censorship; on the day when you promise special facilities and Government support for the Marklake Bill, and again at the end of the Report Stage and Third Reading. The same privilege will be accorded at the end of each stage in the House of Lords, and she will be restored to you on the day following that on which the Bill receives the Royal Assent.

"You will hardly need to be reminded that the Marklake Bill is to be taken on the first Private Member's night after the Recess. Should you fail to give the assurances we require, it will be necessary for us to take such further steps as may seem best calculated to secure the settlement we desire."

It took me some minutes to digest the letter before I was in a condition to offer even the most perfunctory condolence. Now that the blow had been struck, I found myself wondering why it had never been attempted before.

"You've no clue?" I asked.

Rawnsley inspected the letter carefully and held it up to the light.

"Written with a Remington, I should say. And a new one, without a single defect in type or alignment. And the paper is made by Hitchcock. That's all I have to go on."

"What are you going to do?"

"Advise Scotland Yard, I suppose. Then await developments. I don't wish what I've told you this morning to go any further; no good purpose will be served by giving the militants a free advertisement. When I am in town, it is to be understood that Mavis is with her mother at Hanningford; and when I am at Hanningford, Mavis must be at Downing Street."

One has no business in private life to badger ministers with political questions, but I could not help asking what line Rawnsley proposed to take with the Marklake Bill. His grey eyes flashed with momentary fire.

"It won't be taken this session," he declared. "I'm moving to appropriate all Private Members' time for the Poor Law Bill. And that's all, I think; I must be getting back to my wife, she's—a good deal upset. Can you spare Nigel, Roden? I should like to take him if I may. Good-bye, Mr. Merivale. Good-bye, Mr. — Oh, by the way, Roden, remember you're tarred with the same brush. As soon as the Recess is over, you'll have to keep a close watch on your family. Harding's another; I shall have to warn him."

Rawnsley's departure left me with a feeling of anti-climax and vague discomfort. Short of assassination, which would have defeated its own object, a policy of abduction was the boldest and most effective that the militants could devise at a time when—in Joyce's words—all arguments had been exhausted on both sides and war *à outrance* was declared by women who insisted on a vote against men who refused to concede it. I had every reason to think I knew whose brain had evolved that abduction policy; its reckless simplicity and directness were character-istic. Then and now I wondered, and still wonder, whether the author of that policy had sufficient imagination and perspective to appreciate the enormity of her offence, or the seriousness of the penalty attendant on non-success.

"Ber-luddy day!" exclaimed Michael, rejoining us in the library and delicately brushing occasional drops of moisture from his immaculate person. A heavy downpour of rain was starting, and though I looked like being spared initiation into the mysteries of golf—which I am not yet infirm enough to learn—it was not very clear how we were to kill time between meal and meal. Gladys was spending the morning quietly in her room, Philip wandered to and fro like a troubled spirit, and Sylvia had mysteriously departed.

In time Michael condescended to give us the reason. It appeared that while we were closeted with Rawnsley in the library, Robin had decided that rest and relaxation before his Schools could best be secured by the organisation of an impromptu Calico Ball, to be given that night to all who would come. While he sat at the telephone summoning the County of Hampshire to do his bidding, Sylvia had departed in her little white runabout to purchase masks and a bale of calico from Brandon Junction, and scour the neighbourhood in search of piano, violin, and 'cello. The wet afternoon was to be spent by the women of the party in improvising costumes, by the men in French-chalking the floor of the ball-room.

I took the precaution of calling on Gladys to acquaint her with the day's arrangements, and beg her to see that I was not compelled to wear any costume belittling to the dignity of a middle-aged uncle. Then after writing a bulletin to catch my brother at Gibraltar, I felt I had earned rest and a cheroot before luncheon. Brandon Court was one of those admirably appointed houses where you could be certain of finding wooden matches in every room; it was not, however, till I got back to the library that I found companionship and the Seraph. He was lying on a sofa writing slowly and painfully with his left hand.

"If that's volume three," I said, "I won't interrupt. If it's anything else, we'd better smoke and talk. I will do the smoking."

"I'm only scribbling," he answered. "There's no hurry about volume three."

"Your public—*quorum pars non magna sum*—is growing impatient."

"There won't be any volume three," he said quietly.

"But why not? I mean, a mere temporary hitch...."

"It's not that. If it wasn't for this hand I could write like, well, like you *do* write once in a lifetime."

"What's to stop you?"

"Nothing. I only said there wouldn't be a volume three. I shan't publish it."

"Why not?"

His big blue eyes looked up at me thoughtfully for a moment

from under their long lashes. Then he crumpled up the half-covered sheet of paper, remarking—

"There are some things you can't make public."

"But with a *nom de plume*...."

"I might let *you* see it," he conceded.

There we had to leave the subject, as the library was soon afterwards invaded by zealous seekers after luncheon, first Lady Roden and Gartside, then the rest of the party with the single exception of Sylvia. Lady Roden walked over to the window and gazed in dismay at the unceasing downpour.

"Is Sylvia back yet, does anybody know?" she asked.

"She came in about a quarter of an hour ago," volunteered the Seraph.

"Was she very wet?"

"I didn't see her."

Lady Roden bustled out of the room to make first-hand investigation.

"She took a Burberry with her," Robin called out; then springing up he seized an ebony paper knife and advanced on Michael who was reclining decoratively on a Chesterfield sofa. "Talking of Burberries," he went on, with menace in his tone, "what the deuce d'you mean by stealing mine, Michael?"

"Wouldn't be seen dead in your bloody Burberry," Michael responded with delicate languor.

The Roden boys were all much of a size, and on the subject of raided and disputed garments a fierce border warfare raged unintermittently round their bedroom doors. It was so invariable a rule with Michael to meet all direct charges with an equally direct denial that his brothers placed but slight reliance on his word.

"What was it doing in your room, then?" persisted Robin, as he applied the paper-knife to the soles of Michael's feet.

"That was Phil's," said Michael ingenuously.

Robin turned to his elder brother with the suggestion of a

little disciplinary boiling-oil.

"It'll be enough if we just ruffle him," answered the humane Philip. "Keep the door, Pat. Now, Robin!"

The perfect harmony of their attack argued long practice. Almost before I had time to move out of the way, Culling was standing with his back to the door while a scuffling trio on the hearthrug indicated that castigation was already being meted out. Within two minutes the immaculate Michael had been reduced to slim, white nudity, and even as the decorous Gartside proffered a consolatory "*Times'* Educational Supplement," the two brothers and Culling had divided the raiment and taken their centrifugal course through the house, secreting boots, socks, tie and collar in a succession of ingeniously inaccessible places as they went. Then the gong sounded, and Gartside took me in to luncheon.

Such little breezes, as I afterwards discovered, were characteristic of Brandon Court when the three brothers were at home and Philip had forgotten his public dignity. I could have spared the present outbreak, as the inflammatory word "Burberry" had kept me from putting a certain question to the Seraph. At one-thirty he had told Lady Roden that Sylvia had come in about a quarter of an hour before: to be strictly accurate, she had entered the yard as the stable clock struck one-fifteen, and had come into the house three minutes later by a side door and gone straight to her room by a side staircase. The Seraph and I had been sitting in the library since twelve-forty-five. The library looked out over a terrace on to the lawn: stable yard, side door and side staircase were at the diametrically opposite angle of the house. It was impossible for any one, even with the Seraph's uncannily acute senses, to hear a sound from the stable yard; even had it been possible, he could not have identified it as the sound of Sylvia's return.

I put my question in the smoking-room after luncheon, but got no satisfactory answer. Meeting Sylvia in the hall a few minutes later, I took my revenge by setting her to find out.

The afternoon was spent in polishing the ball-room floor. Others worked, I offered advice. At one point, Michael, too, showed a tendency to offer advice, but the threat that his young body would be dragged up and down till the bones cut through the skin and scratched the floor, was effectual in persuading him to swathe his feet in towels and wade through uncharted seas of French chalk to the infinite detriment of the blue colour-scheme he had been forced into adopting for luncheon.

Mrs. Roden, Sylvia and Gladys retired with their three maids and a bale of calico. From time to time one of us would be summoned to have our measurements taken, but no indication was manifested of the guise in which we were to appear. At eight we retired to our rooms with sinking hearts; at eight-thirty a group of sheepish men loitered at the stair-head, waiting for one less self-conscious than the rest to give a lead to the others.

The ball—when it came and found us filled and reckless with dinner—proved an unqualified success. My indistinct memory of it recalls a number of pretty girls who danced well, talked very quickly, and called me—without exception—"my dear." I sat out two with Sylvia, and was cut three times by Gladys, who disappeared with Philip at an early stage. Further, I supped twice with two creditably hungry girls, discussed the lineage of the county with Lady Roden, and smoked a sympathetic cigarette with a nice-looking shy boy of fifteen, who was always being cut by Gladys when he was not being cut by some one else. His name was Willoughby, and I hope some girl has smiled on him less absent-mindedly than my niece.

In my few spare moments I watched Sylvia dealing with her male guests. Culling approached and was rewarded with a smile and one dance. Gartside followed and received an even sweeter, Tristan-und-Isolde smile, and the same proportion of her programme. The Seraph, arm-in-sling, hung unostentatiously on the outskirts of the crowd, and with much hesitation summoned courage to ask if she could spare him one to sit out. She gave him two, and extended it later to three.

I heard afterwards that at the end of the third he prepared to return to the ball-room.

"Who are you taking this one with?" she asked him.

"No one," he told her.

"Why not stay here, then?"

"Haven't you promised it to young Willoughby?"

"He'll survive the disappointment," said Sylvia lightly.

The Seraph shook his head. "May I have one later?" he asked. "You oughtn't to cut Willoughby, he's been looking forward to it."

Sylvia was not accustomed or inclined to dictation from others.

"Have you asked him?" she said, uncertain whether to be amused or angry.

"It wasn't necessary. Haven't you felt his eyes on you while you were dancing? He thinks you're the most wonderful girl in the world. There he's right. He'll treasure up every word you speak, every smile you give him; he'll send himself to sleep picturing ways of saving your life at the cost of his own. And he'll dream of you all night."

The Seraph's tranquil, unemotional voice had grown so earnest that Sylvia found herself growing serious in spite of herself.

"I wish you wouldn't discuss me with boys like that," she said, more to gain time than administer reproof.

"Should I have discussed you?" exclaimed the Seraph. "And would he have told me? Why can't you, why can't any girl understand the mind of a boy of fifteen? You'd make such men of them if you'd only take the trouble. Look at him now, he's thinking out wonderful speeches to make to you...."

"I *hope* not," said Sylvia ruefully.

"He'll forget them all when he meets you. I was fifteen once."

"I wonder if you'll ever be more."

The Seraph made no answer.

"That wasn't meant for a snub," said Sylvia reassuringly.

"I know that."

Sylvia looked at him curiously. "Is there anything you *don't* know?" she asked as they descended the stairs to the ball-room.

"I don't even know if you're going to let me take you in to supper."

"I'm glad there's something."

"That's not an answer."

"Do you want to?"

"You ought to know that without asking."

"I'm afraid there's a great deal about you I *don't* know."

Supper was ended and their table deserted before Sylvia put the question with which I had primed her that afternoon.

"Is there anything I *don't* know? to use your own words," said the Seraph evasively.

"That's not an answer, to use yours."

"It's the only answer I can give," he replied, with that curious expression in his dark eyes that did duty for a smile.

"Why won't you tell me? I'm interested. It's about myself, so I've a right to know."

"But I can't explain; I don't know. It never happened before."

"Never?"

The Seraph thought over his first meeting with her the previous day.

"Never with any one else," he answered.

Sylvia shook her head in perplexity.

"I don't understand," she said. "Either it was just coincidence and you were talking without thinking, or else ... I don't know. It's rather funny. D'you want to smoke? Let's go out on to the terrace."

"The detectives are there."

"No, father said they weren't to appear to-night."

"They're out there."

"How d'you know?"

"I can hear them."

Sylvia looked round at the closed plate-glass windows.

"You *can't*," she said incredulously.

"Will you bet? No, I don't want to rob you. Shall I tell you something else? You opened a fresh bottle of scent to-night when you dressed for dinner. It's Chaminade, the same kind that you were using before, but this is fresher. Had you noticed it?"

The Seraph was considerably less impressed by his powers than Sylvia appeared to be.

"Anything else?" she asked after a pause.

The Seraph wrinkled his brows in thought.

"Gladys Merivale was coughing last night," he said. "Some one passed my door at two o'clock and went into her room. I don't know who it was, but it wasn't you. The coughing stopped for a time, but started again just before three. Then you passed by and went in."

"How do you know?"

"I heard you."

"You may have heard some one; you didn't know it was me. I went once and mother went once. You couldn't tell which was which."

The Seraph lit a cigarette and walked with her to the door of the supper-room.

"Oh, it was your mother?" he said. "Then she went the first time."

"But how do you know?" Sylvia repeated.

"I can't explain, any more than about the car coming back this morning."

Sylvia shook her head a little uneasily.

"You're abnormal," she pronounced.

"Because I...?"

"Go on."

"Because I know a fraction more about you than other people?"

"Do you?"

"Only a fraction. It would take time to understand you."

"How much? I hate to be thought a sphinx."

"However little I wanted, we should be parted before I got it."

"Why? How? How parted?"

The Seraph shrugged his shoulders.

"Don't ask me to read the future," he said with a sigh.

At the end of the ball I found the Roden boys congratulating themselves on the success of the evening. I added my quota of praise, and was pressed to state if I now felt equal to three successive nights at Commemoration.

"Which reminds me!" Robin exclaimed, flying off at his usual tangent. "Where's Sylvia? Sylvia, my angel, what about Commem.?"

His sister looked tired but happy, and in some way excited.

"I'll come if you want me," she answered, putting her arm round Robin's neck and kissing him good-night. "Yes, all right—I will. Oh, Mr. Rawnsley told me this morning that Mavis wouldn't be able to come, so you must get another girl."

Robin dropped his voice confidentially.

"See if you can persuade Cynthia to come. And we're still a man short."

Sylvia looked slowly round the room with thoughtful, unsmiling eyes—past Culling, past Gartside....

"Will you come, Seraph?" she asked.

Less than a day and a half had passed since I had noticed her practice of avoiding Christian names. For some reason I had supposed nicknames to fall into the same category.

CHAPTER V
COMMEMORATION

"Oxford ... the seat of one of the most ancient and celebrated universities in Europe, is situated amid picturesque
environs at the confluence of the Cherwell and the Thames....
Oxford is on the whole more attractive than Cambridge to
the ordinary visitor.... The best time for a visit is the end of
the Summer term.... This period of mingled work and play
(the latter predominating) is named *Commemoration*.... It is
almost needless to add that an introduction to a 'Don' will
greatly add to the visitor's pleasure and profit."
—Karl Baedecker
"Handbook for Travellers: Great Britain."

Of the weeks that passed between my return to London from
Brandon Court and our departure from London to Oxford, I
have only the most indistinct recollection. My engagement
book earned many honourable scars before I carried it away
into my present exile, but for May and the first half of June
there appears a black, undecipherable smudge that my memory
tells me should represent a long succession of late nights and
crowded days. Individual items are blurred out of recogni-
tion; my general sense of the period is that I pretended to be
preternaturally young, and was punished by being made to feel
prematurely old.

It was the busiest part of the London season, and Gladys
appeared to receive cards for an average of three balls a night on
five nights of the week. I accompanied her everywhere, growing
gradually broken to the work and relieved of my more serious
responsibilities by the fact that Philip Roden was too busy at the
House to waste his nights in a ball-room. We seemed to move in
the midst of a stage army, the same few hundred men, women,
and dowagers reappearing in an endless march-past. With the

advent of the big hotels, hospitality had changed in character since the days when I counted myself a Londoner: there was more of it and it was less hospitable. The rising generation, and more particularly the female portion of it, seemed to have taken matters into its own hands.

Regularly each morning, after a late breakfast, Gladys would set me to write a series of common-form letters: "Dear Mr. Blank," I would say, "My niece and I shall be so pleased if you will dine with us here to-night at 8.30 and go on to Lady Anonym's ball." Then Gladys would bring unknowing guest and unknown hostess into communication. "Can I speak to Lady Anonym?" I would hear her call down the telephone. "Oh, good morning! I say, do you think you could *possibly* do with another man for your ball to-night? Honest? It *is* sweet of you. Oh, quite a nice thing—Mr. Incognito Blank, 101, Utopia Chambers, St. James. Thanks, most awfully. Oh no, not *him*, he's the most awful stiff; this is a dear thing. Well, I would have, only he's only just got back to England, he's been shooting big game...."

This was the retail method. In the case of intimate friends, Gladys would be encouraged to send in her own list of desirable invitees. Because I am old-fashioned and unacquainted with English ways, I trust I am not inaccessible to new ideas. I would carry the policy of promiscuity to its logical conclusion. An announcement in the *Times* with draft *ménu*, name of band and programme of music—even a placard outside Claridge's— would save endless postage and stationery, and could not pack the ball-room tighter than on a dozen occasions I remember. Hostesses who believe that numbers are the soul of hospitality, could be certain beforehand of the success of their efforts; superior young men would continue to remark, "Society gettin' very mixed, what?" exactly as they have done ever since I entered my first ball-room at the age of seventeen. Everybody, in short, would be pleased.

We saw a good deal of Sylvia during those weeks, as for

reasons of her own she would frequently drop in at Pont Street and conduct her share of the arrangements over our telephone. Occasionally Gladys would be called in as an accomplice, I would hear "Mr. Aintree's" name added to Lady Anonym's list, and Gladys would remark with fine carelessness, "Oh, just send him the card, if you will; don't bother to say who it comes from." The Seraph may have suspected, but he never had documentary proof of the originating cause of some of his invitations.

In making our arrangements for Commemoration, I decided to take the greater part of my charges to Oxford by road. Robin, of course, was still in residence, and Philip promised to come down by the first possible train. Gladys, Sylvia, the Seraph, and a *pis-aller* of Robin's named Cynthia Bargrave constituted my flock; we motored quietly down to Henley, where we lunched and chartered a houseboat for the Regatta, and arrived in Oxford with ample time for the three girls to have a comfortable rest before dinner. I made rather a point of this, as they were going to have three very tiring days and would naturally wish to look their best; moreover, I wanted to roam round the town with the Seraph.

Even Oxford, that I thought could never alter, had changed during my years of absence. The little, nameless back-street colleges I would gladly sacrifice to the Destroyer, for they serve no purpose beyond that of breeding proctors, and I know we counted it an indignity to be fined by the scion of a college we had to reach by cab. But the High should have been inviolate; there wanted no new colleges breaking through its immemorial sides.... Univ. men, standing at their lodge gate and looking northward, have told me the High already contains one college in excess.

While the Seraph sought out Robin's rooms in Canterbury, I wandered through the college—guiltily, I admit—looking for traces of a popular outbreak that occurred when a ball took place at Blenheim and House men asked in vain for leave to attend it. In time I came to my own old rooms in Tom, and gazed rather in sorrow than anger at the strange new name painted over the door. Twice my fingers went to the handle, twice I told myself that "Mr. R.F. Davenant" had as much right to privacy as I should have claimed in his place.... I wandered out through Tom Gate, across St. Aldates, and down Brewer Street to those pleasant digs in Micklem Hall, where I once spent an all-too-short twelve months. Then I returned to college, crept furtively back to the old familiar door, knocked, listened, entered....

"R.F. Davenant" was far more civil than I should have been at a like intrusion. He showed me round the rooms, offered me whisky and cigarettes, wanted to know when I had been up, whether I was going to the Gaudy.... We were friends in a minute. I liked his fair, neatly-parted hair and clean, fresh colouring; I liked his Meissonier artist proofs; I liked the way the left back leg of the sofa collapsed unless you underpinned it with a Liddle and Scott. Not a thing was changed but the photographs on the mantelpiece. I walked over and surveyed them critically. Then one of those things happened that convince me an idle Quixotic Providence is watching over my least movements: I was staring at the picture of a girl on horseback when he volunteered the information that it was his sister.

"Your married sister?" I suggested.

"Do you know her?"

He fed me on Common-room tea and quarter-pound wedges of walnut cake. Joyce was coming up for two of the three balls I was attending, coming unprovided with partners to chaperone some girl who had captured her brother's wandering fancy. These elder sisters earn more crowns than they are ever accorded; it seemed that Joyce who trampled on the world would stretch herself out to be trampled on by her heedless only brother. I wonder wherein the secret lies.

"Come and dine," suggested Dick Davenant.

I told him of my own party, and lost no time in working the

Cumberland days with his father for all they were worth. What happened to the Seraph I never discovered. As I hurried back to the Randolph for dinner, Robin met me with an apology in advance for the dull evening before me.

"'Fraid you'll have rather a rotten time," he opined. "I wish you had let me find you some old snag or other."

"I shall be all right, Robin," I said.

"There's sure to be bridge *somewhere*. Or look here, what about a roulette-board? Combine business with pleasure—what?"

"I shall be able to amuse myself," I assured him.

Our dinner that night was one of the gayest meals I have eaten; we were all expectant, excited, above our usual form—with the single exception of Philip. If I were a woman, I suppose I should notice these things; as it was I put his silent preoccupation down to overwork. When he approached Robin with other-world gentleness and suggested a stroll up St. Giles after dinner "just to keep me company, old boy," I ought to have suspected something; but it was not till the Seraph, smoking a lonely cigar, murmured something about "*Consul videat ne respublica detrimentum capiat*," that I saw my authority over Gladys was being threatened.

The girls had been despatched for their last mysterious finishing touches, and we had the hall of the Randolph to ourselves.

"What the deuce ought I to do, Seraph?" I asked.

"What *can* you do?"

"I don't know."

"Why do anything?"

That is the question I always ask myself when I have no definite idea what is expected of me.

"I wish he'd had the consideration to wait till my brother came back," I grumbled.

"These little emotional crises never *do* wait till we're ready for them, do they?"

"From the fulness of the heart...."

"Oh, pardon me, I was not speaking of myself."

"I thought you were."

The Seraph shook his head at me.

"No, you didn't. You aren't thinking of me, or Gladys, or Philip, or any one but your own self."

I hypnotised a waiter into taking my order for Benedictine.

"No emotional crises have come *my* way," I protested.

"Something very curious has happened to you since we parted this afternoon."

I accounted for every moment of my time since our arrival in Oxford.

"Why didn't you tell me that before?" he exclaimed when I mentioned my chance meeting with Dick Davenant. "Joyce coming up for the ball? Will you...? No! sorry."

"Will I what?"

"It's no business of mine."

"Why d'you start talking about it, then? Will I what?"

The Seraph knocked the ash off his cigar, finished his coffee, and sat silent. I repeated my question.

"Well...." he hesitated nervously. "Are you going to propose to her to-night?"

"Really, Seraph!"

"You're going to—some time or other...."

"Don't talk nonsense!"

"...I was wondering if it would be to-night."

I felt myself growing rather annoyed and uncomfortable.

"Not very good form to talk like this," I said stiffly. "After all, she's a friend of yours and mine. A joke's all very well...."

"But I'm quite serious!"

"My dear Seraph, d'you appreciate that I've met the girl once—a few weeks ago—and once only since she was a child of five?"

"Oh yes. And do you remember my telling you what was bringing you back to England? Do you remember the impression she made on you that night? If you're going to marry her...."

"Seraph, drop it!"

He withdrew into his shell, and we smoked without speaking until I began to be sorry for snubbing him.

"I didn't mean to be rude," I said apologetically. "But she's a nice girl; I may see her to-night for all I know to the contrary, and this coupling of names.... You see my point?"

The Seraph suddenly developed a nervous, excited earnestness.

"Let me give you a word of advice. If you're going to propose to her—oh, all right; if X. is going to propose to her, he'd better do it now—before the crash comes. There's going to be a very big crash; she's going down under it. If you—if X. proposed now, she might be got out of the way before it's too late. You—X. won't like to see the woman he's going to marry...."

"X. marries her then?" I asked in polite incredulity. "Oh, he should certainly lose no time."

"She may not accept you at once."

"Come and get your coat, Seraph."

"But she will later."

"Come and get your coat," I repeated.

"Ah—you don't believe me—well...."

I gave him my two hands and pulled him out of his chair.

"Can you foretell the future?" I asked with a scepticism worthy of Nigel Rawnsley. "What time shall I breakfast to-morrow? What shall I have for supper to-night? What tie shall I wear next Friday fortnight?"

The Seraph shook his head without answering.

"Very well, then," I said decisively.

"But you don't know either."

Of course he was right.

"I may not know *now*," I said, "but I shall make up my mind in due course, and do whatever I've made up my mind to do—whether it's choosing a tie or...."

"Proposing to Joyce. Exactly. I've never pretended to tell you more than what's in your own mind."

"You talked about the woman X. was going to *marry*, not merely propose to. The last word doesn't lie with X."

"True. But if I know what's passing in Joyce's mind?"

"Does she know herself?"

"No! That's the wonderful thing about a woman's mind, it's so disconnected. She's none of a man's faculty of taking a resolve, seeing it, acting on it.... That's why I said she might not accept you at once."

"You know her mind better than she does?"

As my interest rose, the Seraph became studiedly vague.

"I know nothing," he answered. "I merely suggest the possibility that a woman may form a subconscious resolution and not recognise it as part of her mental stock-in-trade for weeks, months, years.... If you wait for her to recognise it, you may find you come too late; if you come before she recognises it, you may find you've come too early."

I helped him into his coat as the three girls descended the stairs.

"Not a very cheerful prospect for X.," I suggested.

"X. had better help her to recognise her sub-conscious ideas," he answered.

I felt a boy of twenty as we drove down St. Aldates, hurried across Tom Quad, shed our wraps and struggled into the hall. The place was half full already, and the orchestra, with every instrument duplicated and Lorino thundering away at a double grand, had started an opening extra. Youthful stewards, their shirt-fronts crossed with blue and white ribbons of office, hurried to and fro in excessive, callow zeal; bright among the black coats shone the full regimentals of the Bullingdon; while stray followers of Pytchley, Bicester and V.W.H. contributed their colour to the rainbow blaze.

My charges dutifully spilt a drop from their cups in my honour, but at the end of an hour they were free to follow their own various inclinations. There was no sign of Joyce in the ball-room, but I found her at length by the stair-head, gratefully drinking in the fresh air, flushed—or so I fancied—and occasionally passing a hand across eyes that looked tired and strained. I gave her some champagne and led her to her brother's room. Two armchairs that I had purchased in the luxury-loving twenties seemed somehow to have withstood seven undergraduate generations.

"You were quite the last person I expected to find here," I said, after telling her of my meeting with Dick.

"I was quite the last person a lot of people expected to find here," she answered.

"Dick has a lot to be thankful for. So—for that matter—have others."

"Dear old Dick! he has a lot to put up with, if that's what you mean. If he hadn't been a steward, they wouldn't have admitted me. Oh, the staring and the glaring and the pointing and the whispering!"

I now appreciated the reason of the bright eyes and pink cheeks.

"If you *will* espouse unpopular political causes," I began.

"I'm not complaining! *This* was nothing to what I've been through in the past. It's all in the day's work. What are you doing in Oxford?"

I helped myself to one of Dick's cigarettes. He kept them just where I used to keep mine. On second thoughts I put it back and ran my hand along the under-side of the mantelpiece to the hidden shelf where I used to keep cigars maturing. Dick had followed my admirable precedent. I commandeered a promising Intimidad, feeling all the while like the ghost of my twenty-year-old self revisiting the haunts of my affection.

"At the moment I met you, I was feeling very old and miserable," I said, when I had told her of the party committed to my charge. "Time was when I counted for something in this place, porters touched their hats to me, I could be certain of an apple in the back of the neck as I walked through the Quad. Now the hall is filled with young kings who know not Joseph. There are not twelve men or maidens who recognise me."

"Perhaps they don't know you."

"That," I said, "is not very helpful."

"I'm sorry. There are about two hundred people in that hall who know me, but only four recognised me. You were one. I'm grateful."

"But what did you expect?"

"I wasn't sure. You came with the enemy."

It was time for me to define my attitude of political isolation. I told her—what was no more than the truth—that I owed no allegiance to king, country, church, or party. I have never been interested in politics, and twenty years' absence from England have made me nothing if not a citizen of the world. I cared nothing for the great franchise question, it was a matter of indifference to me whether the vote was granted or withheld. On the other hand, I have a great love of peace and comfort, and resent any effort to force me into a position of hostility.

"You won't convert me, Joyce," I said. "No more will the Rodens. I refuse to mix myself up in the miserable business. Friends and enemies, indeed! I have no enemies, but as a friend I wish I could persuade you to accept the *fait accompli*. You're up against *force majeure*, you'll have to give in sooner or later. Why not sooner?"

"Why give up at all?"

"You're striking at an immovable body."

"What happens when an irresistible force meets an immovable body?"

"Is it an irresistible force?"

"Have you seen Mavis Rawnsley the last few weeks?"

The question was asked with fearless, impudent abruptness.

"I don't know her to speak to," I said. "You remember we caught sight of her that night the Seraph took us to the theatre."

"The night I undertook to convert the idlest man in the northern hemisphere? Yes."

"The night that same idler undertook to re-convert you. I've not seen her since."

"Has her father?"

"You must ask him."

"I will. In fact, I have already. 'Where is Miss Rawnsley? A rumour reaches us as we are going to press....' You'll find it all in this week's *New Militant*, I had such fun writing it."

"What was the rumour?"

"We—ell!" Joyce put her head on one side and pretended to spur her memory. "Some one said Mavis Rawnsley had disappeared. Nothing in that, of course; *you*'ve disappeared before now. Then some one else said she was being held to ransom till her father was converted to the suffrage. That interested me. None of the papers said anything about it; you'd have thought Mr. Rawnsley was making a mystery of it. However, I wanted to know, so I'm asking the question in the leading article. Perhaps he'll write and tell me. Do you love me enough to give me a match?"

I lit her cigarette and talked to her for her soul's good.

"As I say, my law's pretty rusty," I told her in conclusion, "but you may take it as quite certain that the penalty for abduction is rather severe."

"Brutally," Joyce assented with unabated cheerfulness. "But you've got to catch your criminal before you can imprison him."

"Or her."

"And you can't catch without evidence."

I wandered round the room in search of two cushions. I found only one, but women do not need cushions to the same extent as men.

"That's the most banal remark I've ever heard from you," I told her. "There never was a criminal yet that didn't think he'd left no traces, never one that didn't think he was equal to the strain of sitting waiting to be arrested. They all end in the same way, get frightened or become reckless—"

"Which am I?"

"Neither as yet. You'll become reckless, because I don't think you know what fear means."

"Reckless! Me reckless! If I have a glass roof put to the editorial room of the *New Militant*, will you climb up and see my moderating influence at work? If it hadn't been for me, we should have been prosecuted over the first number."

"I suppose that's Mrs. Millington?" I hazarded. An echo of her fiery pamphlets and speeches had reached me during the heyday of the arson and sabotage campaign.

"What's in a name?" Joyce asked sweetly.

"Nothing at all. I agree. You tell me there's *some one* who has to be restrained. I tell you you'll be arrested the day after your restraining influence is withdrawn...."

Joyce bowed her assent.

"And that will happen when you're invalided home from the front."

Joyce bowed again. "Me that never had a day's illness in my life," I heard her murmur.

"It'll be a new experience, and you'll have it very shortly if I know anything of what a woman looks like when she's over-worked, over-worried, over-excited. However fit you may be in other ways, you're man's inferior in physical stamina. For the ordinary fatigues of life...."

"But this wasn't!" The interruption came quickly in a tone that had lost its early banter. "Elsie's case comes on at the end of this week. I've been with her, I didn't want to come to-night, but she made me—so as not to disappoint Dick. It's not very pleasant to sit watching any one going through.... However, don't let's talk about it. You were giving me good advice. I love good advice. It's cheap...."

"And so very filling? I'll give no more."

"Don't stop, it's a wonderful index. As long as people give me good advice, I know I need never trouble to ask them for anything more."

I weighed the remark rather deliberately.

"You were nearer being spiteful then than I've ever heard you," I said.

"But wasn't it true? The only three people I can depend on not to give me good advice are Elsie, Dick and the Seraph."

"The only three who'll give you anything more?"

"Among the non-politicals. I've got politicals who'd go through fire and water for me," she declared proudly.

"I can believe it. But only those three among the rest?"

"Those three." She sat looking me in the eyes for a moment, then a mischievous smile of commiseration broke over her face. "My friend, you're not suggesting *yourself*?"

"I'm waiting to be asked."

"It would be waste of time. You've not been living your own sinful selfish life all these years for nothing. If a crash ever came—it's kindly meant, but I should have to put you under instruction for six months before I could be certain of you."

"You won't get six months."

"Then it's hardly worth starting, is it? In any case we shall win without needing to call in outside help. What about getting back to the ball-room?"

I exhibited my unfinished cigar.

"When you're tired of oakum and a plank bed," I began....

"Caught, tried *and* condemned. If you want to be useful, you musn't leave it as late as that."

"The sooner the better."

"I'll come as soon as there's a warrant out."

"Promise?"

"Faithfully. But there won't be any warrant if the cause succeeds."

"I pray you'll fail," was my fervent answer.

Joyce threw her cigarette petulantly into the fireplace.

"You've spoilt *every*thing by that!"

"My help was offered to you, not to your ridiculous cause."

"We can't be separated."

"Will you bet?"

"Yes."

"What?"

"Anything you like!"

She sprang up and faced me with the light of battle in her eyes. The flush had come back to her cheeks, her lips were parted, and the rope of pearls round her neck rose and fell with her quick, excited breathing. I shall not easily forget the picture she presented at that moment. The room was lit by a single central globe, and against the background of dark oak panels her black dress was almost invisible. Standing outside the white circle of light, her slim fragile body was hidden, but through the shadows I could see the shimmer of her spun gold hair and the wonderful line of her gleaming white arms and shoulders.

"Anything you like!" she repeated in confident gay challenge.

"I hold you to that."

Fifteen years ago I bought a scarab-ring in Luxor. After losing it once a day for a fortnight, I had it fitted with ingenious couplings so designed that when I caught it in a glove the couplings drew tight and clamped the ring to the finger. When last I found myself in Egypt, my Arab goldsmith had been gathered to his fathers, and the secret of those couplings is vested in myself. Three London and two Parisian jewellers have told me they could unravel the mystery by cutting the ring to pieces. Short of that, they confessed themselves baffled.

"Hold out your hand, Joyce," I said. "No, the other one.

There!"

I slipped the ring on to her third finger, stepped back to the table, and lit a cigarette. This last was purely for effect.

Joyce looked at the ring and tried to move it.

"No good," I said. "You may cut the ring, which would be a pity because it's unique; and it's not yours till you've won the wager. Or you may amputate the finger, which also would be a pity, as that too ... well, anyway, it won't be yours to amputate if I win the bet."

Again she tried to move the ring, again without success.

"Will you take it off, please?"

I shook my head.

"You said I might fix the wager."

"Take it off, please!" she repeated, frowning disapproval upon me. Unfortunately, like Mrs. Hilary Musgrave, she looks uncommonly well when she disapproves.

"Shall we go back now?" I suggested. "I've finished my cigar."

"A joke may be carried too far," she exclaimed, stamping her foot as I remember seeing her stamp it as a wicked, flaxen-haired child of five.

"Heaven witness I'm not joking!" I protested. "Nothing I could say would move you in your present frame of mind; the wager gave me my chance. It's a ring against a hand, and on the day that sees you separated from your infernal cause, I come to claim my reward. As long as you and the cause remain unseparated you may keep the ring. I'm backing my luck; I always do, and it never fails me."

Joyce gave the ring a last despairing tug, and then with some difficulty drew the finger of her glove over it.

"How long must I wait before I may have the ring cut?" she asked.

I had not considered that.

"Till my death?" I suggested.

"Sooner than that, I hope."

"Oh, so do I. I want to win the wager and get my stakes back."

Joyce passed out before me into the quadrangle, buttoning her glove as she went. I was feeling elated by what had passed, elated and quite deliciously surprised to find how short-lived her anger had been.

"I'm afraid I'm bound up with the cause more intimately than you think," she began with unexpected gentleness. "For—let me see—three years now people have been trying to show me the error of my ways, and I go on just the same. Men and women, friends and relations, a Suffragan Bishop...."

"Quite a proper distinction," I interrupted. "Neither fish, flesh, fowl, nor good red herring."

"...and the only result is that I sink daily deeper into the mire."

"But this is where I come in."

"Too late, I'm afraid. Listen. I used to have a little money of my own. I've sold out every stock and share I possessed to help found the *New Militant*. I'm living on the salary they pay me to edit it. That looks like business, doesn't it?"

I straightened my tie, buttoned the last button of my gloves, and mounted the first step of the Hall stairs.

"Living out in the East," I said, "I have learnt the virtue of infinite patience."

Joyce remained silent. It occurred to me that I had left an important question unasked.

"When I win my wager," I began.

"You won't."

"Assume I do. No one likes losing bets, but would you seriously object to the consequences?"

Joyce gave me the wonderful dawn of a smile before replying.

"I've never given the matter a thought," she answered.

"Subconsciously?" I suggested in a manner worthy of the Seraph.

She shook her head.

"Well, give it a thought now," I begged.

"It wouldn't make much difference whether I objected or not."

"If you honestly object, if you think the whole thing's a joke in questionable taste, I'll take the ring off here and now."

Joyce began to unbutton her glove, then stopped and looked at me. I suppose my voice must have shown I was speaking seriously; her eyes were soft and kind.

"I think any girl 'ud be very lucky...." she began. I bowed, and as I did so an imp of mischief took possession of her tongue. "...very lucky indeed—to engage your roving affection."

"That wasn't what you started to say."

"I never know what I *am* going to say. That's why I'm so good on a platform."

"Shall I take the ring off?"

"I prefer to win it in fair fight."

"If you can," I rejoined, as we pressed our way into the bright warmth of the ball-room.

My charges appeared to be profiting by my absence. Couple after couple floated by with touching heads and dreamy eyes; half-way down the room Philip was whispering in Gladys' ear and making her smile; I caught a glimpse of Robin and Cynthia; then Sylvia and the Seraph glided past.

"Don't they look sweet together?" said Joyce, half to herself, as our faces were subjected to a quick, searching glance.

"What about a turn before supper?" I suggested.

"Am I having it with you?"

"If you will."

"I should like to."

We started round the room, half-way through the waltz. Joyce was a beautiful dancer, easy, light, and rhythmical. It was too good to spoil with talking; I contented myself with one final remark.

"After all," I said, "you may as well start getting used to me."

CHAPTER VI

THE SECOND ROUND

"One sleeps, indeed, and wakes at intervals,
We know, but waking's the main part with us,
And my provision's for life's waking part.
Accordingly, I use heart, head and hand
All day, I build, scheme, study and make friends;
And when night overtakes me, down I lie,
Sleep, dream a little, and get done with it,
The sooner the better, to begin afresh.
What's midnight doubt before the dayspring's faith?
You, the philosopher that disbelieve,
That recognise the night, give dreams their weight—
To be consistent—you should keep your bed,
Abstain from healthy acts that prove you man,
For fear you drowse perhaps at unawares!
And certainly at night you'll sleep and dream,
Live through the day and bustle as you please.
And so you live to sleep as I to wake,
To unbelieve as I to still believe?
Well, and the common sense o' the world calls you
Bedridden,—and its good things come to me."
                              —Robert Browning
                              "Bishop Blougram's Apology."

The Bullingdon Ball took place on the Tuesday night, and
Joyce returned to town the following morning. Her brother may
have mentioned the time, or it may have been pure coincidence
that I should be buying papers and watching the trains when she
arrived at the station with the girl she was chaperoning. We met
as friends and exchanged papers: I gave her the *Morning Post*
and received the *New Militant* in return. As the train slipped

away from the platform, she waved farewell with a carefully gloved left hand. Then Dick and I strolled back to the House.

In drowsy, darkened chamber Robin was sleeping the sleep of the just. As I voyaged round his rooms, I reflected that under-graduate humour changes little through the ages, and in Oxford as elsewhere the unsuspecting just falls easy prey to wakeful, prowling injustice. An enemy had visited that peaceful home of slumber. Half-hidden by disordered bed-clothes, a cold bath prematurely awaited Robin's foot, and on his table was spread a repast such as no right-thinking man orders for himself after two nights' heavy dancing. Moist, indecorous slabs of cold boiled beef, beer for six, two jars of piccalilli and a round of over-ripe Gorgonzola cheese, offered piteous appeal to a jaded, untasting palate. Suspended from the overmantel—that soul might start on equal terms with body—hung the pious aspiration—"God Bless our Home."

"Garton, for a bob!" Robin exclaimed when I described the condition of his rooms.

Flinging the bed-clothes aside, he fell heavily into the bath, extricated himself to the accompaniment of low, vehement muttering that may have been a prayer, and bounded across the landing to render unto Garton the things that were Garton's. I followed at a non-committal distance, and watched the disposal of two pounds of boiled beef in unsuspected corners of Garton's rooms. Three slices were hidden in the tobacco jar, the rest impartially distributed behind Garton's books—to mature and strengthen during sixteen weeks of Long Vacation. Balancing the jug of beer on the door-top—whence it fell and caved in the fraudulent white head of a venerable scout—Robin hastened back to his own quarters and sported the oak.

"I was thinking of a touch of lunch on the Cher," he observed, exchanging his dripping pyjamas for a dressing-gown and making for a window-seat commanding Canterbury Gate, a cigarette in one hand and a Gorgonzola cheese in the other. "If you wouldn't mind toddling round to Phil and the Seraph and routing the girls out, we might all meet at the House barge at one. I'll cut along and dress as soon as I've given Garton a little nourishment. I suppose the pickles 'ud kill him," he added with a regretful glance at the two-pound glass jars.

I communicated the rendezvous to Philip, threw an eye over the "Where is Miss Rawnsley?" article as I crossed the Quad, and dropped anchor in the Seraph's rooms. His quaint streak of femininity showed itself in the bowls of "White Enchantress" carnations with which the tables and mantelpiece were adorned. A neat pile of foolscap covered with shorthand characters indicated early rising and studious method. I found him working his way through the *Times* and *Westminster Gazette* for the last three days.

"I suppose there is no news?" I said when I had told him Robin's arrangements for the day and described the Battle of the Beef.

"Nothing to-day," he answered. "Have you seen yesterday's *Times*?"

I had been far too busy with Joyce and my three wards to spare a moment for the papers. I now read for the first time that the Prime Minister had moved for the appropriation of all Private Members' days. The Poor Law Reform Bill would engage the attention of the House for the remainder of the Session, to the exclusion of Female Suffrage and every other subject.

"That's Rawnsley's answer to *this*," I said, giving the Seraph my copy of the *New Militant*.

"I wonder what the answer of the *New Militant* will be to Rawnsley," he murmured when he had read the article.

"That is for you to say," I told him. "You read the Heavens and interpret dreams and forecast the future...."

"Fortunately I can't."

This was an unexpected point of view.

"Wouldn't you if you could?" I asked.

"Would any one go on living if he didn't cheat himself into believing the future was not going to be quite as black as the present?"

This was not the right frame of mind for a man who had spent two nights dancing with Sylvia—to the exclusion of every one else, and I told him so.

"Come along to the Randolph," he exclaimed impatiently. "To-day, to-night; and to-morrow all will be over. I was a fool to come. I don't know why I did."

We picked up our hats and strolled into King Edward Street.

"You came because Sylvia invited you," I reminded him. "I heard the invitation. Young Rawnsley was not there, but Culling and Gartside were, and a dozen more I don't know by name. Any of them might have been chosen instead, but—they weren't. You should be more grateful for your advantages, my young friend."

"I'm not."

I linked my arm in his, and tried to find out what was upsetting him.

"You've been having some senseless, needless quarrel with her...." I hazarded.

"How can two people quarrel when they've not a single point in common? Our lives are on parallel lines, continue them indefinitely and they'll never meet. Therefore—it's a mistake to bring the parallels so close together that one can see the other."

For a moment I wondered whether he had put his fortune to the test and received a rebuff.

"Does Sylvia think your lives are on parallel lines?" I asked.

"What experience or imagination do you think a girl like that's got? It never occurs to them that everybody's not turned out of the same machine as themselves, with the same ideas, beliefs, upbringing, position, means. D'you suppose Sylvia appreciates that she spends more money on dress in six months than I earn in a year? Can she imagine that I hate and despise all the little conventions that she wouldn't transgress for all the wealth of the Indies? The doctrines she's learnt from her mother, the doctrines she'll want to teach her children—can she imagine that I regard them as so much witchcraft that I wouldn't imperil my soul by asking any sane child to believe? I'm an infidel, a penniless, unconventional Bohemian, and she—well, you know the atmosphere of Brandon Court. What's the good of our going on meeting?"

"Nigel is neither infidel, unconventional, nor Bohemian," I said. "Moreover, he stands on the threshold of a big career...."

"I daresay," said the Seraph as I paused.

"Nigel was not invited. Gartside may be an infidel if he ever troubles to think of such things; he is certainly not penniless or Bohemian. He is a large-framed, large-hearted hero, with every worldly advantage a girl could desire. Gartside was not invited. No more were the others. You were."

"She hadn't known me two days; perhaps two days aren't long enough to find me out."

"Feminine intuition...." I began.

"Feminine intuition's a woman's power of jumping to wrong conclusions quicker than men. Unless you want to get yourself into trouble, you'd better not march into Sylvia's presence with a *New Militant* in your hand."

I thanked him for the reminder, and bequeathed the offending sheet to the Martyrs' Memorial. The heavy type of the headline, "Where is Miss Rawnsley?" reminded me of our earlier conversation.

"I shan't be sorry to get rid of my charges," I remarked. "They're a responsibility in these troublous times."

"Sylvia's in no danger," he answered with great confidence.

"I'm not so sure."

"She's absolutely safe."

"How do you know?"

He looked at me doubtfully, and the confidence died out of

his eyes.

"I don't. It's—just an opinion."

"Even if you're right, there's still Gladys," I said.

"I'd forgotten her."

"She's a fair mark."

"I suppose so."

"Though not as good as Sylvia."

"I assure you Sylvia's in no danger."

"But how do you know?" I repeated.

"I tell you; it's only an opinion."

"But you don't express any opinion about Gladys."

"How could I?"

"How can you about Sylvia?"

He hesitated, flushed, opened his lips and shut them again in his old tantalising way.

"I don't know," he answered as we entered the Randolph, and walked to the end of the hall where the three girls were awaiting us.

Robin had provided an imposing flotilla for our accommodation. His own punt was reserved for Cynthia, himself, and the luncheon-baskets; a mysterious reconciliation had placed Garton's at the disposal of Philip, Gladys, and myself, while Sylvia and the Seraph were stowed away in a Canadian canoe, detached by act of sheer piracy from the adjoining Univ. barge. We took the old course through Mesopotamia and over the Rollers, mooring for luncheon half a mile above the Cherwell Hotel. Hunger and a sense of duty secured my presence for that meal and tea; in the interval I retired for a siesta. Distance, I find, lends enchantment to a chaperon.

It was in my absence that Philip asked Gladys to marry him. On my reappearance at tea-time, Robin shouted the news across a not inconsiderable section of Oxfordshire. I affected the usual surprise, warned Philip that he must await my brother's approval, and shook hands with him avuncularly. Then I watched the orgy of kissing that seems inseparable from announcements of this kind. A mathematician would work out the possible combinations in two minutes, but his calculation would, as ever, be upset by the intrusion of the personal equation, for Robin kissed Gladys not once, but many times, less with a view to welcoming her as a sister than from a reasonable belief that such ill-timed assiduity would exasperate her elder brother.

In time it occurred to some one to make tea, and at six o'clock the flotilla started home. Robin ostentatiously transferred me from Philip's punt to his own, and with equal ostentation announced his intention of starting last so as to round up the laggards. The Canadian canoe shot gracefully ahead, and was soon lost to view; a fast stream was running, and the boat needed little assistance from the paddle. I have no doubt that in the late afternoon sun, and with an accompaniment of rippling water gently lapping the sides of the boat, time passed all too quickly. Fragments of conversation were disinterred for my benefit in the course of the following weeks, to set me wondering anew what sympathetic nimbus I must wear that girls and boys like Sylvia and the Seraph should unlock their hearts for my inspection.

I gather that Sylvia called for the verdict on the success of their expedition to Oxford, and that the Seraph found for her, but with reluctant, qualified judgment.

"You're not sorry you came?" she asked. "Well, what's lacking? I'm responsible for bringing you here; I want everything to be quite perfect."

"Everything *is* perfect, Sylvia."

She shook her head.

"*Some*thing's wrong. You're moody and silent and troubled, just like you were the first time we met. D'you remember that night? You looked as if you thought I was going to bite you. I don't bite, Seraph. Tell me what's the matter, there's still one night more; I want to make you glad you came."

"You can't make me gladder than I am. But you can't find roses without thorns. I wish we weren't all going back to-morrow."

"It's only to London."

"I know, but it'll all be different."

"But why?"

"I don't know, but it *will* be. These three days wouldn't have been so glorious if I hadn't remembered every moment of the time that they were—just three days."

Shipping his paddle, he lay back in the boat and plunged his arms up to the elbow in the cool, reedy water. Sylvia roused him with a challenge.

"Four days would have bored you?"

"Have you ever met the man who *was* bored by four days of your company?"

"Don't you sometimes fancy you know me better than most?"

"I've known you since Whitsun."

"You've known me since...."

She stopped abruptly. The Seraph lifted a wet hand, and watched the water trickling in zigzag rivulets up his arm.

"Shall I finish it for you?" he asked.

"You don't know what I was going to say."

"You've known me since the day I was born."

"Why do you think I was going to say that?"

"You were, weren't you?"

"I stopped in the middle."

"You'd thought out the end."

"Had I?"

"Unconsciously?"

A hand waved in impatient protest.

"If it was unconscious, how should I know?"

The Seraph glanced quickly up at her face, and turned away.

"True," he answered absently.

"No one could know," she persisted.

"*I* knew."

"Guessed."

For answer he picked up his coat from the bottom of the boat, and extracted a closely written sheet of college note-paper. Folding it so that only the last line was visible, he handed it her with the words—

"You'll find it there."

Sylvia read the line, and gazed in perplexity at her companion.

"But I never *said* it," she persisted.

"You were going to."

She turned the paper over without answering.

"What's on the other side?" she asked.

The Seraph extended an anxious hand.

"Please don't read that!" he implored her. "It's not meant for you to see."

"Is it about me?"

"Yes."

"Then why shouldn't I see it?"

"You may, but not now."

"Well, when?"

The Seraph's manner had grown suddenly agitated. To gain time, he produced a cigarette, but his agitation was betrayed in the trembling hand that held the match.

"When we meet again," he answered after a pause.

"We meet again to-night."

"When we meet—after parting."

"We part to dress for dinner."

"I mean a long, serious parting," he replied in a low voice.

Sylvia laughed at his suddenly grave expression.

"Are we going to quarrel?" she asked.

He nodded without speaking.

"Why, Seraph?" she asked more gently.

"We can't help it."

"It takes two to make a quarrel. *I* don't want to."

"We shouldn't—if we were the only two souls in creation."

Sylvia sat silent, fidgeting with a signet ring, and from time to time looking questioningly into the troubled blue eyes before her.

"How do you *know* these things?" she asked at length. "You can't know."

"Call it guessing, but I was right over the unfinished sentence, wasn't I?"

"Perhaps, but how do you know?"

"I don't. It's fancy. Some people spend their lives awake, others dreaming." He shrugged his shoulders. "I dream. And sometimes the dream's so real that I know it must be true."

Sylvia smiled with a shy wistfulness he had not seen on her face before.

"I wish you wouldn't dream we were going to quarrel," she said. "I don't want to lose you as a friend."

"You won't. Some day I shall be able to help you, when you want help badly."

Almost imperceptibly her mouth hardened its lines, and her eyes recovered their disdainful, independent fire.

"Why should I want help?" she asked.

"I don't know," was all he could answer. "You will."

Their canoe had drifted to the Rollers. The Seraph landed, helped Sylvia out of the boat, and stood silently by while it was hauled up and lowered into the water on the other side. As they paddled slowly through Mesopotamia neither was able—perhaps neither was willing—to pick up the threads of the conversation where they had been dropped. In silence they passed the Magdalen Bathing Place, through the shade of Addison's Walk, under the Bridge and alongside the Meadows. Sylvia's mind grappled uneasily with the half-comprehended words he had spoken.

"Do we meet and make it up?" she asked with assumed lightness of tone as the canoe passed through the scummy, winding mouth of the Cher and shot clear into the Isis.

"We meet."

"And make it up?" she repeated.

"I don't know."

"Do you care?"

"Sylvia!"

"What will you do?"

"If we don't?" The Seraph sat motionless for a moment, and then began paddling the boat alongside the barges. "I shall go abroad. I've never been to India. I want to go there. And then I shall go on to Japan, and from Japan to some of Stevenson's islands in the South Seas. I've seen everything else that I want to see."

"And then?"

He raised his eyebrows and shook his head uncertainly.

"Burial at sea, I hope."

"Seraph, if you talk like that we shall quarrel now."

"But it's true."

"There'd be nothing more in life?"

"Not if we quarrelled and never made it up."

"But if we *did*—"

"Ah, that'ud make all the difference in the world."

For a moment they looked into each other's eyes: then Sylvia's fell.

"I don't want to quarrel," she said. "I don't believe we shall, I don't see why we need. If we do, I'm prepared to make it up."

"I wonder if you will be when the time comes," he answered.

We were, with a single, noteworthy exception—a subdued party that night at dinner. Philip and Gladys had much to occupy their minds and little their tongues: Sylvia and the Seraph were silent and reflective: I, too, in my unobtrusive middle-aged fashion, had passed an eventful night and morning. The exception was Robin, who furnished conversational relief in the form of Stone Age pleasantries at the expense of his brother in particular, engaged couples in general, and the whole immemorial institution of wedlock. I have forgotten some of his more striking parallels, but I recollect that each fresh dish called forth a new simile.

"Pity oysters aren't in season, Toby," he remarked. "Marriage is like your first oyster, horrid to look at, clammy to touch, and only to be swallowed at a gulp." "Clear soup for me, please. When I'm offered thick, I always wonder what the cook's trying to hide. Thick soup is like marriage." "Why does dressed crab always remind me of marriage? I suppose because it's irresist-ible, indigestible, and if carelessly mixed, full of little pieces of shell." "Capercailzie is symbolical of married life: too much for one, not enough for two." "Matrimony is like a cigarette before port: it destroys the palate for the best things in life."

No one paid any attention to Robin as he rambled on to his own infinite contentment: he would probably still be rambling but for the arrival of an express letter directed to me in Arthur Roden's writing. We were digesting dinner over a cigar in the hall, and after reading the letter I took Sylvia and the Seraph aside, and communicated its contents. By some chance it was included in a miscellaneous bundle of papers I packed up before leaving England, and I have it before me on my table as I write.

"Private and Confidential," it began—

"My Dear Toby,"

"If this arrives in time, I shall be glad if you will send me a wire to say all is well with Sylvia and the others. We are a good deal alarmed by the latest move of the Militants. You will have seen that Rawnsley got up in the House the other day and moved to appropriate all Private Members' time till the end of the Session, in this way frustrating all idea of the Suffrage coming up in the form of a Private Member's Bill.

"The Militants have made their counterstroke without loss of time. Yesterday morning Jefferson's only child—a boy of seven—disappeared. We left J. out when we were running over likely victims at Brandon: he was away in the *Enchantress* inspecting Rosyth at the time, and I suppose that was how we forgot him. We certainly ought not to have done so, as he has been one of the most outspoken of the anti-militants.

"The child went yesterday with his nurse to Hyde Park. The woman—like all her damnable kind—paid no attention to her duty, and allowed some young guardsman to sit and talk to her. In five minutes' time—she says it was only five minutes—the child had disappeared. No trace of him has been found. Jefferson, of course, is in a great state of worry, but agrees with Rawnsley that no word of the story must be allowed to reach the Press, and no effort spared to convince the electorate of the utter impossibility of considering the claims at present put forward by the Militants. I am arranging a series of meetings in the Midlands and Home Counties as soon as the House rises.

"And that reminds me. Rawnsley received a second letter immediately after the abduction of J.'s boy, telling him his action in respect of Private Members' time had been noted, and that he would be given till the end of the month [June] to foreshadow an autumn session. There may be an autumn session—that depends on the Committee Stage of the Poor Law Bill—but the Suffrage will not come up during its course, and Rawnsley is purposely withholding his announcement till the month has turned.

"For the next ten days, therefore, we may hope to be spared any fresh attack. After that they will begin again, and as my Midland campaign is being announced in the course of this week, it is more than probable that the blow may be aimed at me.

"Please shew this letter to Sylvia and the boys, and explain as much of the Rawnsley affair as may be necessary to make it clear to her. At present she has been told that Mavis is ill in London and may have to undergo an operation. Tell her to use the utmost care not to stir in public without some competent person to escort her. Scotland Yard is increasing its bodyguards, and everything must be done to assist them.

"You will, of course, see the necessity of keeping this letter private.

"Ever yours,

"ARTHUR RODEN."

As I gave the letter to Sylvia and the Seraph to read, I will admit that my first feeling was one of unsubstantial relief that Joyce had been in Oxford when the abduction took place in London. I did not in any way condone the offence, I should not have condoned it even had I known that she was mainly responsible for the abduction. Independently of all moral considerations, I found myself being glad that she was out of town at the time of the outrage. The consolation was flimsy. I concede that. But it is interesting to me to look back now and review my mental standpoint at that moment. I had already got beyond the point of administering moral praise and blame: my descent to active participation in crime followed with incredible abruptness.

I felt the "Private and Confidential" was not binding against the Seraph, as he had been present when Rawnsley described the disappearance of Mavis. While he expounded her father's letter to Sylvia, I gave its main points to Philip and Robin. The comments of the family were characteristic of its various members. Philip shook a statesmanlike head and opined that this was getting very serious, you know. Robin inquired plaintively who'd want to abduct a little thing like him.

"I don't want any 'competent escort,'" Sylvia exclaimed with her determined small chin in the air.

"For less than twenty-four hours," I begged. "I'm responsible for your safety till then. After that you can fight the matter out with your father."

"But I can look after myself even for the next twenty-four hours."

I assumed my severest manner.

"Have you ever seen me angry?" I said.

"Do you think you could frighten me?" she asked with a demure smile.

"I'm quite sure I couldn't," I answered helplessly. "Seraph, can you do anything with her?"

"Nobody can do anything with her...."

"Seraph!"

"...against her will."

"That's better."

I struck at a propitious moment.

"When we leave here," I said to the Seraph, "you're to take her hand and not let go till you're back in the hotel again. I give her into your charge. Treat her...."

I hesitated, and Sylvia interrogated me with a King's Ransom smile.

"Treat her as she deserves," I said. "If she were my wife, ward or daughter, I should slap her and send her to bed. So would you, so would any man worthy of the name."

"Would you, Seraph?"

He was helping her into her cloak and did not answer the question. Suddenly she turned round and looked into his eyes.

"Would you, Seraph?" I heard her repeat.

"I shall treat you—as you deserve to be treated," he answered slowly.

"That's not an answer," she objected.

"What's the good of asking him?" I said as the rest of our party joined us.

In the absence of Joyce I spent large portions of a dull and interminably long night smoking excessive cigarettes and leaning against a wall to watch the dancers. Towards three o'clock I discovered an early edition of an evening paper and read it from cover to cover. Canadian Pacifics were rising or falling, and some convulsion was taking place in Rio Tintos.

The only other news of interest I found in the Cause List. I remember the case of Wylton v. Wylton and Sleabury was down for trial one day towards the end of that week.

CHAPTER VII

A CAUSE CÉLÈBRE

"Conventional women—but was not the phrase tauto-
logical?"

—George Gissing
"Born in Exile."

I always look back with regret to our return to London after
Commemoration. Our parting at the door of the Rodens' house
in Cadogan Square was more than the dispersal of a pleasant,
youthful, light-hearted gathering; it marked out a definite end to
my first careless, happy weeks in England, and foreshadowed a
period of suspense and heart-burning that separated old friends
and strained old alliances. As we shook hands and waved adieux,
we were slipping unconsciously into a future where none of us
were to meet again on our former frank, trustful footing.

I doubt if any of us recognised this at the time—not even
the Seraph, for a man is notoriously a bad judge in his own
cause. Looking back over the last six months, I appreciate that
the seeds of trouble had already been sown, and that I ought to
have been prepared for much that followed.

To begin with, the astonishing acrimony of speech and
writing that characterised both parties in the Suffrage contro-
versy should have warned me of the futility of trying to retain
the friendship of Joyce Davenant on the one hand and the Rodens
on the other. Bitter were their tongues and angry their hearts
in the old, forgotten era of demonstrations and hecklings; the
bitterness increased with the progress of the arson campaign,
and its prompt, ruthless reprisals; but I remember no political
sensation equalling the suppressed, vindictive anger of the days
when the abduction policy was launched, and no clue could be
found to incriminate its perpetrators. I suffered the fate of most

neutral powers, and succeeded in arousing the suspicions of both belligerents.

Again, the Wylton divorce proved—if proof were ever needed—that when English Society has ostracised a woman, her sympathisers gain nothing for themselves by championing her cause. They had better secure themselves greetings in the market-place by leading the chorus of moral condemnation. Elsie Wylton would scarcely have noticed the two added voices, and the Seraph and I might have spared ourselves much unnecessary discomfort. He was probably too young to appreciate that Quixotism does not pay in England, while I—well, there is no fool like a middle-aged fool.

Lastly, I ought to have seen the shadow cast by Sylvia's tropical intimacy with the Seraph at Oxford. She was unquestionably *intriguée*, and I should have seen it and been on my guard. Resist as she might, there was something arresting in his other-world, somnambulant attitude towards life; for him, at least, his dreams were too real to be lightly dismissed. And his sensitive feminine sympathy was something new to her, something strangely stimulating to a girl who but half understood her own moods and ambitions. I have no doubt that in their solitary passage back to Oxford she had unbent and revealed more to him than to any other man, had unbent as far as any woman of reserve can ever unbend to a man. Equally, I have no doubt that in cold retrospect her passionate, uncontrolled pride exaggerated the significance of her conduct, and magnified the moment of unaffected friendliness into an humiliating self-betrayal.

The Seraph—it is clear—had not responded. I know now—indeed, I knew at the time—that Sylvia had made an indelible impression on his receptive, emotional nature. Her wilful, rebellious self-confidence had galvanised him as every woman of strong character will galvanise a man of hesitations and doubts, reservations, and self-criticism. Knowing Sylvia, I find no difficulty in understanding the ascendancy she had established over his mind; knowing him, I can well appreciate his exasperating diffidence and self-depreciation. It never occurred to him that Sylvia could forget his relative poverty, obscurity, and their thousand points of conflict; it never dawned on her that he could be held back by honourable scruples from accepting what she had shown herself willing to offer. The Seraph came back from Oxford absorbed and pre-occupied with haunting memories of Sylvia; with his curious frankness he told her in so many words that she possessed his mind to the exclusion of every other thought. There he had stopped short—for no reason she could see, and it was not possible for her to go further to meet him. Next to the Capitol stands the Tarpeian Rock. I ought to have remembered that with Sylvia it was now crown or gibbet, and that there was no room for platonic admirers.

With his genius for the unexpected the Seraph disappeared from our ken for an entire week after our return to London. Gladys and I were always running over to the Rodens' or receiving visits from Sylvia and Philip; it appeared that he had forsaken Cadogan Square as completely as Pont Street, and the unenthusiastic tone in which the information was volunteered did not tempt me to prosecute further inquiries. On about the fifth day I did pluck up courage to ask Lady Roden if he had yet come to the surface, but so far from receiving an intelligible answer I found myself undergoing rigorous examination into his antecedents. "Who *is* this Mr. Aintree?" I remember her asking in her lifeless, faded voice. "Has he any relations? There used to be a Sir John Aintree who was joint-master of the Meynell."

After a series of unsuccessful inquiries over the telephone, I set out to make personal investigation. Sylvia had carried Gladys off to Ranelagh, and as Robin offered his services as escort to the girls, I felt no scruples in resigning my ward to her charge. For Sylvia, I am glad to say, my responsibility had ceased, and I was at liberty to proceed to Adelphi Terrace, and ascertain why at any hour of the day or night I was met with the news that Mr. Aintree was in town, but away from his flat, and had left no word when he would be back. I called in at the club before trying his flat. The Seraph was not there, but I found the polyglot Culling explaining for Gartside's benefit certain of the more obvious drolleries of the current "Vie Parisienne."

"Where did ye pick up yer French accent, Bob?" I heard him inquire with feigned admiration. "In Soho? I wonder who dropped it there?" Then he caught sight of me, and his face assumed an awful solemnity. "'Corruptio optimi pessima!' I wonder ye've the courage to show yerself among respectable men like me and Gartside."

I inquired if either of them knew of the Seraph's whereabouts, but the question appeared to add fuel to Culling's indignation.

"Where is the Seraph?" he exclaimed. "Well ye may ask! His wings are clipped, there's a dint in his halo, and his harp has its strings broken. The Heavenly Choir—" He paused abruptly, seized a sheet of foolscap and resumed his normal tone. "This'll be rather good—the Heavenly Choir and our Seraph flung out like a common drunk same as Gartside here.

> 'To bottomless perdition, there to dwell—
> Why can't the club afford a decent pen?
> You're our committeeman, Bob, you're to blame.
> I always use blank verse for my complaints.—
> To bottomless perdition, there to dwell
> In adamantine chains and penal fire.'"
>   —John Milton
>   "Paradise Lost, Liber One."

I watched the Heavenly Choir being sketched. In uniform and figure the Archangel Gabriel presented a striking resemblance to any Keeper of the Peace at any Music Hall. An official braided coat bulged at the shoulders with the pressure of two cramped wings, his peaked cap had been knocked over one eye, and his halo—in Culling's words—was "all anyhow." As the artist insisted on a companion picture to show the Seraph's reception in Bottomless Perdition, I turned to Gartside for enlightenment.

"It's been going on long enough to be getting serious," I was told. "A solid week now."

"*What's* been going on?" I exclaimed in despair. "Where are we? Above all, where's the Seraph?"

"Isn't it telling you we are?" protested Culling. "It started on the day you returned from your godless wanderings and prowled through London like a lion seeking whom you might devour. 'Portrait of a Gentleman—well known in Society—seeking whom he may devour,'" he murmured to himself, stretching forth a hand for fresh foolscap. "And it's been going on ever since. And nobody's had the courage to speak to him about it. There you have the thing in a nutshell."

I turned despairingly to Gartside, and in time was successful in extracting and piecing together an explanation of his dark references to the Seraph. "Once upon a time," he began.

"When pigs were swine," Culling interrupted, "and monkeys chewed tobacco."

"Shut up, Paddy! Once upon a time a girl named Elsie Davenant married a man called Arnold Wylton. Perhaps she knows why she did it, but I'm hanged if anybody else did. She was a nice enough girl by all accounts, and Wylton—well, I expect you've heard some queer stories about him, they're all true. After they'd been married—how long was it, Paddy?"

"Oh, a few years—by the calendar," said Culling, eagerly taking up the parable. "It's long enough she must have found 'em! Wylton used to work in little spells of domesticity in the intervals of being horse-whipped out of other people's houses, and disappearing abroad while sundry little storms blew over. Morgan and Travers took in a new partner and started a special 'Wylton Department' for settling his actions out of court...."

"This is all fairly ancient history," I interposed.

"It's the extenuating circumstance," said Gartside.

Culling warmed oratorically to his work.

"In the fulness of time," he went on in the manner of the Ancient Mariner, "Mrs. Wylton woke up and said, 'This is a one-sided business.' Toby, ye're a bachelor. Let me tell you that married life is a *mauvais quart d'heure* made up of exquisite week-ends. While Wylton dallied unobtrusively in Buda Pesth, giving himself out to be the Hungarian correspondent of the *Baptist Family Herald*, Mrs. Wylton spent her exquisite week-end at Deauville."

He paused delicately.

"Girls will be girls," sighed Gartside.

"A gay cavalry major, with that way they have in the army, made a flying descent on Deauville. He'd been seen about with her in London quite enough to cause comment. Good-natured friends asked Wylton why he was vegetating in Pesth when he might be in Deauville; he came, he saw, he stayed in the self same hotel as his wife...."

"Which curiously enough had been already chosen by the gay cavalry major."

Culling shook his head over the innate depravity of human nature.

"You see the finish?" he inquired rhetorically. "They say the senior partner in Morgan and Travers had a seizure when Wylton had finished the last batch of cases in his own department, and strolled into the private office to instruct proceedings for a petition."

"Six days ago, decree nisi was granted," said Gartside.

"Scene in Court: President expressing sympathy with Petitioner," murmured Culling, with quick pencil already at work on the blotting-pad.

I lit a cigar to clear my head.

"Where does the Seraph come in?" I persisted like a man

with an *idée fixe*.

"In the sequel," said Gartside. "There is a right way of doing everything, also a wrong. When one is divorced, one hides one's diminished head...."

"I always do," said Culling.

"One grows a beard and goes to live in Kensington. Mrs. Wylton is making the mistake of trying to brazen things out. 'You may cut me,' she says, 'but ye canna brek me manly sperrit.' Consequently in every place where she can be certain of attracting a crowd, Mrs. Wylton is to be found in the front row of the stalls, very pretty, very quiet and so unobtrusively dressed that you're almost tempted to damn her as respectable."

He lit a cigarette and I took occasion to remind him that we had not yet come in sight of the Seraph.

Culling took up the parable.

"Is she alone?" he asked in a husky whisper. "Sir, she is not! Who took her to dinner last night at Dieudonné's, the night before at the Savoy, the night before that at the Carlton? Who has been seen with her at the Duke of York's, the Haymarket, the St. James'?"

"Who rides with her every summer morning in the Park?" cut in Gartside. "It is our Seraph. Our foolish Seraph, and we lay at your door the blame for his demoralisation. Seriously, Toby, somebody ought to speak the word in season. He's getting talked about, and that sort of flying in the face of public opinion doesn't do one damn's worth of good. The woman's got to have her gruel and take her time over it. She'll only put people's backs up by going on as she's doing at present. Mind you, I'm sorry for her," he went on more gently. "In her place I'd have done precisely the same thing, and I'd have done it years ago. But I should have had the sense to recognise I'd got to face the consequences."

I wondered for a short two seconds if it would be of the slightest avail to proclaim my belief in Elsie Wylton's innocence. A glance at Culling and Gartside convinced me of the futility.

"Where's the Seraph now?" I asked.

"With her. Any money you like. She lives with her sister in Chester Square; you'll find him there."

I sent a boy off to telephone to Adelphi Terrace. Until his return with the announcement that the Seraph was still away from home, Gartside suggested the lines on which I was to admonish the young offender.

"The gay cavalry major's prudently shipped himself back to India," he said, "and he was a pretty shadowy figure to most people as it was. What the Seraph has to understand is that he'll get all the discredit of being an 'and other' if he ties himself to her strings in this way. I only give you what everybody's saying."

I promised to ponder his advice, and after being reminded that Gladys and I were due at his musical party the following week, and reminding him that he was expected to lunch on my house-boat at Henley, we went our several ways.

Wandering circuitously round the smoking-rooms and library on my way to the hall, I had ample corroboration of what—in Gartside's words—everybody was saying. The Wylton divorce was the one topic of conversation. For the most part, I found Gartside's own tolerance to the woman representative of the general feeling in the club: his strictures on the folly of the Seraph's conduct had a good many echoes, though two men had the detachment to praise his disinterested behaviour. Of the rest, those who did not condemn opined that he was too young to know any better.

The one discordant note was struck when I met Nigel Rawnsley in the hall. Elsie Wylton was shot hellwards in one sentence and the Seraph in another, but the burden of his discourse was reserved for the sacramental nature of wedlock and the damnable heresy of divorce. I was subjected to a lucid exposition of the Anglican doctrine of marriage, initiated into the mysteries of the first three (or three hundred) General Councils of the Church, presented with thumbnail biographies of Arius and S. Athanasius, and impressed with the necessity of unfrocking all priests who celebrated the marriage of divorced persons. It was all very stimulating, and I found that half my most prosaic friends were living in something that Rawnsley damningly described as "a state of sin."

It was tea-time before I arrived at Chester Square. I suppose I had never taken Gartside very seriously: the moment I saw Elsie and the Seraph, my lot was unconditionally thrown in with the publicans and sinners. She greeted me with the smile of a woman who has no care in the world: then as she turned to ring the bell for tea, I caught the expression of one who is passing through Purgatory on her way to Hell. The Seraph's eyes were telegraphing a whole code-book. I walked to the window so that she could not see my face, nor I hers.

"I thought you wouldn't mind my dropping in," I said as carelessly as I could. "It was tea-time for one thing, and for another I wanted to tell you that you've done about the pluckiest thing a woman can do. Good luck to you! If there's anything I can do...."

Then we shook hands again, and I found her death-like placidity a good deal harder to bear than if she had broken down or gone into hysterics. I do not believe the Davenant women know how to cry: Nature left the lachrymal sac out of their composition. Yet on reflection I can see now that she was suffering less than in the days six weeks before when the anticipation of the divorce lowered menacingly over her head and haunted every waking moment. It is curious to see how suspense cards down a woman's spirit while the shock of a catastrophe seems actually to brace her and call forth every reserve of strength. From this time till the day of my departure from England, Elsie was indomitable.

"It's hard work at present," she said with a gentle, tired smile, "but I'm going through with it."

That was what her father used to say when I climbed with him in Trans-Caucasia. He would say it as we crawled and fought and bit our way up a slippery face of rock, sheer as the side of a house. And he was five and twenty years my senior.

"What are you doing to-night?" I asked.

"We were trying to make up our minds when you came in," said the Seraph.

"Dinner somewhere, I suppose, and a theatre? What's on, Seraph? I'm all alone to-night, and I want you and Elsie to dine with me."

Elsie was sitting with closed eyes, bathing her forehead with scent.

"Make it something that starts late," she said wearily. "I don't feel I can stand many hours."

After a brief study of the theatrical advertisements in the *Morning Post* the Seraph went off to make arrangements over the telephone. I took hold of Elsie's disengaged hand and tried in a clumsy, masculine fashion to pump courage into her tired spirit.

"You must stick it out to the end of the Season," I told her. "It's only a few more weeks, and then you can rest as long as you like. Don't let people think they can drive you into hiding. If you do that, you'll lose pride in yourself, and when you lose pride in yourself, why should any one believe in you?"

"How many people believe in me now?"

"Not many. That's why I admire your pluck. But there's Joyce for one."

"Yes, Joyce," she assented slowly.

"And the Seraph for another."

"Yes, the Seraph."

"And me for a third."

I felt her trying to draw her hand away.

"I wonder if you do, or whether it's just because I'm a bit—

hard hit."

I let go the hand as she rose to blow out the spirit lamp. Standing erect—blue-eyed, pale faced and golden haired—she was wonderfully like Joyce, I thought, with her slim, black-draped figure and slender white neck, but a Joyce who had drunk deep of tribulation.

"It's a pity you weren't ever at a boys' school," I said.

"Why?"

"If you had been, you'd know there are some boys who simply can't keep themselves and their clothes clean, and others who can't get dirty or untidy if they try. In time the grubby ones usually get cleaner, but the boy who starts with a clean instinct never deteriorates into a grub. The distinction holds good for both sexes. And it applies to conduct as much as clothes. The Davenants can't help keeping clean. I've known three in one generation and one in another."

I said it because I meant it. I should have said it just the same if Elsie had had no sister Joyce.

The Seraph came back with Dick Davenant, and I tried to get him to join us, but he was already engaged for dinner. Shortly afterwards I found it was time to get home and change my clothes. In the hall I found Joyce and pressed her into our party. It was a short, hurried meeting, as she was saying good-bye to two colleagues or fellow-conspirators when I appeared. I caught their names and looked at them with some interest. One was the formidable Mrs. Millington, a weather-beaten, stoutish woman of fifty with iron-grey hair cut short to the neck, and double-lensed pince-nez. The other was an anæmic girl of twenty—a Miss Draper—with fanatical eyes that watched Joyce's every movement, and a little dry cough that told me her days of agitation were numbered. When next we met she wiped her lips after coughing.... Mrs. Millington I never saw again.

That night was my first effort in the vindication of Elsie Wylton. I believe we dined at the Berkeley and went on to Daly's.

The place is immaterial; wherever we went we found—or so it seemed to our over-sensitive, suspicious nerves—a slight hush, a movement of turning bodies and craning necks, a whispered name. Elsie went through it like a Royal Duchess opening a bazaar; laughing and talking with the Seraph, turning to throw a word to Joyce or myself; untroubled, indifferent—best of all, perfectly restrained. The hard-bought actress-training of imme-morial centuries should give woman some superiority over man....

We certainly supped at the Carlton in a prominent position by the door. I fancy no one missed seeing us. The Seraph knew everybody, of course, and I had picked up a certain number of acquaintances in two months. We bowed to every familiar form, and the familiar forms bowed back to us. When they passed near our table we hypnotised them into talking, and they brought their women-folk with them....

When supper was ended we moved outside for coffee and cigars, so that none who had entered the supper room before us should leave without running the gauntlet. We had our share of black looks and noses in air, directed I suppose against Joyce as much as against her sister; and many a mild husband must have submitted to a curtain lecture that night on the text that no man will believe political or moral evil of any woman with a pretty face. The older I get the truer I find that text; I cannot remember the day when I was without the instinct underlying such a belief.

At a quarter-past twelve Elsie began to flag, and we started our preparations for returning home. As I waited for my bill— and swore a private oath that Gartside should translate his sympathy into acts, and join our moral-leper colony before the week was out—an unexpected party emerged from the restau-rant and passed us on their way to collect cloaks. Gladys and Philip, Sylvia and Robin, driven home from Ranelagh by the impossibility of securing a table for dinner, had eaten sketchily at Cadogan Square, hurried to the Palace, and turned in to the

Carlton to make up for lost food.

The Seraph of course saw them first, rose up and bowed. I followed, and both of us were rewarded by a gracious acknowledgment from Sylvia. Then she caught sight of Joyce and Elsie, and her mouth straightened itself and lost its smile. The change was slight, but I had been expecting it. Another moment, and the straight lines broke to a slight curve. Every one bowed to every one—Robin with his irrepressible, instinctive good-humour, Philip more sedately, as befitted a public man, the eldest son of the Attorney-General, and an avowed opponent of the Militant Suffrage Movement. Then Sylvia passed on to get her cloak, I arranged with Philip to take Gladys home, we bowed again and parted.

The whole encounter had taken less than two minutes. It was more than enough to make Elsie say she must decline my invitation to Henley.

"A public place is one thing, and a houseboat's another," she said. "You wouldn't invite two people to stay with you if you knew the mere presence of one was distasteful to the other."

"You've got to go the whole road," I said. "If the Rodens know me, they've got to know my friends."

"We mustn't be in too much of a hurry," she answered. "I'm right, aren't I, Joyce? There's no scandal about Joyce, but she's given up visiting with the Rodens. It was beginning to get rather uncomfortable."

The matter was compromised by the Seraph inviting Elsie to come to Henley in an independent party of two. They would then secure as much publicity as could be desired without causing any kind of embarrassment to a private gathering.

I saw nothing of Sylvia until Gartside's Soirée Musicale three nights later. The Seraph dined with us, and when Philip snatched Gladys from under my wing almost before the car had turned into Carlton House Terrace, I retired with him into an inviting balcony and watched the female side of human nature at work.

Sylvia stood twelve feet from us, looking radiant. Instinctive wisdom had led her to dress—as ever—in white, and to wear no jewellery but pearls. Her black hair seemed silkier and more luxuriant than ever; her dark eyes flashed with a certain proud vitality and assurance. Nigel Rawnsley was talking to her, talking well, and paying her the compliment of talking up to her level. I watched her give thrust for thrust, parry for parry; all exquisite sword play.... His enemies called Nigel a prig, even his friends complained he was overbearing; I liked him, as I contrive to like most men, and only wish he could meet more people of his own mental calibre. He had met one in Sylvia; there was no button to his foil when he fenced with her.

"Thus far and no farther," I murmured.

The Seraph looked up, but I had only been thinking aloud. I was wondering why she painted that sign over her door when Nigel approached. A career of brilliant achievement and more brilliant promise, her own chosen faith and ritual, ambition enough and to spare—Nigel entered the lists well armed, and she was the only one who could humanise him. I wondered what gulf of temperamental antipathy parted them and placed him without the pale....

They talked till Culling interposed his claim for attention, preferring the request with triplicated brogue. From time to time Gartside strayed away from his other guests and shivered a lance in deferential tourney. As I watched his fine figure, and looked from him to the irrepressible Culling, and from Culling to Rawnsley's clear-cut, intellectual face, I asked myself for the thousandth time what indescribable affinity could be equally lacking in three men otherwise so dissimilar.

With light-hearted carelessness she guarded the sword's length of territory that divided them. It was adroit, nimble fencing, but I wondered how much it amused her. Not many women can resist the age-long fascination of playing off one admirer against another; but I should have written Sylvia down among the exceptions. She did not want admiration.... Then I remembered Oxford and read into her conduct the first calculated stages in the Seraph's castigation. If this were her object, it failed; the Seraph was ignorant of the very nature of jealousy. In the light of their subsequent meeting, I doubt if this were even her motive.

We had both received a distant bow as we entered the room, but not a word had been vouchsafed us. I am afraid my nature is too indolent to be greatly upset by this kind of neglect. The Seraph, I could see, grew rather unhappy when his presence was overlooked every time he came within speaking distance. It was not till the end of the evening that she unbent. I had promised to take Gladys on to a ball, and at eleven I came out of hiding and went in search of her. Culling had just been told off to find Robin, and Sylvia stood alone.

"Are you going on anywhere?" she asked the Seraph when they had the room to themselves.

"It's the Marlthrops, isn't it?" he asked.

"And Lady Carsten. Robin and I are going there. Are you coming?"

The Seraph's hand went to his pocket and made pretence of weighing three or four invitations in the balance. Finally he selected the Carsten card and glanced at it with an air of doubt.

"Will my presence be welcome?" he asked.

"You must ask Lady Carsten, she's invited you."

"Welcome to you?"

"It depends on yourself."

"What must I do?"

Sylvia pursed up her mouth and looked at him with head on one side.

"Be a little more particular in the company you keep."

"I usually am."

"With some startling lapses."

"I'm not aware of any."

Sylvia drew herself up to her full height.

"How have you spent the last week?"

"In a variety of ways."

"In a variety of company?"

"The same nearly all the time."

She nodded.

"This is my objection."

"If *she* doesn't object...." A dawning flush on Sylvia's cheek warned him to leave the sentence unfinished.

"I'm giving you advice for your own sake because, apparently, you've no one else to advise you," she said with the slow, elaborate carelessness of one who is with difficulty keeping her temper. "You've spent the last week thrusting yourself under every one's notice in company with a woman who's just been divorced from her husband. Every one's seen you, every one's talking about you. If you like that sort of notoriety...."

"Can it be avoided?"

"You can drop the woman."

"She's none too many friends."

"She's one too many."

"I cannot agree."

"Then you put yourself on her level."

"I should be proud to rank with her."

Sylvia paused a moment to steady her voice.

"I've got a temper," she remarked with exaggerated indifference, "it's never wise for anybody to rouse it, and many people would be annoyed if you talked to them as you're talking to me. I—simply don't think it's worth it, but can you wonder if I ask you to choose between her and me?"

The Seraph's face and voice were grave.

"The choice seems unnecessary," he said.

"You must take it from me that I have no wish to be seen about with a man who allows his name to be coupled with a woman of that kind."

"What kind, Sylvia?"

"You know my meaning."

"But your meaning is wrong."

"I mean an ugly word for an ugly sin. A woman of the kind that breaks the Seventh Commandment."

The Seraph began tearing his card in narrow strips.

"Elsie Wylton didn't," he said quietly.

"She told you so?"

"I didn't need telling."

Sylvia's expression implored pity on the credulity of man. The Seraph was still nervously fingering his card, but no signs of emotion ruffled her calm. The face was slightly flushed, but she bent her head to hide it.

"Part friends, Seraph," she said at last, "if you're not coming to the Carstens'. Think it over, and you'll find every one will give you the same advice."

"I dare say." He pocketed the torn card and prepared to accompany her. "What would you do in my place if you believed the woman innocent?"

Sylvia shirked the question.

"Innocent women don't get into those positions."

"It is possible."

"How can she prove her innocence?"

"How do you prove her guilt?"

"I don't attempt to go behind what the Court finds."

At the door the Seraph hesitated.

"To-night's only an armistice, Sylvia," he stipulated. "I must have time to think. I'm not committed either way."

She gave him her old friendly smile.

"If you like." Then the smile melted away. "My ultimatum comes in force to-morrow morning, though. You must make up your mind then."

CHAPTER VIII

HENLEY—AND AFTER

"We shall find no fiend in hell can match the fury of a disappointed woman."

—Colley Cibber
"Love's Last Shift."

Henley Regatta was something of a disappointment to me. I had furbished up the memories of twenty years before—which was one mistake—and was looking forward to it—which was another. In great measure the glory had departed from the house-boats, every one poured into the town by train or car, and the growth of *ad hoc* riverside clubs had reduced the number of punts and canoes on the river itself. Being every inch as much a snob as my neighbour, I regretted to find Henley so deeply democratised....

I think, in all modesty, my own party was a success. Our houseboat was the "Desdemona," a fair imitation of what the papers call "a floating hotel": we brought my brother's cook from Pont Street and carried our cellar with us from town. And there was a pleasant, assiduous orchestra that neither ate nor slept in its zeal to play us all the waltzes we had grown tired of hearing in London. A Mad Hatter's luncheon started at noon and went on till midnight. Any passing boat that liked the "Desdemona's" looks, moored alongside and boarded her: no one criticised the food or cigars, many dropped in again for a second or third meal in the course of the afternoon, and if they did not know Gladys or myself, they no doubt had a friend among my guests or waiters.

Both those that slept on board and those that visited us at their stomachs' prompting were cheery, light-hearted, out to enjoy themselves. I admit my own transports were moderated by the necessity of having to dance attendance on Lady Roden. The air became charged with Rutlandshire Morningtons, and our conversation showed signs of degenerating into a fantastic Burke's Auction Bridge. Two earls counted higher than three viscounts; I called her out with one marquis, she took the declaration away with a duke, I got it back again with a Russian prince: she doubled me.... Apart from this, I enjoyed myself. All the right people turned up, except Gartside who was kept in town discussing Governorships with the India Office.

There were Rodens to right of us, Rodens to left of us: in a field behind us, unostentatiously smoking Virginia cigarettes, loitered a watchful Roden bodyguard. The Regatta started on July 3rd and on the previous day Rawnsley had given the House its time-table. There would be no Autumn Session, but the House would sit till the end of the third week in August to conclude the Third Reading of the Poor Law Bill; no fresh legislation would be introduced. The New Militants had their answer without possibility of misconstruction, and the families of Cabinet Ministers moved nowhere without a lynx-eyed, heavy-booted, plain-clothes escort.

I summoned Scotland Yard out of its damp, cheerless meadow, gave it bottled beer and a pack of cards, and told it to treat the "Desdemona" as its own and to ring for anything likely to contribute to its comfort. Though we had never met before and were only to meet once again, I felt for those men as I should feel for any one deputed to bear up the young Rodens lest at any time they dashed their feet against stones....

Sylvia was laconic and decisive. She had engaged and defeated her father, met and routed her brothers. Any one who guarded her reckless person did so at their peril; she declined to argue the point. I fancy Lady Roden accepted a detective more or less as part of her too-often-withheld due; Philip was constitutional, guided by precedent, anxious to help peace and order in the execution of their arduous duties. The only active molestation came from Robin: left to himself he would have ignored the detectives' very existence, but at the fell suggestion of Culling I discovered him whiling away the morning by bursting into the guard-room at five-minute intervals with hysterical cries of "Save me! Oh, my God! save me!"

The saturnine, enigmatic Michael pursued his own methods. How he had escaped from Winchester in the midst of the terminal examinations, I never discovered. His telegram said, "What about me for Henley, old thing? Michael." I wired back, "Come in your thousands," and he came in a dove-grey suit, grey socks and buckskin shoes, grey tie, silk handkerchief and Homburg hat. I appreciated Michael more and more at each meeting. Of a detached family he was the most detached member. Observing me staring a trifle unceremoniously at his neck-tie, he produced a note-book and pencil and invited my written opinion. "On Seeing my New Tie" was inscribed on the front page, and the comments—so far as I remember the figures—were:—

> (1) "Oh, my God!" (40%).
> (2) "*Have* you seen Michael's tie?" (40%).
> (3) "Michael *darling*!" (Sylvia's *cri de cœur*, 10%).
> (4) "It's a devilish good tie" (my own verdict, perhaps not altogether sincere). (10%.).

"Come and shew yer ticket o' leave," urged Culling with derisory finger outstretched to indicate the forces of law and order.

"No bloody peelers for this child," Michael answered in a voice discreetly lowered to keep the offending epithet from his sister's ears.

I noticed an exchange of glances between Culling and himself, but was too busy to think much of it at the time. Eleven minutes later, however, the majesty of Scotland Yard had been incarcerated in its own stronghold. Culling sat outside their door improvising an oratorio on an accordion. "The Philistines are upon thee," I heard him thunder as I passed that way. Michael was lying prone on the deck of the house-boat, dangling at safe distance the key of the cabin at the end of a Japanese umbrella.

"*Quis custodiet ipsos custodes?*" he asked, as an official hand shot impotently out of the cabin window. The question may have been imperfectly understood.

"Sanguineos quis custodes custodiet ipsos?" he ventured.

As there was still no answer, common humanity ordained that I should possess myself of the key and hold a gaol delivery. The detectives were near weeping with humiliation, but I comforted them in some measure, won a friendship that was to serve me in good stead, and was at length free to resume my duties as host.

From time to time perfunctory racing took place, without arousing either interest or resentment. We all had our own ways of passing the time between meal and meal; one would study the teeth and smile of a musical-comedy star, another would watch Culling at the Three Card Trick, a third would count the Jews on a neighbouring house-boat.... There was no sign of Elsie or the Seraph, but that was only to be expected. He was to provide her with luncheon and publicity at Phyllis Court, and give the "Desdemona" a wide berth. Those, at least, were his sailing orders if he came; but Elsie had been over-tired and over-excited for some weeks past, and I should not have been surprised to hear she had stayed in town at the last moment.

It is one thing to set a course, and another to steer it—of Henley this is probably truer than of any other stretch of water in the world. When half the punts are returning from island to post after luncheon, and the other half paddle down stream to look at the house-boats, the narrow water midway between start and finish becomes hopelessly, chaotically congested. One or two skiffs and dinghies—which should never be allowed at any regatta—make confusion worse confounded till a timely collision breaks their sculls, or the nose of a racing punt turns them turtle; and with the closing of the booms, three boats begin to sprout where only one was before.

Through a forest of dripping paddles, I watched punt, dinghy and canoe fighting, pressing, yielding; up-stream, down-stream, broad side on, they slid and trembled like a tesselated pavement in an earthquake. The fatalists shipped their poles and paddles, and abandoned themselves to the line of least resistance. Faces grew flushed, but tempers remained creditably even....

"Mary, mother of God! it's our sad, bad, mad Seraph!"

Having exhausted the possibilities of the Three Card Trick, and being unable to secure either a pea or two thimbles, Paddy Culling had wandered to my side and was watching the crowd like a normal man.

I followed the direction of his eyes. The Seraph had turned fatalist and was being squeezed nearer and nearer the "Desdemona." A last vicious thrust by a boatload of pierrots jammed the box of his punt under our landing-stage. He waved a hand to me and began distributing bows among my guests.

"Droppit sthraight from Hiven," cried Culling with unnecessary elaboration of his already strong brogue. "The tay's wet, Mrs. Wylton, and we waiting for some one would ask a blessing. Seraph, yer ambrosia's on order."

They would not leave the punt, but we brought them tea; and a fair sprinkling of my guests testified to the success of our last few weeks' campaign by coming down to the raft and being civil to Elsie. There was, of course, no commotion or excitement of any kind; of those who lingered on deck or in the saloon, fully half, I dare say, were unconscious of what was going on below. Such was certainly the case with Sylvia. While Paddy and I served out strawberries to the crew of the punt, she had been washing her hands for tea, and as we crowned a work of charity with a few cigars and a box of matches, she came out onto the raft for assistance with the clasp of a watch-bracelet.

Paddy volunteered his services, I looked on. Her eyes travelled idly over the crowded segment of river opposite my boat, and completed their circuit by resting on the punt and its occupants. Elsie bowed and received a slight inclination of the head in return. The Seraph bowed, and was accorded the most perfect cut I have ever witnessed. Sylvia looked straight through him to a dinghy four yards the other side. It was superbly, insolently done. I have always been too lazy to cultivate the art of cutting my friends, but should occasion ever arise, I shall go to Sylvia for the necessary tuition.

As soon as the congestion was in some measure relieved, the Seraph waved good-bye to me and started paddling up stream towards Henley Bridge. Elsie had seen all that was to be seen in the cut, and—womanlike—had read into it a variety of meanings.

"I hope you're not tired," the Seraph said, as they landed and walked down to the station.

"I've had a lovely time," she answered. "Thanks most awfully for bringing me, and for all you've done these last few weeks. And before that." She hesitated, and then added with a regretful smile, "We must say good-bye after to-day."

"You're not going away?"

"Not yet; but you've got into enough trouble on my account without losing all your friends," she answered.

"But I haven't."

"You're risking one."

"On your account?"

She nodded.

He had not the brazenness to attempt a direct denial.

"Why should you think so?" he hedged.

"Seraph, dear child, I couldn't help seeing the way she took your bow. I got you that cut."

"She doesn't cut Toby," he objected. "And he and I are equally incriminated."

"There is a difference."

"Is there?"

"She's quite indifferent how much *he* soils his wings."

The Seraph was left to digest the unspoken antithesis. His face gradually lost the flush it had taken on after their encounter at the raft, his eyes grew calmer and his hands steadier; on the subject of their contention, however, he remained impenitent.

"I shan't say good-bye till you honestly tell me you don't want to see me again."

"You know I can't say that, Seraph."

"Very well, then."

"But it isn't! The good you do me is simply not worth the harm you do yourself. It didn't matter so much till Sylvia came to be reckoned with."

The Seraph shifted impatiently in his corner.

"Neither Sylvia Roden nor any other woman or man in the world is going to dictate who I may associate with, or who I mayn't."

"You must make an exception to the rule in her case."

"Why should I?"

"Every man has to make an exception to every rule in the case of one woman."

His chin achieved an uncompromising angle.

"To quote the Pharisee of blessed memory," he said, "I thank God I am not as other men."

Elsie was well enough acquainted with his moods to know nothing was to be gained by further direct opposition.

"I should like you to come to Chester Square," she compromised; "but you mustn't be seen with me in public any more."

"I shall ride in the Park to-morrow as usual," he persisted.

"I shan't be there, Seraph."

A surprise was awaiting me when Gladys and I returned to Pont Street in the early hours of Sunday morning, after waiting to see the fireworks—by immemorial tradition—extinguished by a tropical downpour. Brian notified me by wireless that he was on his way home and halfway through the Bay. He was, in fact, already overdue at Tilbury, but had been held up while the piston of a high-compression cylinder divested itself of essential portions of its packing.

"Who's going to tell him about Phil?" Gladys asked in consternation when I read her the message. We were getting on so comfortably without my brother that I think the natural affection of us both was tinged with resentment that he was returning by an earlier boat than he had threatened.

"As you are the offender," I pointed out.

"You were responsible for me."

"Why not leave it to Phil?" I suggested, with my genius for compromise.

"That's mean."

"Well, will you tell him yourself? No! I decline to be mixed up in it. I shan't be here. The day your parents land, I shall shift myself bag and baggage to an hotel. Isn't the simplest solution to break off the engagement? Well, you're very hard to please, you know."

I really forget how we settled the question, but the news was certainly not broken by me. The Seraph dropped in to dinner on the last night of my guardianship, and I asked him whether he thought I could improve on the Savoy as my next house of entertainment.

"But you're coming to stay with *me*," he said.

"My dear fellow, you've no experience of me as a guest. I don't know how long I'm staying in London."

"The longer the better, if you don't mind roughing it."

I knew there would be no "roughing it" in his immaculate mode of living, but the question was left undecided for the moment as I really felt it would be better for us both to run independently. Ten weeks of domesticity shared even with Gladys gave me a sensation of clipped wings after my inconsiderate, caravanserai existence, and—without wishing to be patronising—I had to remember that he was a man of very moderate means and would feel the cost of housing me more than I should feel it myself. The following afternoon I called round at Adelphi Terrace to acquaint him with my decision, but something seemed to have upset him; he was gazing abstractedly out of the window and I had not the heart to bother him with my own ephemeral arrangements. At the door of the flat his man apologetically asked my advice on the case; his master was eating, drinking, and smoking practically nothing, wandering about his room instead of going to bed, and gazing out into space instead of his usual daily writing.

I thought over the symptoms on my way to the Club, and decided to employ a portion of the afternoon in playing providence with Sylvia. It is a part for which I am unfitted by inclination, instinct, experience, and aptitude.

Some meeting of political stalwarts was in progress when I arrived at Cadogan Square, but I was mercifully shewn into Sylvia's own room and allowed to spend an interesting five minutes inspecting her books and pictures. They formed an illuminating commentary on her character. One shelf was devoted to works of religion, the rest to lives and histories of the world's great women. Catherine of Siena marched in front of the army, Florence Nightingale brought up the rear; in the ranks were queens like Elizabeth, Catherine of Russia, and Joan of Arc, the great uncrowned; writers from Madame de Sévigné to George Eliot, actresses from Nell Gwyn to Ellen Terry, artists like Vigée le Brun, reformers like Mary Woolstonecraft. It was a catholic library, and found space for Lady Hamilton among the rest. My inspection was barely begun when the door opened and Sylvia came in alone.

"'Tis sweet of you to come," she said. "Have you had tea? Well, d'you mind having it here alone with me? I'm sure you won't want to meet all father's constituents' wives. I hope I wasn't very long."

"No doubt it seemed longer than it was," I answered. "Still, I've had time to look at some of your books and make a discovery about you. If you weren't your father's daughter, you'd be a raging militant."

From the sudden fire in her eyes I thought I had angered her, but the threatening flame died as quickly as it had arisen.

"There's something in heredity after all, then," she said with a smile. "Do I—look the sort of person that breaks windows and burns down houses?"

So far as looks went the same question might have been asked of Joyce Davenant. That I did not ask it was due to a prudent resolve to keep my friendship with Rodens and Davenants in separate watertight compartments.

"You look the sort of person that has a great deal of ability and ambition, and wants a great deal of power."

"Without forgetting that I'm still a woman."

"Some of the militants are curiously feminine."

"'Curiously,' is just the right adverb."

"Joan of Arc rode astride," I pointed out.

"Florence Nightingale didn't break windows to impress the War Office."

"As an academic question," I said, "how's your woman of personality going to make her influence effective in twentieth-century England?"

"Have you met many women of personality?"

"A fair sprinkling."

"So I have; you could feel it as if they were mesmerising you, you had to do anything they told you. But they'd none of them votes."

The arrival of tea turned our thoughts from politics, and at the end of my second cup I advanced delicately towards the purpose of my call.

"You like plain speaking, don't you, Sylvia?" I began.

"As plain as you like."

"Well, you're not treating the Seraph fairly."

I leant back and watched her raising her little dark eyebrows in amused surprise.

"Has he sent you here?" she asked.

"I came on my own blundering initiative," I said. "I don't know what the trouble's about."

"But whatever it is, I'm to blame?"

"Probably."

Sylvia was delighted. "If a man doesn't think highly of women I do like to hear him say so!"

"As a matter of fact I'm not concerned to apportion blame to either of you. You're both of you abnormal and irrational; as likely as not you're both of you wrong. I wanted to tell you something about the Seraph you may not have heard before."

In a dozen sentences I told her of my first meeting with him in Morocco.

"Thanks to you," I said, "he's pretty well got over it. Remember that I saw him then, and you didn't; so believe me when I tell you he was suffering from what the novelists call a 'broken heart.' He won't get over it a second time."

"You're sure it was broken?" she asked dispassionately. "Um. It sounds to me like a dent; press the other side, the dent comes out."

I produced a cigarette case, and flew a distress signal for permission.

"I should like you to be serious about this," I said.

"I? Where do I come in?"

I searched vainly for matches, and eventually had to use one of my own.

"He's in love with you," I said.

Sylvia dealt with the proposition in a series of short sentences punctuated by grave nods.

"Gratifying. If true. Seems improbable. Irrelevant, anyway. Unless I happen to be in love with him."

"I was not born yesterday," I reminded her. "Or the day before."

"You might have been."

I bowed.

"I mean, you're so deliciously young. Do you usually go about talking to girls as you've been talking to me?"

I buttoned up my coat, preparatory to leaving. "Being a friend of you both," I said, "if a word of advice—"

"But you haven't given it."

Literally, I suppose that was true.

"Well, if your generosity's greater than your pride, you can apologise to him: if your pride's greater than your generosity, waive the apology and sink the past. I've a fair idea what the quarrel's about," I added.

"I see." Sylvia brought flippancy into her tone when speaking of something too serious to be treated seriously: the flippancy was now ebbing away, and leaving her implacable and unyielding. "Is there any reason why I should do anything at all?" she asked.

I stretched out my hand to bid her good-bye. "I've not done it well," I admitted, "but the advice was not bad, and the spirit was really good."

"Admirable," she answered ironically. "I should be glad of such a champion. Have you given *him* any advice?"

"What d'you suggest?"

Sylvia knelt on the edge of a sofa, clasping her hands lazily behind her head.

"I ride in the Park every morning," she began. "I ride alone because I prefer to be alone. My father objects, and Phil doesn't like it, because they don't think it's safe. I think I'm quite capable of taking care of myself, so I disregard their objection. Your friend also rides in the Park every morning, sometimes with a rather conspicuous woman and the last few mornings alone. I don't know whether it's design, I don't know whether it's chance—but he rides nearer me than I like."

I waited for her to point the moral, mentioning incidentally that England was a free country and the Park was open to the public.

"He may have the whole of it," she answered, "except just that little piece where I happen to be riding at any given moment."

"I'm afraid you can't keep him out of even that."

Her eyes broke into sudden blaze. "I can flog him out of it as I'd flog any man who followed me when I forbade him."

There was nothing more to be said, but I said it as soon as I dared.

"We're friends, Sylvia?" She nodded. "And I can say anything I please to you?"

"No one can do that."

"Anything in reason? Well, it's this—you're coming a most awful cropper one of these fine days, my imperious little queen."

"You think so?"

"I do. You're half woman, and half man, and half angel, and three-quarters devil."

Sylvia had been counting the attributes on her fingers.

"When I was at school," she interrupted, "they taught me it took only two halves to make a whole."

"I've learnt a lot since I left school. One thing is that you're the equivalent of any three ordinary women. Now I really am going. Queen Elizabeth, your most humble servant."

Her hand went again to the bell, but I was ready with a better suggestion.

"It would be a graceful act if you offered to show me down-stairs," I said. "It'll be horribly lonely going down two great long flights all by myself."

She took my arm, led me down to the hall, and presented me with my hat and stick.

"Are you walking?" she asked as we reached the door. "If not, you may have my private taxi. Look at him." She pointed to an olive-green car at the corner of the Square. "I believe I must have made a conquest, he's always there, and whenever I'm in a hurry I can depend on him. I think he must refuse to carry any one else. It's an honour."

I ran through my loose change, and lit upon a half-sovereign, which I held conspicuously between thumb and first finger.

"He'll carry me," I said.

"I doubt it."

"Will you bet?"

"Oh, of course, if you offer to buy the car!"

"You haven't the courage of your convictions," I said severely. "Good-bye, Queen Elizabeth."

It was well for me she declined the wager. I walked to the corner and hailed the taxi; but the driver shook his head.

"Engaged, sir," he said.

"Your flag's up," I pointed out.

"My mistake, sir."

Nonchalantly pulling down the flag, he retired behind a copy of the *Evening News*. I was sorry, because his voice was that of an educated man, and I am always interested in people who have seen better days; they remind me of my brother before he was made a judge. I had only caught a glimpse of dark eyes, a sallow complexion and bushy black beard and moustache. England is so preponderatingly clean-shaven that a beard always arouses my suspicions. If the wearer be not a priest of the Orthodox Church, I like to think of him as a Russian nihilist.

After dinner the following night I mentioned to the Seraph that I had run across Sylvia, and hinted that his propinquity to her in the Park each day was not altogether welcome.

"So she told me this morning," he said.

"I thought you wouldn't mind my handing on an impression for what it was worth," I added with vague floundering.

"Oh, not at all. I shall go there just the same, though."

"You'll annoy her."

He shrugged his shoulders resignedly. "That's as may be. This is not the time for her to be running any unnecessary risks."

"You can hardly kidnap a grown woman—on horseback—in broad daylight—in a public park," I protested.

"The place is practically deserted at the hour she rides."

The following day the Seraph rode as usual. Sylvia entered the Park at her accustomed time; saw him, cut him, passed him. For a while they cantered in the same direction, separated by a hundred and fifty yards; then the Seraph gradually reduced the distance between their horses. His quick eyes had marked a group of men moving furtively through a clump of trees to the side of the road. Their character and intentions will never be known, for Sylvia abruptly drew rein—throwing her horse on his haunches as she did so—then she turned in her own length, and awaited her gratuitous escort. The Seraph had to swerve to avoid a cannon. As he passed, her hand flashed up and cut him across the face with a switch; an instinctive pull at the reins gave his horse a momentary check and enabled her to deal a second cut back-handed across his shoulders. Then both turned and faced each other.

Sylvia sat with white face and blazing eyes.

"It was a switch to-day, and it will be a crop to-morrow," she told him. "It seems you have to be taught that when I say a thing I mean it."

The Seraph bowed and rode away without answering. Physically as well as metaphorically he was thin-skinned, and the switch had drawn blood. Three weeks passed before his face lost the last trace of Sylvia's castigation. A purple wale first blackened and then turned yellowish green. When I saw him later in the day, his face was swollen, and the mark stretched diagonally from cheekbone to chin, crossing and cutting the lips on its way. He gave me the story quietly and without rancour.

"I can't go again after this," he concluded, "but somebody ought to. If you've got any influence with her, use it, and use it quickly. She doesn't know—you none of you know—the danger she's in at present!"

He jumped up to pace the room in uncontrollable nervous excitement.

"What's going to happen, Seraph?" I asked, in a voice that was intended to be sympathetic, sceptical, and pacifying at one and the same moment.

"I don't know—but she's in danger—I know that—I know that—I'm certain of that—I know that."

His overstrung nerves betrayed themselves in a dozen different ways. It occurred to me that the less time he spent alone in his own society the better.

"I'll see if I can do anything," I said in off-hand fashion. "Meantime, I dropped in to know if your invitation held good for a bed under your hospitable roof-tree."

"Delighted to have you," he answered; and then less conventionally, "it's very kindly intended."

"Kindness all on *your* side," I murmured, pretending not to see that he had plumbed the reason for my coming.

The old, absent thought-reading look returned for an instant to his eyes.

"All my razors are on my dressing-table," he said. "Don't hide them. I shan't commit suicide, but I shall want to shave. I never keep firearms."

I had intended to supervise my removal from Pont Street in person; on reflection I thought it would be wiser to send instructions over the telephone, and give the Seraph the benefit of my company for what it was worth.

CHAPTER IX
THE THIRD ROUND

"When we two parted
In silence and tears,
Half broken-hearted
To sever for years,
Pale grew thy cheek and cold,
Colder thy kiss;
Truly that hour foretold
Sorrow to this."

—Lord Byron
When We Two Parted.

Though the flat in Adelphi Terrace became my home from this time until the end of my residence in England, I saw little of the Seraph for the week following my change of quarters. I think he liked my company at meals, and whenever we were together I certainly worked hard to distract his mind from the unhappy quarrel with Sylvia. But I will not pretend that I sat by him day and night devising consolatory speeches; I am no good at that kind of thing, he would have seen through me, and we should speedily have got on one another's nerves. For the first day or two, then, I purposely measured out my companionship in small doses; later on, when he had got used to my presence, I became more assiduous. Those were the days when I could see reflected in his eyes the fast approaching nightmare of his dreams.

My one positive achievement lay in persuading him to resume the curious journal he had started at Brandon Court and continued in Oxford. I called—and still call—it the third volume of Rupert Chevasse's life, or, more accurately, "The Child of Misery"; for though it will never be published, its literary parentage is the same, and its elder brothers are Volumes One and Two. I count it one of the great tragedies of the book-world that—at least in his life-time—the third volume will never be given to the public; in my opinion—for what that is worth—it is the finest work Aintree has ever accomplished. At the same time I fully endorse his resolution to withhold it; it has been a matter of lasting surprise that even I was allowed to read the manuscript.

He worked a great many hours each day as soon as I had helped the flywheel over dead-point. Half-way through the morning I would wander into the library and find a neat manu-script chapter awaiting me; when I had finished reading, he would throw me over sheet after sheet as each was completed. It was an interesting experience to sit, as it were, by an obser-vation hive and watch his vivid, hyper-sensitive mind at work. I had been present at half the scenes and meetings he was describing. I had heard large fragments of the dialogue and allowed my imagination to browse on the significance of each successive "soul-brush." Yet—I seemed to have heard and seen less than nothing! His insight enabled him to depict a psycho-logical development where I had seen but a material friendship. It was one-sided, of course, and gave me only the impression that a vital, commanding spirit like Sylvia's would leave on his delicate, receptive imagination. When at a later date Sylvia took me into her confidence and showed me reverse and obverse side by side, I felt like one who has assumed a fourth dimension and looked down from a higher plane into the very hearts of two fellow-creatures. It was a curious experience to see those souls stripped bare—I am not sure that I wish to repeat it—there comes a point where a painful "study of mankind is man."

While the Seraph worked, I had plentiful excuse for playing truant. Decency ordained that after my twenty years' respite I should spend a certain amount of time with my brother and his wife, and since Sylvia's edict of banishment, I was the sole channel of communication between Cadogan Square and Adelphi Terrace. It was noticeable—though I say it in no carping spirit—that Philip sought my company a shade less assiduously when I ceased to watch over the welfare of Gladys. Finally, I devoted a portion of each day to Chester Square. Elsie adhered to her decision that the Seraph must be no more seen in company with her in public, and even a private call at the house was impossible so long as his face carried the marks of Sylvia's resentment.

The burden of the publicity-campaign fell on my shoulders, though it came to be relieved—to his honour be it said!—by Gartside. I gave him my views of Elsie's behaviour, brought the two of them together at dinner, and left his big, kind heart to do the rest. He responded as I knew he would, and his adhesion to our party was matter of grave offence to Elsie's detractors, for his name carried more weight with the little-minded than the rest of us put together. Culling enrolled himself for a while, but dropped away as he dropped out of most sustained efforts. Laziness brought about his defection more than want of faith or the pressure of orthodox friends; indeed I am not sure that his strongest motive in joining us was not a passing desire to confound Nigel Rawnsley. In this as in other things, we never treated him seriously; but with Gartside it was different. At a time when Carnforth's resignation of the Bombay Governorship was in the hands of the India Office—and it was an open secret that Gartside's name stood high on the list of possible successors—it required some courage to incur the kind of notoriety that without doubt we both of us did incur. He ought to have been lunching with Anglo-Indians and patting the cheeks of Cabinet Ministers' children, instead of trying to infect Society with his belief in a divorced woman's innocence.

In the course of the campaign I began to see a little, but only a little, more of Joyce than I had been privileged to do during the time when I was supposed to be watching over the destiny of Gladys. I am not sure that I altogether enjoyed my new liberty of access to her house; it worried me to see how overworked and tired she was beginning to look, though I had the doubtful satisfaction of knowing that nothing I could say or do would check her. She risked her health as recklessly as she had been risking her liberty since the inauguration of the New Militancy. I had to treat her politics like a cold in the head and allow them to run their nine days' course. Though I saw she was still cumbered with my scarab ring, we never referred to our meeting in Oxford. I am vain enough to think that she did not regard me even at this time with complete disfavour, but I will atone for my vanity by saying I dared do next to nothing to forward my suit. My foothold was altogether too precarious; an attempt to climb higher would only have involved me in a headlong fall.

And yet, before I had been a week at Adelphi Terrace, I made the attempt. Elsie telephoned one evening that she was going out, but would have to leave Joyce who was too tired to face a restaurant and theatre. She would be dining alone; if I had nothing better to do, would I look in for a few minutes and see if I could cheer her up? I had promised to dine with Nigel, but it was a small party and I managed to slip away before ten. Joyce was half asleep when I was shown into the drawing-room; she did not hear me announced, and I was standing within two feet of her before she noticed my presence.

"I've run you to earth at last," I said.

Then I observed a thing that made me absurdly pleased. Joyce was looking very white and tired, with dark rings round the eyes, and under either cheekbone a little hollow that ought not to have been there. When she opened her eyes and saw me, I could swear to a tiny flush of pleasure; the blue eyes brightened, and she smiled as children smile in their sleep.

"Very nearly inside it," she answered, with a woebegone shake of the head. "Oh, Toby, but I'm so tired! Don't make me get up."

I had no thoughts of doing so. Indeed, my mind was solely concerned with the reflection that she had called me Toby; it was the first time.

"What have you been doing to get yourself into this state?" I asked severely.

"Working."

"There you are!" I said. "Something always happens when people take to work. I shall now read you a short lecture on female stamina."

"You're sure you wouldn't prefer to smoke?"

"I can do both."

"Oh, that's not fair."

Joyce Davenant and Sylvia Roden have only two character-istics in common; one is that I am very fond of both, the other, that I can do nothing with either. I capitulated, and selected a cigarette.

"A live dog's worth a good many dead lions," I reminded her as a final shot.

"Are *you* trying to convince me of the error of my ways?"

"I am not your Suffragan Bishop," I answered in the tone Robert Spencer adopted in telling a surprised House of Commons that he was not an agricultural labourer.

"I'm so glad. I couldn't bear an argument to-night."

The effort she had made on my arrival had spent itself, and I was not at all certain whether I ought to stay.

"Look here," I said, "if you're too tired to see me, I'll go."

"Please, don't!" she laid a restraining hand on my sleeve. "I'm all right if you don't argue or use long words; but I've had such a headache the last few days that I haven't been able to sleep, and now I don't seem able to fix my attention properly, or remember things."

I had met these symptoms before; the first time in India with men who were being kept too long at work in the hot weather.

"In other words, you want a long rest."

She nodded without speaking.

"Why don't you take it?"

"I simply can't. I've put my hand to the plough, and you know what we are. Obstinate, hard-mouthed brutes, the whole family of us. I've got other people to consider, I mustn't fail them."

"And the benighted, insignificant people who don't happen to be your followers? Some of them may cherish a flickering interest in your existence."

"Oh! they don't count."

"Thank you, Joyce."

She held out a pacifying hand. "I'm sorry. I didn't mean to be ungracious. But those women— You know, you get rather attached to people when you've spoken and fought and been imprisoned side by side with them. I always feel rather mean; any one of them 'ud die for me, and I'm not at all sure I'd do the same for them. Everything's been different since Elsie got her freedom; it's easier to fight for a person than a principle."

"Are you weakening?"

"Heavens! No! I'm just showing you I should be honour-bound to stand by my fellows even if I lost all faith in the cause. I say, don't go on smoking cigarettes; ring the bell and make Dick give you a cigar. He's in the house somewhere. I heard him come in a few minutes ago."

"I came to see you," I pointed out.

"But I'm dreadfully poor company to-night."

"I take you as I find you, in sickness and health, weal and woe—"

"Mr. Merivale!"

Her voice was very stern.

"You remember our wager?" I said, with a shrug of the shoulders.

"It was a joke," she retorted. "And not in very good taste. Oh, I was as much to blame as you were."

"But I was quite serious."

"Did you seriously think I should give up the Cause?"

"I offered very long odds. A twopenny ring—but you remember what they were."

"Are you any nearer winning?"

"I should like to think so."

"Because we haven't answered Mr. Rawnsley's time-arrangements in the House?"

"Oh, I've no doubt the reply has been posted."

She nodded significantly. "And they haven't found their hostages yet."

"But they've paid no ransom."

"It's an indurance test."

I got up to find myself a match. As I did so, I caught a glimpse of her left hand, wearing the scarab-ring; it disappeared for a moment, and to my surprise reappeared without the ring.

"Suppose we call the bet off?" she suggested. "It was all rather silly."

"Odds offered and taken and horses running. It's too late now. How did you find out the secret?"

"I didn't. My finger shrank and the ring came off three days ago when I was washing my hands."

"You didn't pull?"

"No."

"Show me."

"It was like this," she began, slipping the ring back on to the third finger. "Rather loose—"

I tightened the couplings before she saw what I was about.

"That's soon remedied. Come to me when the finger's nice and plump again, and I'll let it out."

A shadow of annoyance crossed her face.

"Now I shall have it cut," she said.

"You could have had that done three weeks ago. You could have thrown the thing away three days ago. You didn't do either."

A smile dimpled its way into her cheeks. "How old are you? Over forty?"

"What a way of looking at things!" I exclaimed. "Marlborough was fifty before he started his campaigns, Wren nearer fifty than forty before ever he put pencil to paper. You don't know the possibilities of virgin soil."

"I was wondering how long it was since you left school."

I got up and dusted the flecks of cigarette ash from my shirt.

"I'm going now," I said. "It's time you were in bed. Just one word before I go. You want to win this wager, don't you? So do I. Well, if you don't give yourself a holiday, you're going to break down and lose it."

Smiling mischievously, she got up and took my proffered hand.

"It'll be an ill-wind, then—"

"Damn the wager!" I burst out. "I don't want to win it at that price. Joyce, if I say I'm beaten, will you be a good girl and go to bed and stay there? Win or lose, I can't bear to see you looking as ill as you are now."

She shook her head a little sadly. "I can't take a holiday now."

"You'll lose the wager."

She looked up swiftly into my face, and lowered her eyes.

"I don't know that I mind that much."

"Joyce!"

"But I can't take a holiday," she repeated.

I opened the door, and on the threshold waved my hand in farewell.

"Won't you wait till Elsie comes back?" she asked.

"I will wait for no one."

"But where are you off to?"

I scratched my chin, as one does when one wishes to appear reflective.

"I am going to break the Militant Suffrage Movement."

"A good many people have failed," she warned me.

"They never tried."

"How will you begin?"

I walked downstairs thoughtfully, weighed Dick's tall hat in the balance, and decided in favour of my own.

"I have no idea," I called back to the figure at the stair-head.

The Seraph had marked his confidence in me by the bestowal of a latch-key. I let myself in at Adelphi Terrace and wandered round the flat in search of him. He was not in the library or dining-room, but at length I discovered him in pyjamas sitting in the balcony outside his bedroom, and gazing disconsolately out over the river. He knew where I had been before I had time to tell him, and was able to make a fairly accurate guess at the nature of my conversation with Joyce. Perhaps there was nothing very wonderful in that, but it fitted in with the rest of his theory: I remember he summarised her mental condition by saying that a certain sub-conscious idea was coming to be consciously apprehended. It was a cumbrous way of saying that both Joyce and I had made rather an important discovery; what puzzled me then, and puzzles me still, is that at my first meeting with her either of us should have given him grounds for forming any theory at all. Even admitting that I may have been visibly impressed, I could see no response in her; but I have almost given up trying to understand the Seraph's mind or mode of thought.

"You've not got her yet," he warned me.

"No one knows that better than I do."

"Her mind's still very full of her cause."

"Yes, damn it."

"Almost as full of it as of you. She's torn between you, and you'll have to fight if you want to keep your foothold."

I told him, as I had told Joyce, that I proposed to break the Suffrage movement.

"How?" he asked.

"I thought you might be able to help. What *is* going to be the end of it?"

He shook his head moodily, and picked up a cigarette.

"I'm not a prophet."

"You've prophesied to some purpose before now," I reminded him.

He paused to look at me with the cigarette in one hand and a lighted match in the other.

"Guesswork," I heard him murmur.

"But it worked out right?"

"Coincidence."

"*You* don't think that."

"I may think the world's flat if it amuses me," he answered, blowing out the match.

The abruptness of his tone was unusual.

"What's been worrying you, Seraph?" I asked.

"Nothing. Why?"

I lay back in my chair and looked him up and down.

"You've forgotten to light your cigarette," I pointed out. "You're shaking as if you'd got malaria, and wherever your mind may be, it's not in this room and it's not attending to me."

"I'm sorry," he apologised, sitting down. "I'm rather tired."

To belie his words he jumped up again and began pacing feverishly up and down before the open balcony window.

"Let's hear about it," I urged.

"You can't do any good."

"Let *me* judge of that."

He paused irresolutely and stood leaning his head against the frame of the window and looking out at the flaming sky-signs on the far side of the river.

"It won't do any good," he repeated over his shoulder. "Nobody 'ud believe you, but—I don't know, you might try. She must be warned. Sylvia, I mean. She's absolutely on the brink, and if some one doesn't save her, she'll be over. I can't interfere, I should only precipitate it. Will you go, Toby? She might listen to you. It's worth getting your face laid open to keep her out of danger. Will you go?"

He turned and faced me, wild-eyed and excited. His lips were white, and his fingers locked and unlocked themselves in uncontrollable nervous restlessness.

"What's the danger?" I asked, with studied deliberation.

"I don't know. How should I? But it's there; will you go?"

"I don't mind trying," I answered, taking out my watch.

"You must go now!"

It was a quarter to one, and I told him so. Nobody can be less sensitive than I to the charge of eccentricity, but I refuse to disturb a Cabinet Minister's household at one in the morning to proclaim that an overstrung nervous visionary has a premonition that peril of a vague undefined order is menacing the daughter of the house.

"We must wait till Christian hours," I insisted.

"Ah, you don't believe it; no one does!"

At eleven o'clock next morning—as soon, in fact, as I had drunk my coffee and was comfortably shaved and dressed—I drove round to Cadogan Square in search of Sylvia. I had no very clear idea what warning I was to give her when we met; indeed I felt wholly ridiculous and slightly resentful. However, my word had gone forth, and I was indisposed to upset the Seraph by breaking it. I left him in the library, silent and pale, writing hard and accumulating an industrious pile of manuscript against my return. By morning light no trace remained of his overnight excitement.

To my secret relief Sylvia was not in when I arrived. The man believed she was shopping and would be out to luncheon, but if I called again about three I should probably find her at home. It hardly seemed worth my while to return to Adelphi Terrace, so I ordered some cigars, took a turn in the Park, lunched at the Club, and talked mild scandal with Paddy Culling. At three I presented myself once more in Cadogan Square.

The door stood open, and Sylvia appeared in sight as I mounted the steps.

"Worse and worse!" she exclaimed as she gave me a hurried shake of the hand. "I was so sorry to be out when you called this morning. Look here, will you go inside and tell mother you're coming to dinner to-night."

"But I'm dining out already."

"Oh, well, when will you come? Ring up and fix a night. I must simply fly now."

"It won't take a minute."

"Honestly I can't wait! I've got to go down to Chiswick of all unearthly places! My poor old darling of a fräulein's been taken ill and she's got no one to look after her. I *must* just see she's got everything she wants. It's horribly rude, but you will forgive me, won't you? She rang up at half-past twelve, and I've only just got back."

Touching my hand with the tips of her fingers, she flashed down the steps before I could stop her. The bearded Orthodox Church retainer was waiting at the kerb, and I heard her call out "Twenty-seven, Teignmouth Road, Chiswick," as he slammed the door and clambered into his seat. I caught my last glimpse of her rounding the corner into Sloane Street, the same black and white study that I had admired when I first visited Gladys— white dress, black hat; white skin, dark hair, and soft unfathomable brown eyes; a splash of red at the throat, a flush of colour in her cheeks. Then I hailed a taxi on my own account and drove back to Adelphi Terrace.

The Seraph was still in the library, sitting as I had left him more than four hours before. An empty coffee cup at his elbow marked the only visible difference. He was writing quicker than I think I have ever seen a man write, and allowed me to enter the room and drop into an armchair by the window without raising his eyes or appearing to notice my presence. I had been there a full five minutes before he condescended—still without looking up from his writing—to address me.

"You couldn't stop her, then?"

"No."

"But you saw her?"

"Just for a moment."

"'Just for a moment.' Those were the words I had used."

He stopped writing, drew a line under the last words, blotted the page and threw it face-downwards on the pile of manuscript. Then for the first time our eyes met, and I saw it was only by biting his lips and gripping the arms of the chair that he could keep control over himself.

"You'd like some tea," he said, in the manner of a man recalling his mind from a distance. "Can you reach the bell?"

"Is this the end of the chapter?" I asked as he tidied the pile of manuscript and bored it with a paper fastener.

"It's the end of everything."

"How far does it carry you?"

"To your parting from Sylvia."

"Present time, in fact?"

"Forty minutes ago."

I checked him by my watch. "And what now?" I asked.

He looked up at me, looked through me, I might say, and sat staring at the window without answering.

The next two hours were the most uncomfortable I have ever spent. If in old age my guardian angel offers me the chance of living my whole life over again, I shall refuse the offer if I am compelled to endure once again that silent July afternoon. The Seraph sat from four till six without speech or movement. As the sun's rays lengthened, they fell on his face and lit it with cold, merciless limelight. He had started pale and grew gradually grey; the eyes seemed to darken and increase in size as the face became momentarily more pinched and drawn. I could see the lips whitening and drying, the forehead dewing with tiny beads of perspiration.

I made a brave show of noticing nothing. Tea was brought in; I poured him out a cup, drank three myself, and ostentatiously sampled two varieties of sandwich and one of cake. I cut my cigar noisily, damned with audible good humour when the matches refused to strike, picked up a review and threw it down again, and wandered round the room in search of a book, humming to myself the while.

At six I could stand it no longer.

"I'm going to play the piano, Seraph," I said.

"For pity's sake don't!" he begged me, with a shudder; but I had my way.

When the *City of Pekin* went down in '95 as she tried to round the Horn, one of my fellow-passengers was a gigantic, iron-nerved man from one of the Western States. I suppose we all of us found it trying work to sit calm while the boats were lowered away: no one knew how long we could keep our heads above water and we all had a shrewd suspicion that the boat accommodation was insufficient. We should have been more miserable than we were if it had not occurred to the Westerner to distract our minds. In spite of a thirty-degree list he sat down to the piano and I helped hold him in position while we thundered out the old songs that every one knows without consciously learning—"Clementine," "The Tarpaulin Jacket," "In Cellar Cool." We were taking a call for "The Tavern in the Town" when word reached us that there was room in the last boat.

I set myself to distract the Seraph's mind, and gave him a tireless succession of waltzes and ragtimes till eight o'clock. Then the bell of the telephone rang, and I was told Philip Roden wished to speak to me.

"It's about Sylvia," he began. "She hasn't come back yet, and we don't know where she is. The man says you had a word with her as she started out: did she say where she was going?"

I told him of the message from Chiswick, and repeated the address I had heard her give the chauffeur.

"I don't know what the matter was," I added. "Sylvia may have found the woman worse than she expected. Hadn't you better inquire who took the message and see if he or she can throw any light on the mystery?"

I was half dressed for dinner when Philip rang me up again, this time with well-marked anxiety in his voice.

"I say, there's something very fishy about this," he began. "I've just rung up the Chiswick address and the Fräulein answered in person. She wasn't ill, she hadn't been ill, and she certainly hadn't sent any message to Sylvia."

"Well, but who—?" I started.

"Lord knows!" he answered. "It might be any one. The address is a boarding house with a common telephone: any one in the house could have used it. You said twelve-thirty, didn't you? The Fräulein was out in Richmond Park at twelve-thirty."

"What about Sylvia?" I asked.

"That's the devil of it: Sylvia hadn't been near the place. When was it exactly that you saw her? Three-five, three-ten? And she turned into Sloane Street? North or South? Well, North's the Knightsbridge end. And that's all you can say?"

I mentioned the invitation she had given me, and asked if I could be of any assistance in helping to trace her. Philip told me he was going at once to Chiswick to investigate the mystery of the telephone, and promised to advise me if there was anything fresh to report. Then he rang off, and I gave a *résumé* of our conversation to the Seraph. He had just come out of the bath and was sitting wrapped in a towel on the edge of the bed. I remember noticing at the time how thin he had gone the last few weeks: he had always been slightly built, but the outline of his collarbones and ribs was sharply discernible under the skin.

"I think it would be rather friendly if I went round after dinner to see if there's any news of her," I concluded.

"There won't be," he answered.

"Well, that of course we can't say."

"*I* can. They won't have found her, they don't know where she is."

"Philip may hear something in Chiswick; it looks like a silly practical joke."

"But you know it isn't."

"I don't know what to think," I answered, as I returned to my room and the final stages of my toilet. I soon came back, however, to tie my tie in front of his glass and propound a random question. "I suppose *you* don't know where she is?"

"How should I?"

"You sometimes do."

"So do other people."

"You sometimes know where she is when other people don't—and when you've no better grounds for knowing than other people."

He was still sitting on the bed in *déshabille*, his hands clasped round his bare knees and his head bowed down and resting on his hands. For a moment he looked up into my face, then dropped his head again without speaking.

"You remember what happened at Brandon Court?" I persisted.

"Guess-work," he answered.

"Nonsense!"

"Well, what other explanation do you offer?"

"I don't know; you've got some extra sensitiveness where Sylvia's concerned. Call it the Sixth Sense, if you like."

"There *is* no Sixth Sense. I thought Nigel disposed of that fallacy at Brandon."

"Not to my satisfaction—or yours."

The Seraph jumped up and began to dress.

"Well, anyway I don't know where she is now," he observed.

"Meaning that you did once?"

"You *say* I did."

"You know you did."

"There's not much sign of it now."

"May be in abeyance. It may come back."

I watched him spend an unduly long time selecting and rejecting dress-socks.

"It won't come back as long as the connection's broken at her end," I heard him murmur.

CHAPTER X
THE ZEAL THAT OUTRUNS DISCRETION

"Selina! The time has arrived to impartThe covert design of my passionate heart.No vulgar solicitudes torture my breast,No common ambition deprives me of rest....My soul is absorbed in a scheme as sublimeAs ever was carved on the tablets of time.To-morrow, at latest, through London shall ringThe echo and crash of a notable thing.I start from my fetters, I scorn to be dumb,Selina! the Hour and the Woman are come...Hither to the rescue, ladies!Let not fear your spirits vex.On the plan by me that made isHangs the future of your sex...Shall she then be left to mourn herIsolation and her shame?Come in troops round Hyde Park Corner,Every true Belgravian dame."

—Sir George Otto Trevelyan
"The Modern Ecclesiazusæ."

I ought to have known better than to go round to Cadogan Square next morning. Bereaved families, like swarming bees, are best left alone; and I knew beforehand that I could render no assistance. At the same time, I felt it would be unfriendly to treat Sylvia's disappearance as part of the trivial round and common task, especially after my overnight conversation with Philip. And if I could bring back any news to the Seraph, I knew I should be more than compensated for my journey.

Save for its master and mistress, I found the house deserted. Philip had organised himself into one search party, Robin into another: Nigel Rawnsley appeared to be successfully usurping authority at Scotland Yard, and from Sloane Street and Chiswick respectively Gartside and Culling paced slowly to a central place of meeting. Every shopkeeper, loafer, postman, and hawker along the route was subjected to searching inquisition: the car, its passenger, and black-bearded driver were described and re-described. My two detective friends from Henley, as I afterwards found out, passed a cheerful day at headquarters, drinking down unsweetened reprimands and striving to explain the difficulties of protecting a young woman who refused to be shadowed.

I admired the way Arthur Roden took punishment. When armchair critics scoff at a generation of opportunist politicians, I think of him—and of Rawnsley, who suffered first and longest. Their public pronouncements never wavered; the Suffrage must be opposed and defeated on its own merits or demerits, and no attacks on property, no menaces to person could shake them from what they regarded as a national duty. Even if I chose to think old Rawnsley's mechanical, cold-blooded inhumanity extended to the members of his own family, it would be impossible to charge Jefferson with indifference to his only child, or Roden with want of affection towards his only daughter. I know of no girl who exacted as much admiring devotion from the members of her own family as Sylvia: or one who repaid the exaction so generously.

Their wives were even more uncompromising than the Ministers. I have no doubt the New Militants thought to strike at the fathers through the mothers, and the reasoning seemed tolerably sound. I admit I expected at first to find Mrs. Rawnsley and Mrs. Jefferson calling for quarter before their husbands, and if the New Militants miscalculated, I miscalculated with them. I had not expected their policy of abduction to arouse much active sympathy, but the bitter, uncompromising resentment it evoked far surpassed my anticipations. Had the perpetrators been discovered, I believe they would have been lynched in the street; and without going to such lengths, I feel confident that the mothers themselves would have sacrificed their own children rather than yield a single inch to women who had so outraged every maternal instinct. Had their own feelings inclined to surrender, Rawnsley, Jefferson, and Roden would have surrendered only over their wives' bodies.

"We shall go on exactly as before," Arthur told me when I asked his plans. "The enemy has varied its usual form of communication; this is what I have received."

He threw me a typed sheet of paper.

"We shall be glad to know *within the next ten days* (expiring Saturday) when the Government will guarantee the introduction of a bill to give women the parliamentary vote on the same terms as it is enjoyed by men."

"How are you answering this?" I asked.

"My campaign in the Midlands is all arranged," was the reply, "and will go forward in due course."

"And Sylvia?"

"Anything that can be done will be done. I am offering two thousand pounds reward...."

"Are you making the whole thing public?"

"It's more than half public already. We tried to keep it secret, as you know. To avoid giving them a free advertisement. However, they've advertised themselves by broad hints in the *New Militant*; the gutter-press has taken it up until half England knows and the other half suspects. Rawnsley's seeing the *Times*, and you'll have the whole story in to-morrow's papers. I shall confirm it at Birmingham next week." He paused, and drummed with his fingers on the library table. "I can't answer for the men, but there's not a mother in the length and breadth of the land who won't be on our side when the story comes out."

The ultimate collapse of the whole New Militant campaign has proved his sagacity as a prophet.

"You've got no traces yet of Mavis Rawnsley and the Jefferson boy?" I asked.

"So far the police are completely baffled. They're clever, these women, very clever."

"No clue?"

"Nothing you could take into court. We're not even sure where to look for the perpetrators."

"You've no suspicions?" I ventured to ask.

"Oh, suspicions, certainly." He looked at me shrewdly and with a spice of disfavour. "Candidly, I suspect your friend Miss Davenant."

"Why her in particular?" I asked carelessly.

"By a process of exclusion. The old constitutional agitators, the Blacks and the Campions and that lot, are out of the question; they've publicly denounced the slightest breach of the law. I acquit the Old Militants, too—the Gregorys and Haseldines and Ganons. They're too stupid, for one thing; they go on burning houses and breaking windows in their old fatuous way. And for another thing they haven't the nerve...."

"There are a good many Hunger-Strikers among them," I interposed, probably with the dishonest intention of spreading his suspicions over the widest possible area.

"Less than before," he answered. "And their arch-Hunger-Striker, the Haseldine woman, carried meat lozenges with her the last time she visited Holloway. No, they're cowards. If you want brain and courage you must look to a little group of women who detached themselves from the Old Militant party. Mrs. Millington was one and Miss Davenant was another."

"The eminently moderate staff of the ultra-constitutional *New Militant*," I said as I prepared to leave.

"If you've any influence with either of those women and want to save them a long stretch of penal servitude, now's your time to warn them."

"Good Heavens! you don't suppose I'm admitted to their counsels!"

"You could advise them as a friend."

"When you tell me there's not enough suspicion to carry into court? I fear they wouldn't listen."

"They might prefer to stop play before their luck turns," he answered as he accompanied me to the door. "Their quiescent state is the most significant, most suspicious, most damning thing about them. If a house-breaker opened a religious book-shop, you might think he had reformed. Or you might think he was preparing an extra large coup. Or you might think he sold sermons by day and cracked cribs by night."

"What cynics you public men are!" I exclaimed as I ran down the steps and turned in the direction of Chester Square.

I have said that "Providence" is not one of my star *rôles*, and I had every reason to know that my eloquence was unavailing when set to the task of converting Joyce from her militant campaign. However, I have seen stones worn away by constant dripping.... And in any case I had not been near the house for nearly two days.

"I'm afraid you can't see Joyce," Elsie told me as we shook hands. "She wouldn't go to bed when the doctor told her, and now she's really rather bad."

I was more upset by the news than I care to say, but Elsie hastened to assure me.

"It's nothing much so far," she said. "But she's got a temperature and can't sleep, and worries a good deal."

"Can't we get her away?" I exclaimed impatiently.

Elsie shook her head.

"I've tried, but she simply won't leave town."

"But what's to keep her?"

"There's the paper every week."

It always annoys me to find any one thinking the world will come to an end unless run on his or her own favourite lines.

"If she died, some one else would have to edit it," I pointed out. "Who's doing it now?"

"Mrs. Millington. I'm afraid it's no use telling people that till they *are* dead."

"And then it's a little late in the day," I answered irritably.

Elsie proceeded to give me the real reason for Joyce's obstinacy.

"When you're dead you don't have to take responsibility for

your deputy's mistakes."

"That's it, is it? Mrs. Millington setting the Thames on fire?"

"Her zeal sometimes outruns her discretion," said Elsie with a smile. "That's what's chiefly worrying Joyce."

I picked up my hat and stick and moved towards the door.

"And Joyce is losing her nerve?" I hazarded.

"She's not up to her usual form," was all Elsie would answer.

"Give her my love," I said at the door, "and best wishes for a quick recovery. If she isn't well in two days' time, I shall carry her off by main force and put her into a nursing home."

Then I went off to lunch at the Club, and found fault with the food, the wine, the cigars and all creation. Paddy Culling opened a subscription list to buy me a box of liver pills. The Seraph—after I had been two minutes at Adelphi Terrace—said he was sorry Joyce was no better.... I thanked him for his sympathy, and sat down to read the current copy of the *New Militant*.

In my careless, hot-blooded youth I made a collection of inanimate journalistic curiosities. It was my sole offence against the wise rule that to collect anything—from wives up to postage stamps—is a mark of incipient mental decay. There was the *Punch*, with the cartoon showing the relief of Khartoum; and I remember I had a copy of the suppressed issue of the *Times*, when the compositors usurped control of Empire and edited one of Harcourt's Budget speeches on lines of their own. There was also a pink *Pall Mall Gazette*, bought wet from the machine at a shilling the copy, when paper ran out and they borrowed the pink reserve rolls of the *Globe*. I had a copy of another journal that described in moving language the massacre of the Peking Legations. The Legations were, in fact, never massacred, but they should have been on any theory of probability, and, for aught I know, the enterprising journalist may have believed with Wilde that Nature tends to copy Art.

I also had several illustrated weeklies depicting—by the pen of Our Special Artist—that first Coronation Ceremony of

Edward the Seventh, and the verbal account of it given by "A Peeress" who had been present. More lately I acquired the original American paper which sent the *Titanic* to her grave with the band playing "Nearer, my God, to Thee."...

I am half sorry the collection is dispersed. I should have liked to add the one historic number of the *New Militant* that appeared under Mrs. Millington's fire-and-brimstone editorship. To the collector it is curious, as being the last issue of the paper; by the mental pathologist it is regarded as an interesting example of what is by common consent called "Militant Hysteria." The general public will remember it as the documentary evidence which at last enabled the police to secure a warrant of arrest against the "proprietors, printers and publishers of the newspaper called and known as the *New Militant*," to raid the printing office in Clerkenwell, and lay bare the private memoranda of the New Militant organisation.

My own copy did not survive my departure from England, and I could not do Mrs. Millington the injustice of trying to reproduce her deathless periods. I remember there was a great deal of "Where is Miss Rawnsley? Where is Master Jefferson? Where is Miss Roden?" Such questions implicated no one, and only annoyed inconsequential persons like myself, who detest being set conundrums of which I do not know the answer by some one who obviously does. The practice is futile and vexatious.

The incriminating words came heavy-typed in the last paragraph of the leading article, and contained an unmistakable threat that the policy of abduction would continue until female suffrage had been secured.

After dinner that night I strolled round to the Club to hear what people were saying.

"They've done for themselves this time," Gartside told me with much assurance when I ran across him in the hall. "Don't ask me where I got it from, and don't let it go any further, but there's a warrant out against some one."

I was conscious of a very uncomfortable sensation of hollowness.

"Is it indiscreet to ask who?"

"I can't tell you, because I don't know. I fancy you proceed against the whole lot, printers included."

"They've not wasted much time," I said.

It was Tuesday night. The *New Militant* went to press at midday and was on sale next morning throughout the country. In London, of course, it could be obtained overnight, and I had secured an early copy by calling at the office itself.

I stood in the middle of the hall wondering exactly what I could do to prevent the arm of the law stretching out and folding Chester Square in its embrace. I was still wondering when Paddy Culling bounded up the steps and seized Gartside and myself by either hand.

"It's yourself should have been there," he panted, momentarily releasing my arm in order to mop a red, dripping forehead. His broken collar and caved-in hat suggested a fight: his brogue reminded me that the offer of a golden throne in heaven will not avail to keep an Irishman out of a brawl. "Down Clerkenwell way ut was, the War of the Woild Women. The polis...."

He was settling down to a narrative of epic proportions. The Irish are this world's finest raconteurs as they are its finest fighters, riders and gentlemen. It was an insult, but I could not wait.

"Have they raided the place, Paddy?" I asked.

"They have." His eyes reproached me for my interruption. "The polis...."

"Did they get any one?"

"Am I telling ye or am I not? Answer me that."

"I know, Paddy," I said with all the contrition at my command. "But I've got to go, and I just wanted the main outline...."

"They got Mrs. Millington," he began again, "and she

fighting the way ye'd say she'd passed her born days being evicted. There was one had the finger bitten off him and another scratched in the face till the gutters ran blood. Five strong men held her down and stamped out the life of her, and five more dragged her down the road by the hair of her head and droppit her like a swung cat over the railings of the common mortuary. The vultures...."

"Did they get any one else?" I interrupted.

"It's the fine tale ye're spoiling," he complained.

"But just tell me that," I pleaded.

"They did not," he answered with ill-concealed disgust. "Unless ye'd be calling a printer's devil one of God's fine men and women. But the polis...."

I hurried down the steps and jumped into a taxi. I thought first of calling to warn them at Chester Square. Then I decided to communicate by telephone. If Joyce had not already been arrested, and if I was to be of any assistance later on, I could not afford to be discovered in the incriminating neighbourhood of her house.

I gave the Seraph the heads of my story as I looked up the number and waited for my call.

"You're through," the Exchange told me after an interminable delay.

"Hallo, hallo!" I kept calling, for what seemed like half an hour. "Will you give another ring, please, Exchange?"

A further age dragged its course, and I was told that there did not seem to be any one at the other end.

"Now will you tell me what we're to do, Seraph?" I exclaimed.

We sat and stared at each other for the best part of five minutes. Then the decision was taken out of our hands. I saw him prick up his ears to catch a sound too faint for my grosser senses.

"Some one coming upstairs," he whispered. "It's a woman, and she's coming slowly. Now she's stopped. Now she's coming on again."

I rose from my chair and tiptoed across the room.

"Can it be Joyce?" I asked, sinking my own voice to a whisper.

"She's going on to the next floor," he answered with a shake of the head; and then with sudden excitement, "Now she's coming back."

"She mustn't ring the bell," I cried, running out into the hall.

"It's all right, there's nobody here but ourselves," he called out as I opened the door and ran out onto the landing.

Ten feet in front of me, leaning back against the banisters, stood Joyce Davenant. One hand covered her eyes and the other was pressed to her heart. She was trembling with fever and panting with the exertion of climbing four flights of stairs. A long fur coat stretched down to bare feet thrust into slippers, her head was covered by a shawl, though the hair fell loosely inside her coat. At the neck I could see the frilled collar of a nightdress.

"Joyce!" I exclaimed.

She uncovered her face and showed eyes preternaturally bright, and white cheeks lit by a single spot of brilliant colour.

"I said I'd come when there was a warrant out," she panted with game, gallant attempt at a smile. Then I caught her in my arms as she fell forward, and carried her as gently as I could inside the flat.

I left it to the Seraph to take off her coat and lay her in his own bed. He did it as tenderly as any woman. Then we went to the far side of the room and held a whispered consultation. I am afraid I could suggest nothing of value, and the credit of our arrangement lies wholly at his door.

"We must get a nurse," he began. "Elsie mustn't be seen coming near the place or the game's up. What about that woman who helped you bring Connie Matheson home from Malta this spring? Can you trust her? Have you got her address? Well, you must see if you can get her to-night. No, not yet. We want a doctor. Her own man? No! It would give us away at once. Look out Maybury-Reynardson's address in the telephone book, somewhere in Cavendish Square. He's a sportsman; he'll do it if you say it's for me. You must go and see him in person; we don't want the Exchange-girls listening. Anything more? I'll square my man and his wife when they come in. Oh, tell your nurse the condition this poor child's come in; say it's a bachelor establishment and we haven't got a stitch of anything, and can't send to Chester Square for it. Tell her to bring...."

He paused to listen as heavy feet ascended the stairs. The noise was loud enough even for me this time. There was a ring at the door.

"Wine cellar. Locked. Haven't got key," he whispered turning out the light and locking himself inside the room with Joyce.

I opened the front door and found myself faced with the two Roden detectives I had corrupted with bottled beer at Henley.

"Why, this is like old times!" I said. "Have you been able to find any trace of Miss Roden?"

They had not, and I see now that my question was singularly tactless. They bore no resentment, however, and told me they had called on other business. There was a warrant out against Miss Davenant. She was not to be found at the Clerkenwell printing office, and while Chester Square was being searched, a woman had slipped out of the house by a side door, entered a car and driven away.

"Could you follow her?" I asked, with all the Englishman's love of the chase.

That, it appeared, had been difficult, as the number of the car seemed to have been wilfully obscured.

"That's an offence, isn't it?" I asked.

It was, and the driver—if traced—would find himself in trouble. They had followed a likely-looking car and seen it turn southward out of the Strand. When they reached Adelphi Terrace, however, there was only one car in sight, drawn up outside our door and presenting a creditably clear number-plate. Its driver had vaguely seen another car, but had not particularly noticed it. They called on chance, as this was the only suite with lights in it. Had I seen or heard anything of the car or a woman getting out of it?

"I've only just come in myself," I told them. "Half an hour, to be exact. That was possibly my taxi you saw outside. I didn't notice the number. How long ago did you see your suspected car turn into Adelphi Terrace? Ten minutes? Oh, then I should have seen any one who came up here, shouldn't I? Would you like to look round to make sure?"

The senior man stepped back and glanced up at the name painted over the door.

"It's Mr. Aintree's flat," I explained. "I'm staying with him."

The man hesitated uncertainly.

"I haven't any authority," he began.

"Oh, hang the authority!" I said. "Mr. Aintree wouldn't mind. Dining-room, wine-cellar, library.... Won't you come in? Not even for a drink? Sure? Well, good-night. Oh, it's no trouble."

Detectives—or such few of them as I have met—remind me of Customs-house officials: if you offer your keys and go out of your way to lay bare your secrets before their eyes, they will in all probability let you through without opening a single trunk. They are perverse as women—and simple as children.

I tapped at the Seraph's door and told him I had disposed of the police without uttering a single falsehood. It was almost the last time I was able to make that boast. We gave our friends ten minutes' start, and I then set out in search of nurse and doctor. Joyce looked shockingly ill when I left, but her breathing was peaceful. Occasionally she moved or moaned in her sleep; as I turned at the door for a last look, the Seraph was rearranging her pillow and smoothing the hair back from her face.

I had to walk into the Strand to find a taxi. Outside the Vaudeville I met my brother and his wife, and was bidden to sup with them at the Savoy. I refused for many reasons, the first being that a man who starts a career of crime at the age of forty-two must not for very decency be seen eating in company with a judge of the High Court. My meeting did good in giving me the idea of establishing a succession of *alibis*. When I had made the necessary arrangements with Maybury-Reynardson and the nurse, I looked in once more at the Club.

Culling, Gartside and Nigel Rawnsley had the north smoking-room to themselves. They seemed to be discussing some plan of campaign, and the rescue of Sylvia was its object. Perhaps I should not say "discussing": Nigel was holding forth in a way that made me think he must have been a Grand Inquisitor in some previous incarnation. The ruthlessness of a Torquemada was directed by Napoleonic statecraft and brought down to date by the terrorism of a brow-beating counsel. The combination was highly impressive; his own contribution consisted in an exquisite choice of epithets.

"Talk to the Chief," I heard him say in summary of his plan of campaign. "Get him to arrange for Merivale, J., to try the case, and you'll find the woman Millington will exhibit surprising celerity in imparting whatever information she may have gathered in respect of the whereabouts of Mavis and Sylvia and the Jefferson boy."

"King's Evidence, d'you mean?" asked Gartside. "Not she!"

"Inconceivably less ornate than that. I agree with you that she might withhold her consent. It is therefore more expedient to coax her into the confessional without implicating her fellow conspirators. If you were being tried by Merivale and saw seven years' penal servitude stretching in pleasing prospect before you, you'd want to start the day on terms of reasonable amity with your judge. If you knew Merivale's daughter was engaged to marry a man whose sister had been spirited away, would you not strive to acquire merit in the eyes of your judge's family by saying where the sister could be found? It is approximately equivalent to a year's reduction of sentence."

Paddy Culling scratched his head thoughtfully with a paper knife.

"If Miss Davenant's afther hiding herself in one of the coops where the other little chicken's stored away...." he began.

"She's not," Nigel interrupted decisively. "The risk's too considerable; she wouldn't want to betray herself and her hostages at the same moment. She's in London...."

"Is she?" asked Gartside.

"She was to-day at lunch-time, because her doctor called at the house. Of course, the police in their infinite sagacity must needs start searching at the wrong end and afford her opportunities of escape."

"Out of London if she wanted to," persisted Gartside.

"Not by train," said Nigel. "Every station's watched...."

"By car."

"By airship, equally. The woman's seriously ill; you'd kill her."

Paddy Culling looked at his friend a little enviously.

"You know a lot about the inside of that house," he said.

"By the simple expedient of the sovereign in season to the kitchen-maid, who, like the rest of her class, was unquestionably loyal, but more unquestionably impecunious. The woman Davenant's in London, and they'll find her in three days. Where she is, I can't tell you. I may know more when I've seen the officers' reports to-morrow morning. Sylvia I'll undertake to find within a week. The woman Millington will give her away, and if she doesn't, the woman Davenant will have to."

"When you've caught her," said Culling quietly.

"Not even when you've caught her," said Gartside with greater knowledge. "I know the breed. It's pedigree stock."

Nigel lit a cigarette with ostentatious elaboration.

"Even pedigree stock has its less spirited moments," he said. "For example, when it's seriously ill. I fancy I could make the woman Davenant tell me all I wanted in three minutes."

The tone was extraordinarily sinister. I seemed to realise in a flash why Sylvia, with a woman's quicker, deeper insight, kept the speaker at a distance.... However, I had come to the Club to establish an *alibi,* not to reflect on the character of Sylvia's admirers. And I wanted to get back to Adelphi Terrace as soon as my purpose was effected.

"I was sorry to run away in the middle of your story, Paddy," I said. "I'd promised to meet a man, and I was rather late as it was. You'd got as far as the disposal of Mrs. Millington's body in the common mortuary and the arrest of a poor, mean printer's devil. What happened then? Was any one else caught?"

Paddy looked at me almost with affection, his eyes alight with oratorical fire.

"It's yourself should have been there to see it," he began, grasping my arm with one hand and making his points with the other. "The polis and red coats was there, and the newspaper men in their thousands, and the gravediggers in their tens of thousands...."

CHAPTER XI
THE AMATEUR DETECTIVE

"My mind ... rebels at stagnation. Give me problems, give me work, give me the most abstruse cryptogram, or the most intricate analysis, and I am in my own proper atmosphere.... I crave for mental exaltation. That is why I have chosen my own particular profession, or rather created it, for I am the only one in the world ... the only unofficial consulting detective.... I am the last and highest court of appeal in detection.... I examine the data, as an expert, and pronounce a specialist's opinion. I claim no credit in such cases. My name figures in no newspaper. The work itself, the pleasure of finding a field for my peculiar powers, is my highest reward."

—Sir A. Conan Doyle
"The Sign of Four."

Premonitions—so far as my gross person is concerned—are a matter of digestion, nerves and liver. If I woke up on the morning after Joyce's flight to Adelphi Terrace with a dull sense of impending disaster, I ascribe it to the fact that I had passed a more than ordinarily hideous night. Unlike the Seraph, who never went to bed, I had sufficient philosophy to turn in when the doctor had left and the nurse was comfortably established. It had been made clear to me that I could do no manner of good by staying up and getting in people's way....

I started in my own room, but quickly took refuge in the library. If there are two sounds I cannot endure, one is that of a crying child, and the other of a woman—or man for that matter—moaning in pain. Even in the library I could hear Joyce suffering. Maybury-Reynardson had told us she was all right, and there is no point in calling in experts if you are going to disbelieve them. But I do not want to experience another night of the same kind.

And in the morning the papers were calculated to heighten the horror of the worst premonitions I could experience. I opened the *Times*, noted in passing that Gartside had fulfilled popular expectation by being appointed to the Governorship of Bombay, and turned to the account of the Clerkenwell raid. Culling was right in saying Mrs. Millington's had been the only arrest of importance; but he had left the battlefield at the end of the fighting, and had not waited to see the conquerors march into the citadel.

I felt myself growing chilled and old as I read of the discoveries in the printing office. Mrs. Millington would stand charged with incitement to crime and public threat of abduction; serious enough, if you will, but her debt was discharged as soon as she had paid the penalty for a single article in a single paper. Her threats were embryonic, not yet materialised. Joyce stood to bear the burden of the three abductions carried out to date....

I am no criminologist, and can offer neither explanation nor theory of the mental amblyopia that leads criminals to leave one weak link, one soft brick, one bent girder, to ruin a triumph of design and construction. They always do—men and women, veterans and tiros—and Joyce was no exception. When the police broke open the safe in her editorial office, the first document they found was the half sheet of Chester Square notepaper that the journalists agreed to christen "The Time Table."

It was written in Joyce's hand, and her writing could be identified by a short-sighted illiterate at ten yards' distance. I have forgotten the dates by this time, and can only guess at them approximately; words and names have been added in full where Joyce put only initials. This was the famous Time Table:—

500, Chester Square, S.W.
May 8. Rejection of W. (women's) S. (suffrage) Amendment.
May 9. M.R. (Mavis Rawnsley) letter R. (Rawnsley).
~~June 16. R.'s (Rawnsley's) Time Table.~~ [This was ruled
    through.]

June 17. P. (Paul) J. (Jefferson) Letters R. and J. (Rawnsley and Jefferson).

June 30. R. (Rawnsley) to decide re A.S. (Autumn Session).

July 2. R. (Rawnsley) in H. (House). No A.S. (Autumn Session).

July 9. S. (Sylvia) R. (Roden). Letters R. (Rawnsley) & R. (Roden).

July 19. R. (Rawnsley) to reply re facilities.

July 20. W.G. [I am not sure whether this refers to Walter Greatorex, the ten-year-old son of the President of the Board of Agriculture and Fisheries, or Lady Winifred Gaythorne, daughter of the Marquis of Berwick—of the India Office. Both Greatorex and Berwick were opposed to the franchise, but in a mild, unoffending fashion. The invariable typed challenge does not help me to decide, as only one letter was to be sent, the usual Letter R. (Rawnsley)].

"So far the police have been unable to discover the where-abouts of Miss Davenant," the article concluded. That was the sole, poor consolation I could offer to a white, tired Seraph as I threw him the paper and went back to my gloomy premonitions.

As he read, I thought over my last *alibi* in the north smoking-room at the Club. I wondered what story my friends, the Henley detectives, were concocting in their report, and what action Nigel Rawnsley would take when he had digested it.

It is not entirely my "wisdom after the event" that made me select Nigel as our most formidable opponent, nor altogether my memory of the lead he had taken in the discussion overnight; I was beginning to appreciate his character. When he is Prime Minister of England, like his father before him, it will be in virtue of the same qualities. A brain of steel and a ruthless, iron resolution will force the οἱ φύσει ἀρχόμενοι to follow and obey him. He will be feared, possibly even hated, but the hatred will leave him indifferent so long as power is conceded him. I have met no young man so resolute or successful in getting his own way; few who give me the impression of being so ruthless and, perhaps, unscrupulous in their methods. He is still preserved from active mischief by his astonishing self-consciousness and lack of humour; when he has outgrown these juvenilities, he will be really formidable. His wife—when she comes—will have my sympathy, for what that is worth; but there will be many women less discerning than Sylvia to strive for the privilege.

It was noon before the Amateur Detective invaded us. The Seraph's man—who had already been admitted to our secret, and would at any time have been crucified head-downwards for his master—flung open the library door with the words—

"Mr. Nigel Rawnsley, Lord Gartside, Mr. Culling, Mr. Philip Roden."

The Seraph rose and offered chairs. You could to some extent weigh and discriminate characters by the various modes of entry. Nigel refused to be seated, placed his hat on the table and produced a typewritten transcript of the two detectives' reports in the traditional manner of a stage American policeman— which in passing, I may say, is nothing like any American policeman I have ever met anywhere in America or the civilised world. Philip and Gartside were self-conscious and uncomfortable; Culling strove to hide his embarrassment by more than usual affability.

"It's ill ye're looking, Seraph," he remarked, as he accepted a cigarette. "And has this great ugly brute Toby been slashing the face off you?"

Then the inquiry began, with Philip as first spokesman.

"Sorry to invade you like this, Seraph," he began, "but it's about my sister. You know she's disappeared? Well, we were wondering if you could help us to find her."

"I'll do anything I can...." the Seraph started.

"Do you know where she is?" Nigel cut in.

"I'm afraid I don't."

"Do you know any one who does?" Philip asked.

"I don't know that I do."

Philip hesitated, started a sentence, and closed his lips again without completing it. Nigel took up the examination.

"You know Miss Davenant, I believe?"

"Yes."

"Does she know where Sylvia and Mavis are?"

"I have no idea. You must ask her."

"I propose to."

The Seraph turned to Philip, glancing at the clock as he did so.

"I'm afraid the limits of my utility are soon reached. If there's anything I can do...."

"You can tell us where Miss Davenant is hiding," said Nigel.

"Can I?"

"You can and will."

The Seraph treated him to a long, unhurried scrutiny, starting from the boots and working up to the freckled face and sandy hair. Then he turned away, as though the subject had no further interest for him.

Nigel tried to return the stare, but broke into a blush and took refuge in his typewritten transcripts.

"I have here," he said, "a copy of the reports of the two detectives who watched Miss Davenant's house in Chester Square last night. They saw a woman, with her hair loose, and a long coat over whatever clothes she was wearing, jump into a car and drive to Adelphi Terrace."

"They were certain of the identity of the car?" I asked.

"Perfectly."

"They weren't when I talked to them last night," I said. "No number—no nothing. They thought it was the same car and called in on chance, as there was a light here, to see if we knew anything. I offered to show them round, but they wouldn't come in, so we prayed for mutually sweet dreams and parted."

Nigel tapped his papers.

"I have here their sworn statement that the car which left Chester Square was the car that turned into Adelphi Terrace."

"Perjury—like joy—cometh in the morning," I observed.

"That is as may be. I happen to know that Miss Davenant is seriously ill; I imagine, wherever she has gone, she has not gone far. The number of houses within easy reach of Chester Square—houses that would take her in when there's a warrant out for her arrest—is limited. These considerations lead me to believe that the statement of these men is not perjured."

"I will apologise when next we meet," I said. When a young man like Nigel becomes stilted and dignified, I cannot repress a natural inclination to flippancy.

Philip intervened before Nigel could mature a crushing repartee.

"Look here, Seraph," he began. "Just as a favour, and not because we have any right to ask, will you say whether Miss Davenant's anywhere in this flat? If you say she is, I'm afraid we shall have to tell the police; if you say she isn't, we'll go away and not bother you any more."

"You must speak for yourself," Nigel interposed, before the Seraph could answer.

We sat for a moment in silence. Then Nigel continued his statement with unmistakable menace in his tone.

"If once the police intervene, the question becomes more serious and involves any one found harbouring a person for whom a warrant of arrest has been issued. I naturally do not wish to go to extremes." He turned to me: "You offered to show the detectives round these rooms last night; will you make me the same offer?"

I pointed to the Seraph.

"They aren't my rooms. I'm only a guest. I took it upon myself to make the offer in the Seraph's absence."

He repeated his request in the proper quarter, but was met with an uncompromising refusal.

"May I ask your reason?" he said.

"It is a question of manners," answered the Seraph.

"Then you wish me to apply for a search-warrant?"

"I am entirely indifferent. If you think it worth while, apply for one. As soon as it is presented, the police—are—welcome—to—any— discoveries—they—may—make."

The Seraph spoke with the quiet scorn of injured innocence. I saw a shadow of uncertainty settle on Nigel's face. The Seraph must have seen it, too; we preserved a strategic silence until uncertainty had matured into horrid doubt. I felt sorry for Nigel, as I feel sorry for any successful egoist in the toils of anticipated ridicule.

"It would be quicker to clear the matter up now," he said.

"My whole day is at your disposal."

"But mine is not. What is that room?"

"A spare bedroom, now occupied by Toby, if you ask for information."

Nigel started to cross the room.

"I like to check all verbal information," he remarked.

The Seraph had shorter distance to cover, and was standing with his back to the door when Nigel got there.

"I allow no unauthorised person to search my rooms without my leave," he said.

"You cannot always prevent it."

"I can in this case."

"We are four to one."

"You are one to two."

"My mistake, no doubt." He waved a hand round the room to indicate his allies.

"Assuredly your mistake, if you think Toby will stand by and let you search my rooms without my leave, or that any one of the others would raise a finger to help you."

Not one of his three allies had moved a step to support him. Nigel was impressed. Without retreating from his position he tried the effect of bluff.

"You forget the circumstances are exceptional. My sister has been spirited away, and so has Phil's. If we think you know the whereabouts of the woman who kidnapped them, we shall neither of us hesitate to employ timely physical force on you, perhaps inflict salutary physical pain."

"You may try, if you like."

"If I try, I shall succeed."

"You don't really think that, you know."

Gartside felt it was time to restore the peace. Walking up to Nigel, he led him firmly back to his place at the table and motioned the Seraph to his old position in the armchair by the fireplace. There was a long, awkward silence. Then Culling crossed the room, and sat on the arm of the Seraph's chair.

"Ye're white and ill, Seraph," he said, "and ye know I'm not the man would badger you. We're in a hole, and maybe ye can give us a hoist out of it. Do ye, or do ye not, know where Miss Davenant's hiding herself?"

The Seraph looked him steadily in his eyes.

"Yes."

"Well, is she, or is she not, in these rooms?"

"Would *you* like to search them?"

"Damn it, no, man! Give us yer word, and that's enough."

For a fraction of time the Seraph gazed at the faces of Culling, Philip and Gartside, weighing the characters and measuring the men.

"It's not enough for Rawnsley," he said.

"It'ull have to be."

"He likes to check all verbal information."

Culling shook his clenched fists in the air and involved us all in a comprehensive curse. The Seraph lit himself a cigarette, blew out the match with a deliberation Nigel could not have surpassed, and addressed the company.

"We seem to have reached a deadlock," he began. "Shall I

offer a solution? The four of you come here and charge me with harbouring the woman who is supposed to have made away with Miss Rawnsley and Miss Roden. Very good. Every man is free to entertain any suspicions he likes, and to ventilate them—provided he doesn't forget his manners. Three of you behaved like gentlemen, the fourth followed his own methods. I should like to oblige those three. Rawnsley, you have menaced me with personal violence, and threatened me with a search warrant. You have done this in my own library. If you will apologise, and undertake not to enter these rooms again or to molest me here or anywhere else, and if you will further undertake not yourself to apply—or incite any one else to apply—for a warrant to search the flat, I shall have pleasure in accompanying Gartside wherever he chooses to go, unlocking any doors that may be locked, and offering him every facility in inspecting every nook and cranny in these rooms. As you may not accept verbal information even from him, I shall have pleasure in extending my offer to Culling. The one will be able to check the other."

He blew three smoke-rings and waited for an answer.

There was another moment of general discomfort. Nigel jibbed at the idea of apologising, Gartside and Culling would have done anything to avoid accepting the offer; from Philip's miserable fidgeting I could see that he had been persuaded into coming against his better judgment. For myself, I waited as a condemned man waits for the drop to fall. It was bound to come in a few seconds' time, but—illogically enough—I had ceased to dread it. My one fear was that Joyce should betray herself by one of those pitiful moans that had mingled with my dreams and vexed my sleep throughout the night. To this hour I can remember thinking how horror-stricken I should be if that sound broke out again. It had begun to get on my nerves.... The discovery itself was inevitable; I could imagine no trick or illusion that would enable the Seraph to steer his inquisitors past one of the principal rooms in the flat.

"I apologise for any offence I may have given, and I undertake all that you ask."

It was not gracefully done, but the Seraph accepted the words for the spirit.

"Come on, and let's get it over!" Culling exclaimed, jumping up and cramming his hat on the back of his head. With sinking heart I saw the three of them framed in the doorway, Gartside's huge form towering over the other two.

"Devilish sorry about the whole business," I heard him begin as the door closed. It was opened again for a moment as the Seraph reminded me where the drinks were kept, and suggested I should compound a cocktail. Then it closed finally.

Outside in the hall Culling added his contribution to the general apology.

"Come quietly," was all the Seraph would answer. "I hope she's sleeping."

Both men paused abruptly and gazed first at the Seraph and then at each other. He returned their gaze unwaveringly, surprised apparently that they should be surprised. Then he led them wide-eyed with expectation across the hall; wide-eyed they watched him bend and listen, tap and gently open a bedroom door. The nurse rose from her chair at the bedside and placed a finger on her lips—

"Praise God, she's sleeping!" murmured Paddy Culling, with instinctive reverence removing his hat. Gartside looked for a moment at the flushed cheeks and parched lips, then turned away as the Seraph closed the door.

"Mustn't go back yet," he said. "We'd better look at one or two more rooms just to fill in time."

One of the shortest recorded councils of war was held in the bathroom. Culling, with his quick, superficial sympathy had already made up his mind, but Gartside stood staring out of the window with head bent and hands locked behind his back, struggling and torn between an unwillingness to hurt Joyce and a deep hungry desire to bring Sylvia safely out of her unknown hiding-place.

"You'll kill her if you move her," the Seraph remarked, dispassionately but with careful choice of time. Gartside's foot tapped the floor irresolutely. "Toby's engaged to marry her," he added softly.

With a sigh and a shrug of the shoulders Gartside turned to Culling, nodded without speaking, and linked arms with the Seraph.

"You're a good little devil," he said with a forced smile. "When this poor girl's better, get her to say where Sylvia is. She'll tell you. And let me know when the whole damned thing's straightened out. I'm off to Bombay in ten days' time. And it isn't very cheerful going off without knowing where Sylvia is. Now we've been out long enough," he added in firm, normal tones.

All three of us looked up quickly as the door opened. Culling's hat was once more on his head, and he was trying to pull on a pair of gloves and light a cigarette at the same time.

"All over but the cheering," he began abruptly. "High and low we've searched, and not found enough of a woman would make a man leave Eden, and she the only woman in the world."

"You've searched every room?" asked Nigel with a suspicious glance at the Seraph.

"Cellar to garret," answered Culling serenely, "and no living creature but a pair of goldfinches, and one of them dead; unless you'd be counting the buxom matron that the Seraph dashes my hopes by sayin' has a taste for drink like the many best of us, and she married already, and the mother of fourteen brace of twins and a good plain cook into the bargain."

Nigel picked up his papers and turned to Gartside for corroboration.

"We searched every room," he was told, "and Miss Davenant's not here. Seraph, we owe you...."

The apology was cut short, as speaker and listeners paused

to catch a sound that floated through the silent hall and in at the open library door. A long, troubled moaning it was, the sound I had heard all night and dreaded all the morning.

"I shall have to check the verbal information after all," said Nigel as he put back his hat and papers on the table.

"Where are you off to?" asked Gartside as he approached the door.

"It seems I must search the house myself."

"You undertook to accept our finding."

"I thought I could trust you."

"I have said Miss Davenant is not in these rooms," said Gartside in a warning voice.

"If you said it a hundred times I should still disbelieve you. Let me pass, please."

He raised a hand to clear himself a passage, but in physical strength he had met more than his match. Seizing both wrists in one hand and both ankles in the other, Gartside carried him like a child's doll across the room to the open library window, thrust him through it, and held him for ninety seconds stretched at arm's length three storeys above the level of the street. The veins stood out on his forehead, and I heard his voice rumbling like the distant mutter of thunder.

"When I say a thing, Nigel, you have to believe me. The moon's of green cheese if I tell you to believe it, and when I say Miss Davenant's not in this flat, she's not and never has been, and never will be. You see?"

Stepping back from the window, he dropped his burden on a neighbouring sofa. Nigel straightened his tie, brushed his clothes, and once more gathered up his hat, his papers, and the remains of his dignity.

"Culling says there is no woman but a cook in the house," he began, with the studied tranquillity of an angry man. "He clearly lies. Gartside says Miss Davenant is not in the flat. He probably lies, but it is always possible that the sound we heard may have come from some woman Aintree thinks fit to keep in his rooms. In either event, I do not feel bound by the under-taking I have given." He pulled out a note-book and pretended to consult it. "To-day's Wednesday. If my sister and Sylvia have not been restored to their families by midday on Monday, I shall apply for a warrant to have these rooms searched. They will, of course, be watched in the interval. If Lord Gartside or any other person presumes to lay a finger on me, I shall summon him for assault."

Pocketing the note-book he passed out of the flat with the air I suspect Rhadamanthus of assuming, when he is leaving the court for the luncheon interval, and has had a disagreeable morning with the prisoners. Culling accompanied him to prevent a sudden bolt at a suspicious-looking door, Philip followed with the Seraph, I brought up the rear with Gartside. All of us were smarting with the Englishman's traditional dislike of a "scene."

"I never congratulated you on the Bombay appointment," I said, with praiseworthy design of scrambling onto neutral terri-tory. "How soon are you off?"

"Friday week," he answered.

"It's little enough time—nine days."

"Oh, I've known for some little while beyond that. It was only made public to-day."

"It's a pleasant post," I said reflectively. "In a tolerably pleasant country. I shall probably come to stay with you; I'm forgetting what India's like."

"I wish you would," he said warmly.

"How are you going? P. and O. I suppose?"

"No, I shall go in my own yacht."

Culling turned round to reprove me for my forgetfulness.

"We Gartsides always take our own yachts when we cross the ocean to take up our new responsibilities of Empire," he explained.

"Where do you sail from?" I ask. "Marseilles?"

"Southampton. Are you coming to see me off?"

"I might. It depends whether I can get away. Half London will be there, I suppose?"

Candidly I cannot say whether my questions were prompted by what the Seraph would call a sub-conscious plan of campaign. Gartside undeniably thought they were, and met me gallantly.

"I'm eating a farewell dinner every night till I sail," he said. Then, sinking his voice, he added, "You know the yacht—she's roomy, and there will be only my two aide-de-camps and myself. No one will be seeing me off, because I haven't told them when I'm sailing. It's the usual route—anywhere in the Mediterranean. But I can't sail before Friday week."

"I see. Well," I held out my hand, "if I *don't* see you again, I'll say good-bye."

"Good-bye. Best of luck!" he answered, and waved a hand as I walked back and rejoined the Seraph in the hall.

He was so white that I expected every moment to see him faint, and his clothes were wet with perspiration. I, who am not so fine-drawn, had found the last hour a little trying.

"You're going to bed in decent time to-night," I told him. "I'm going to see Nurse, and find out if she knows of any one she can trust to come and help her. And I'm going to keep you out of the sick-room at the point of a bayonet if you've got one."

I had expected a protest, but none came. He sat with closed eyes, resting his head on his hand.

"I suppose that will be best," he assented at last.

"And now you're coming to get something to eat," I said, leading him into the dining-room.

"I'm not hungry," he complained.

"But you're going to eat a great deal," I said, pushing him into his chair and selecting a serviceable, sharp-pronged pickle-fork.

After luncheon I had my usual siesta, prolonged rather beyond my usual hour. It was five o'clock when I awoke, and I found the Seraph playing with a sheet of paper. He had written "Thursday, Friday, Saturday, Sunday, Monday" on it, and after "Monday," "12.0 P.M."

"What's all this?" I asked.

"Our days of grace."

I added "Friday week" to the calendar.

"If we can get Joyce well enough to move away from Nigel's damned cordon of police," I said, "and if we can hide her somewhere till Friday week, friend Gartside's yacht is going to solve a good many problems."

"It's not going to find Sylvia," he answered.

That was unquestionably true.

"I don't know how that's going to be managed," I said.

We sat without speaking until dinner-time, and ate a silent dinner. At eleven o'clock he left the room, changed out of his dress clothes into a tweed suit, and put on a hat and brown walking boots.

"Where are you off to?" I asked when he came back.

"I'm going to find Sylvia."

The expression in his eyes convinced me—if I wanted any convincing—that the strain of the last few days had proved too much for him.

"Leave it till the morning," I said in the tone one adopts in talking to lunatics and drunken men.

"She wants me now."

"A few hours won't make any difference," I urged. "You'll start fresher if you have a night's rest to the good."

The Seraph held out his hand.

"Good-bye. You think I'm mad. I'm not. No more than I ever am. But Sylvia wants me, and I must go to her."

"Where is she?" I asked.

"I don't know."

"Then how are you going to find her?"

"I don't know."

"Well, where will you start looking?"

"I don't know."

He was already halfway across the hall. I balanced the rival claims of Joyce and himself. She at least had a doctor and nurse, and a second nurse was coming in the morning. He had no one.

"Damn you, Seraph!" I said under my breath, and then aloud: "Wait a bit and I'll come too."

"Hurry up then!" he answered chafing visibly at the delay.

I spoke a hurried word to the nurse, took a last look at Joyce, changed my clothes and joined him on the landing.

"Which way first?" I asked, and received the answer I might have expected.

"I don't know."

CHAPTER XII
THE SIXTH SENSE

"There was no sound at all within the room. But ... he saw a woman's face.

"He saw it quite clearly for perhaps five seconds, the face rising white from the white column of the throat, the dark and weighty coronal of the hair, the curved lips which alone had any colour, the eyes, deep and troubled, which seemed to hint a prayer for help which they disdained to make—for five seconds, perhaps, the illusion remained, for five seconds the face looked out at him ... lit palely, as it seemed, by its own pallor, and so vanished."

—A.E.W. Mason
"Miranda of the Balcony."

Neither by inclination nor habit am I more blasphemous or foul-mouthed than my neighbour, but I should not relish being ordered a year in Purgatory for every occasion on which I repeated "Damn you, Seraph!" in the course of the following nineteen or twenty hours.

It was nearly midnight when we left Adelphi Terrace, and I had in my own mind fixed one hour as the maximum duration of my patience or willingness to humour a demented neurotic. Thirty minutes out, thirty minutes back, and then the Seraph would go to bed, if I had to keep him covered with my revolver. *En parenthèse*, I wish I could break myself of the habit of carrying loaded firearms by night. In the settled, orderly Old Countries it is unnecessary; in the West it is merely foolish. I should be the richer by the contents of six chambers before I had time to draw on the quick, resourceful child of a Western State.... Nevertheless, my revolver and I are inseparable.

We started down the Strand, along the Mall, past Buckingham Palace, and through Eaton Square to the Cadogan Estate. This was what I ought to have expected, if I had had time to sort out my expectations. The Seraph stood for a few minutes looking up at the Rodens' slumbering house, and then walked slowly eastward into Sloane Street.

"Shall we go back now?" I suggested, in the voice one uses to deceive a child.

"I'm not mad, Toby," he answered, like a boy repeating a lesson. "I must find Sylvia."

He wandered into Knightsbridge, hesitated, and then set out at an uncertain three miles an hour along the border of the park towards Kensington. I realized with a sinking heart that he was heading for Chiswick.

"Better leave it till the morning, Seraph," I urged, with a hand on his shoulder. "She'll be in bed, and we mustn't disturb her."

He shook me off, and wandered on—hands in pocket and eyes to the ground. Twice I thought he would have blundered into an early market-cart, but catastrophe was averted more by the drivers' resource than any prudence on his own part. As we left Kensington and trudged on through the hideous purlieus of Hammersmith, I began to visualize our arrival at the Fräulein's house, and my stammering, incoherent apologies for my companion's behaviour.

The deferential speech was not required. On entering Chiswick High Street we should have turned to the right up Goldhawk Road, and then taken the second or third turning to the left into Teignmouth Terrace. The Seraph plodded resolutely on, looking neither to the right nor left, through Hounslow, past the walls of Sion Park and the gas-works of Brentford, into Colnbrook and open country. There was no reason why he should not follow the great road as far as the Romans had built it—and beyond. Night was lifting, and the stars paled in the blue uncertain light of early dawn.

I gripped him by the shoulders and made him look me in the face.

"We're going back now," I said.

"*You* can."

"You're coming with me."

"I must find Sylvia."

"If you'll come back now, I'll take you to her in the morning."

"I'm not a child, Toby, and I'm not mad."

"You're behaving as if you were both."

"I must find Sylvia," he repeated, as though that were an answer to every conceivable question.

"If you're sane," I said, "you can appreciate the insanity of walking from London to Bath in search of a girl who may be in Scotland or on the Gold Coast for all you know. She's as likely to be in the Mile End Road as on the Bath Road. Why not look there? It's nearer Adelphi Terrace, at all events."

He looked at me for a moment reproachfully, as though his last friend had failed him, then turned and plodded westward....

"God's truth!" I cried. "Where are you off to?"

"I must find Sylvia," he answered.

"But where? Where?"

"I don't know."

"Why this God-stricken road rather than another?"

"She came along here."

"How do you know?"

He raised his eyebrows and shrugged his shoulders.

"She did," was all he would answer.

It was near Langley that I threatened him with personal injury. He had quickened his pace and shot slightly ahead of me. I have never been of a fleshy build, and with the exception of excessive cigar-smoking, my tastes are moderate. On the other hand, I never take exercise save under compulsion, or walk a mile if I can possibly ride, drive, or fly. We had covered some twenty miles since leaving home, my feet seemed cased in divers' boots, my mouth was parched with thirst, and I was ravenously hungry.

"Are you sane?" I asked, as I caught him up.

"As sane as I ever am."

"Then you will understand my terms. We are going to leave the main road and walk straight to Langley Station. We are going to take the first train back to town, and we are...."

"You can," he interrupted.

"You will come with me. Don't tell me you have to find Sylvia, because it will be waste of breath. I have here a six-chambered revolver, loaded. Unless you come to the station with me, here and now, I shall empty one chamber into each of your legs. And if any one thinks I'm murdering you, I shall say I'm in pursuit of a dangerous lunatic. And when they see you, they'll believe me."

He looked at me for perhaps half a second, and then walked on. It was, I suppose, the answer I deserved.

It came as a surprise to me when he accepted my breakfast proposition at Slough. I put his assent down to sheer perversity, for I should have breakfasted in any case. My mind was made up. I would ask him for the last time to accompany me back to London, and if he refused I would return to Adelphi Terrace and bed, leaving him to follow the sun's path till he pitched head-foremost into the Bristol Channel....

I breakfasted unwashed, unshaven, dusty, at full length on a sofa in a private room, simmering with grievance and irritability.

"*Now* then," I said, as I lit a cigar, threw the Seraph another, and turned to a Great Western time-table.

"I must be getting on," he answered, giving me back my cigar.

"Just a moment," I said. "Up-trains, Sundays. Up-trains, week-days. Ten-fifteen. Horses and carriages only. Ten-thirty; that'ull do me. I'll walk with you as far as the cross-roads."

I was so angry with myself and him that we parted without a word or shake of the hand. I watched him striding westward in the direction of Salt Hill, and carried my temper with me towards the station. The first twenty yards were covered at a swinging, resolute pace, the second more slowly. I was still far from the station when an absurd, irritating sensation of shame brought me to a standstill. Mad, unreasonable as I knew him to be, the more I thought of the Seraph, the less I liked the idea of leaving him in his present state. The sight of a garage, with cars for hire, decided me. I ordered one for the day, with the option of renewing on the same terms as long as I wanted it.

"Take the money while you can get it," I warned the proprietor, with the petulance of a tired man. "With luck you'll next hear of me from the inside of a padded cell. Now!" I said to the driver, "listen very carefully. I'm about as angry as a man can be. Here are two sovereigns for yourself; take them, and say nothing, whatever language you may hear me use. I want you to drive along the Bath Road until you see a young man in a grey tweed suit walking along with his eyes on the ground. You're to keep him in sight wherever he goes. *He's* mad, and *I'm* mad, and *everybody's* mad. Follow him, and address a remark to me at your peril. I've been up all night, I've walked from London to Slough, and I'm now going to sleep."

My orders called forth not so much as the lift of an eyebrow. The difference between eccentricity and madness may be measured in pounds sterling. A rich man is never mad in England, unless, of course, his heirs-at-law cast wistful glances at the pounds sterling. In that case there will be an Inquisition and a report to the Masters.... My driver left me to slumber undisturbed.

I slept only in snatches. The car would run a mile, pass the Seraph, pull up, wait, start forward and stop again. Once I invited him to come aboard, but he shook his head. I dozed, and dreamed, and woke, asking the driver what had come of our quarry.

"He's following, sir," he told me.

I was struck with an ingenious idea.

"At the next cross-roads," I said, "turn off to the right or left, drive a hundred yards and pull up. If he follows, we'll lead him round in a circle and draw him back to London."

We shot ahead, turned and waited. In time a dusty figure came in sight trudging wearily on. At the cross-roads he came for a moment into full view, and then passed out of sight along the Bath Road without so much as throwing a glance in the direction of the car.

"Damn you, damn you, damn you, Seraph!" I said, as I ordered the driver to start once more in pursuit.

At Taplow the dragging feet tripped and brought him down. Through a three-cornered tear in the leg of his trousers I could see blood flowing freely; his hands were cut and his forehead bruised, but he once more rejected my offer of a seat in the car. Opposite Skindles he stumbled again, but recovered himself and tramped on over the bridge, into Maidenhead, and through the crowded, narrow High Street. Passers-by stared at the strange, dusty apparition; he was too absorbed to notice, I too angry to be resentful.

It was as we mounted Castle Hill and worked forward towards Maidenhead Thicket that I noticed his pace increasing. A steady four miles an hour gave way to intermittent spells of running. I heard him panting as he came alongside the car, and the rays of a July afternoon sun brought beads of sweat to glisten dustily on his lips and forehead.

"Wait here," I said to the driver as we came to the fringe of the Thicket. To our right stretched the straight, white Henley Road; ahead of us lay Reading and Bath.

The Seraph trotted up, passed us without a word or look, and stumbled on towards Reading.

"Forward!" I said to the driver, and then countermanded my order and bade him wait.

Twenty yards ahead of us the Seraph had come to a standstill, and was casting about like a hound that has overshot the scent. I watched him pause, and heard the very whimper of a hound at fault. Then he walked back to the fork of the road, gazed north-west towards Henley, and stood for a moment on tiptoe with closed eyes, head thrown back and arms outstretched like a pirouetting dancer.

I waited for him to fall. I say "waited" advisedly, for I could have done nothing to save him. I ought to have jumped out, called the driver to my aid, tied hands and feet, and borne my prisoner back to London and a madhouse. Throughout the night and morning, well into the afternoon, I had cursed him for one lunatic and myself for another. My own madness lay in following him instead of shrugging my shoulders and leaving him to his fate. His madness ... as I watched the strained pose of nervous alertness, I wondered whether he was so mad after all.

With startling suddenness the rigid form relaxed, eyes opened, head fell forward, arms dropped to the body. He ran fifty yards along the road, hesitated, plunged blindly through a clump of low gorse bushes, and fell prone in the middle of a grass ride.

"Stop where you are!" I called to the driver as I ran down the road and turned into the bridle-path.

The Seraph was lying with one foot caught in a tangle of bracken. He was conscious, but breathed painfully. I helped him upright, supported him with an arm round the body, and tried to lead him back to the car.

"This way!" he gasped, pointing down the ride. Half a mile away I caught sight of a creeper-covered bungalow—pictur- esque, peaceful, inanimate, but with its eastern aspect ruined by the presence of a new corrugated iron shed. I judged it to be a garage by the presence of green tins of motor spirit.

"She's there—Sylvia!" he panted, slowly recovering his breath as we walked down the bridle-path. "Go in and get her. Make them give her up!"

I looked at his torn, dusty clothes, his white face and dizzy eyes. At the fork of the road I had come near to being converted. It was another matter altogether to invade a strange house and call upon an unknown householder to yield up the person of a young woman who ought not to be there, who could only be there by an implied charge of felonious abduction, who probably was not there, who certainly was not there.... I am at heart conventional, decorous, sensitive to ridicule.

"We can't," I said weakly. "It's a strange house; we don't know that she's there; we might expose ourselves to an action for slander...."

He walked to the gate of the garden, freed himself from the support of my arm, and marched up to the front door. I took inglorious cover behind a walnut-tree and heard him knock. There was a pause. A window opened and closed; another pause, and the sound of feet approaching. Then the door opened.

"I have come for Miss Roden," I heard him say.

"Roden? Miss Roden? No one of that name lives here."

The voice was that of a woman, and I tried to catch sight of the face. I had heard that voice before, or one suspiciously like it.

"I will give you two minutes to produce Miss Roden."

The answering voice quivered with sudden indignation.

"You must be intoxicated. Take your foot out of the door and go away, or I'll call a man and have you given in charge."

The voice, rising in shrill, tremulous excitement, would have added something more, but was silenced by a fit of coughing. I left my walnut-tree, pushed open the gate, and arrived at the bungalow door as the coughing ceased and a handkerchief dabbed furtively at a fleck of bright red froth.

"Miss Draper, I believe?" I said.

She looked at me in surprise.

"That is my name."

"We met at Miss Davenant's house in Chester Square. Don't

apologize for not remembering me, we were never introduced. I just caught your name. We have called...."

"Is this person a friend of yours?" she asked, pointing a contemptuous finger at the Seraph.

"He is. We have called for Miss Roden."

"She is not here."

"One minute gone," said the Seraph, watch in hand.

Miss Draper turned her head and called to some one inside the house. I think the name was "John."

"I am armed," I warned her.

She paid no attention.

"One minute and a half," said the Seraph.

I put my hand out to cover the watch, and addressed Miss Draper.

"I don't think you appreciate the strength of our position," I began. "You are no doubt aware that the office of the *New Militant* has been raided; your friend Mrs. Millington has been arrested, and there is a warrant out against your other friend, Miss Davenant."

"They haven't caught her," said Miss Draper, defiantly.

I could almost forgive her when I saw the look of doglike fidelity that the mention of Joyce's name brought into her eyes.

"Do you know where she is?" asked the Seraph.

"I shan't say."

"I think it probable that you do *not* know," I answered. "Miss Davenant is critically ill, and is lying at the present time in my friend's flat."

"You expect me to believe that?"

"It doesn't matter whether you believe it or not. The flat is already suspected and watched."

"Why don't they search it?"

"Because England is a corrupt country," I said, boldly inventing. "I have what is called a friend at Court. Miss Davenant's sister—Mrs. Wylton—is an old friend of mine, and

I wish to spare her the pain of seeing Miss Davenant arrested—
in a critical condition—if it can be avoided. My friend at Court
has been persuaded to suspend the issue of a search-warrant, if
Miss Roden and the others are restored to their families before
midnight to-night. I may say in passing that if Miss Davenant
were arrested, tried and imprisoned, it would be no more than
she richly deserved. However, I do not expect you to agree with
me. Out of regard to Mrs. Wylton we have come down here. I
need not say how we found Miss Roden was being kept here—"

"She is not."

I sighed resignedly.

"You wish Miss Davenant to be given up?"

"You don't know where Miss Davenant is, and I do."

It was bluff against bluff, but we could go on no longer on the
old lines. I produced my revolver as a guarantee of determination, pocketed it once more, pushed my way past her as gently
as I could, waited for the Seraph to follow, and then closed the
door.

"I am now going to search the house," I told Miss Draper.
"This is your last chance. Tell me where Miss Roden is, and I
will compound a felony, and let you and every one else in the
house escape. Put a single obstacle in my way, and I will have
the lot of you arrested. Which is it to be?"

She started to tell me again that Sylvia was not there. I made
a step across the room and saw her cover her face with her
hands. The battle was over.

"Where is she?" I demanded, thanking God that it has not
often been my lot to fight with women.

Miss Draper pointed to a door on the left of the hall; the key
was in the lock.

"No tricks?" I asked.

She shook her head.

"You had better make yourself scarce."

Even as I put my hand to the door she vanished into the

back of the house. I heard the sound of an engine starting, and rushed out to see if I had even now been outwitted. The garrison was driving out hatless and coatless, stripped of all honours of war; in the driving-seat sat my friend the bearded priest of the Orthodox Church, his beard somewhat awry. Miss Draper was beside him; there was no one else.

I returned to the hall—where the Seraph was sleeping upright against the wall—opened the door and entered a darkened room. As my eyes grew accustomed to the subdued light, I traced the outline of a window, and drew back the curtains. The sun flooded in, and showed me that I stood in a bedroom. A table with an untasted meal stood against one wall; by the other was a camp bedstead. At length on the bed, fully dressed but blindfolded, gagged, and bound hand and foot, lay Sylvia Roden.

I cut the cords, tore away the bandages, and watched her rise stiffly to her feet. Then I shut the door and stood awkwardly at the window, while she buried her face in her hands and sobbed.

It was soon over, but she was the better for it. I watched her drink three tumblers of water and seize a crust of dry bread. It appeared that she had conducted a hunger-strike of her own for the last twenty-four hours; and I think she looked it. Her face was white with the whiteness of a person who has been long confined in a small, dark room. A bruise over one temple showed that her captors had had to deal with a woman of metal, and her wrists were chafed and cut with the pressure of the cords. Worst of all was her change of spirit; the voice had lost its proud ring of assurance, the dark eyes were frightened. Sylvia Roden was almost broken.

"You didn't expect to see me, Sylvia," I said, as I buttered the stale crusts to make them less unappetizing.

She shook her head without answering.

"Did you think no one was ever coming?"

She looked at me still with the frightened expression in her eyes.

"No."

The uncertainty of her tone made me wonder whom she had been expecting. My question was answered before I could ask it.

"How did you find me?"

"The Seraph brought me here."

Her pale cheeks took on a tinge of colour.

"Where is he?" she asked.

"Outside."

"I must go to him!" she exclaimed, jumping up and then swaying dizzily.

I pressed her back into her chair.

"Wait till you've had some food," I said, "and then I'll bring him in."

"But I don't want any more."

"Sylvia," I said firmly, "if you're not a good girl we shan't rescue you another time."

She ate a few slices of bread and butter while I gave her an outline of our journey down from London. Then we went out into the hall. The Seraph had collapsed from his upright position, and was lying in a heap with his head on the floor. I carried him out of the hall and laid him on the bed in Sylvia's prison. His heart was beating, but he seemed to have fallen into a deep trance. Sylvia bent down and kissed the dusty forehead. Then her eyes fell on a faint red mark running diagonally from one cheek-bone, across the mouth, to the point of the chin. She had started crying again when I left the room in search of brandy.

I stayed away as long as I thought necessary to satisfy myself that there were no other prisoners in the house. When I came back, the tears were still wet on her cheeks, and she was bathing his face and waiting for the eyes to open.

"Your prison doesn't run to brandy," I told her. "We must get him to Maidenhead, and I'll give him some there. I've got a car waiting about half a mile away. Will you look after him while I fetch it?"

"Don't be long," she said, with an anxious look at the white, still face.

"No longer than I can help. Here's a revolver in case any one wants to abduct either of you. It's loaded, so be careful."

I placed the revolver on the table and picked up my hat.

"Sylvia!" I said at the door.

"Yes?"

"Can you be trusted to look after him properly?"

She smiled for the first time since her release from captivity.

"I think so," she said. Then the voice quavered and she turned away. "He's rather precious."

The car was brought to the door, and the driver—who, after all, had been paid not to be surprised—looked on unemotionally as we carried the Seraph on board. I occupied an uncomfortable little seat backing the engine, while Sylvia sat in one corner and the Seraph was propped up in the other.

On the way back I was compelled to repeat *in extenso* the whole story of our search, from the hour we left Adelphi Terrace to the moment when Miss Draper bolted with the Orthodox Church priest and I forced my way into the darkened prison cell.

Sylvia's face was an interesting study in expression as the narrative proceeded.

"But how could he *know*?" she asked in a puzzled tone when I had ended. "You must explain that. I don't see how it's possible."

"Madam, I have provided you with a story," I replied in the manner of Dr. Johnson; "I am not obliged to provide you with a moral."

As a matter of fact I had reversed the natural order, and given the moral before the story. The moral was pointed when I drank a friendly cup of tea in Cadogan Square; the day before she marked his cheek with its present angry wale.

Of course, if you point morals before there's a story to hang them from, you must expect to see them disregarded.

CHAPTER XIII
OR THE OBVIOUS ALTERNATIVE

"If one puts forward an idea to a true Englishman—
always a rash thing to do—he never dreams of considering
whether the idea is right or wrong. The one thing he considers
of any importance is whether one believes it oneself.... The
inherited stupidity of the race—sound English common
sense...."

—Oscar Wilde
The Picture of Dorian Gray.

If the Seraph's quest for Sylvia was one of the strangest
experiences of my life, I count our return to London among its
pleasantest memories. Almost before I had time to cut the cords
round her wrists and ankles, I was telling myself that Joyce now
lay free from the menace of an inquisition at Adelphi Terrace.
Thursday afternoon. She had eight days to pick up sufficient
strength for Maybury-Reynardson to say I might smuggle her
to Southampton and convey her on board the S.Y. *Ariel*.... I hope
I was not heartless or ungrateful in thinking more of her than
of the white, unconscious boy in front of me; there was nothing
more that I could do, and if there had been, Sylvia would have
forestalled me.

I count the return a pleasant memory for the light it threw on
Sylvia's character. Passion and pride had faded out of her dark
eyes; I could no longer call her Queen Elizabeth; but she was
very tender and remorseful to the man she had injured. This was
the Sylvia of an Oxford summer evening; I could recognise her
from the Seraph's description. I treasure the memory because it
was the only glimpse I ever caught of this side of her character;
when next we met—before her last parting from the Seraph—
she had gone back to the earlier hard haughtiness, and though I
loved Sylvia at all times, I loved her least when she was regal.

And lastly I dwell on this memory for the way she talked to me when my tale was done. It was then she showed me the reverse side of her relations with the Seraph, and filled in those spaces that the manuscript narrative in Adelphi Terrace left blank. I remember most of what she told me; their meetings and conversations, her deepening interest, rising curiosity, growing attachment.... I had watched the Sixth Sense as a spectator; she gave me her own curiosity—uneasiness— belief and disbelief— ultimate uncertainty. I realised then what it must have meant to such a girl to find a man who was conscious of her presence at a distance and could see the workings of her mind before they were apparent to herself in any definite form. I learned to appreciate the thrill she must have experienced on discovering a soul in sympathy with her own restless, volatile, hungry spirit.

I remember it all, but I will not be guilty of the sacrilege of committing it to paper. No girl has ever spoken her heart to me as Sylvia then spoke it; I am not sure that I want to be again admitted to such confidences. It is all strange, and sad, and unsatisfactory; but above all it is sacred. Her imprisonment had taken the fire out of Sylvia's blood; and her meeting with the Seraph had worked on her emotions. At another time she would have been more reticent. As after our return from Oxford, I sometimes think we were punished by an extreme of cold for having been injudiciously admitted to bask in an extreme of heat. That is the way with the English climate, and with a certain number of reserved, proud girls who grow up under its influence....

I dropped Sylvia at Cadogan Square without going in, and carried the Seraph straight back to Adelphi Terrace. Maybury-Reynardson was paying Joyce an evening visit; the report was satisfactory so far as it went, but indicated that we must exercise great patience before a complete cure could be expected. I asked—on a matter of life and death—whether she could be moved in a week's time. He preferred to give no opinion, and reminded me that I must not attempt to see or speak to the patient. Then I turned him over to the Seraph, ordered myself some dinner, and went to bed.

In the morning a telephone message informed me that Arthur Roden would like us both to go round to Cadogan Square. I answered that it was out of the question so far as the Seraph was concerned; and it was not till late on the Saturday afternoon that I felt justified in letting him get out of bed and accompany me. He still looked perilously white and ill, and though one strain had been removed by the discovery of Sylvia, and another by the departure of the search-warrant bogey, I could see no good purpose in his being called in to assist at an affecting reconciliation, and having to submit to a noisy chorus of congratulation.

We were spared both. I suppose I shall never know the true reason for the reception that awaited us, but I distribute the responsibility in equal shares between Lady Roden and Nigel Rawnsley. And of course I have to keep reminding myself that I had been present at the search, while they were not; that they were plain, matter-of-fact materialists with a rational cause for every effect, while I—well, I put myself out of court at once by asking them to believe in an absurdity called a Sixth Sense.

I find it hard, however, to forgive Nigel his part in the scene that followed; so far as I can see he was actuated first by jealousy on Sylvia's account, secondly by personal venom against the Seraph as a result of the unauthorised search-party, and lastly by the obstinate anger of a strong-willed, successful egoist, who has been driven to dwell even temporarily in the shade of unsuccess. Lady Roden, it must never be forgotten, had to sink the memory of Rutlandshire Morningtons, and the quarterings and armorial devices of an entire Heralds' College, before she could be expected to do justice to a man like the Seraph.

We were shown into the library, and found Arthur, Nigel and Philip seated before us like the Beasts in Revelation. Lady Roden and Sylvia entered later and sat to one side. There was much bowing and no hand-shaking.

The story of the search was already known—Sylvia had told it as soon as she got home, probably in my own words; and in the first, fine, careless rapture, I have no doubt she had spoken of the Seraph in the strain I had heard in the car. If this were the case, Lady Roden's eyes must have been abruptly and painfully opened. I felt sorry for her. Rutlandshire Morningtons frowned sour disfavour from the walls at the possibility of her daughter— with her daughter's faith and wealth—allying herself with an infidel, unknown, relationless vagrant like Lambert Aintree. Rationalism in the person of Nigel Rawnsley was called in to discredit the story of the search and save Sylvia from squandering herself on a common adventurer.

"You remember the terms of our agreement last Wednesday?" he began. "I undertook to suspend application for a search warrant...."

"If we discovered Sylvia," I said. "Yes?"

"And my sister Mavis."

I hope Nigel did not see my jaw drop. Save for the moment when I looked casually through the other rooms in the Maidenhead bungalow I had completely forgotten the Mavis stipulation. Every plan and hope I had cherished in respect of Joyce had been cherished in vain.

"The time was to expire on Monday, at noon," said the Seraph.

"Exactly. I thought I would remind you that only half the undertaking had been carried out. That is all."

Nigel would make an admirable proctor; he is to the manner born. I had quite the old feeling of being five shillings the poorer for straying round the streets of Oxford at night without academical dress.

I caught the Seraph's eye and made as if to rise.

"One moment," said Arthur. "There is a good deal more to come."

I folded my arms resignedly. Any one may lecture me if it amuses him to do so, but the Seraph ought to have been in bed instead of having to submit to examination by an old K.C.

"The question is a good deal wider," Arthur began. "You, Aintree, are suspected of harbouring at your flat a woman who is wanted by the police on a most serious charge...."

"I thought we'd cleared all this up on Wednesday," I said, with an impatient glance at Nigel.

"No arrangement you may have made on Wednesday is binding on me."

"It was binding on your son, who sits on one side of you," I said, "and on Mr. Nigel Rawnsley, who sits on the other."

Arthur drew himself up, no doubt unconsciously.

"As a Minister of the Crown I cannot be a party to any connivance at crime."

"Philip and Nigel," I said. "As sons of Ministers of the Crown, I hope you will take that to heart."

"What I have to say—" Arthur began.

"One moment!" I interrupted. "Are you speaking as a Minister of the Crown or a father of a family? Sylvia's been restored to you as the result of your son and Nigel conniving at what you hope and believe to be a crime. You wouldn't have got her back without that immoral compromise."

"The flat would have been searched," said Nigel.

"It was. Paddy and Gartside searched it and declared themselves satisfied...."

"They lied."

"Will you repeat that to Gartside?" I asked invitingly. "I fancy not. They searched and declared themselves satisfied. I offered to show the detectives round ten minutes after—by all accounts—this woman ought to have taken refuge there. Anybody could have searched it if they'd approached the owner properly."

He ignored my implied reproof and stuck to his guns.

"There was a woman there when Gartside said there was not."

"Gartside only said Miss Davenant wasn't there."

It was the Seraph speaking, slowly and almost for the first time. His face flushed crimson as he said it. I could not help looking at Sylvia; I looked away again quickly.

"There was *some* woman there, then?" said Nigel.

My cue was plain, and I took it.

"Miss Davenant is the only person whose name is before the house," I interposed. "Gartside said she was not there. Were you satisfied, Phil? I thought so. It's no good asking you, Nigel; you won't be satisfied till you've searched in person, and that you can't do till after Monday. Every one who agreed to Wednesday's compromise is bound by it till Monday midday. If after that Nigel *still* thinks it worth while to conduct Scotland Yard over the flat, of course we shan't attempt to stop him. As for any one who was not present or personally bound by Wednesday's compromise, that is to say, you, Arthur—do you declare to win by 'Father of a Family' or 'Minister of the Crown'? You must take one or the other."

"The two are inseparable," he answered shortly.

"You must contrive to separate them. If you declare 'Father of a Family,' you must hold yourself bound by Phil's arrangement. If you declare 'Minister of the Crown,' you oughtn't to have profited by the compromise, you oughtn't to have allowed us to restore Sylvia to you. Common schoolboy honour tells you that. Incidentally, why haven't you had the flat searched already? As a Minister of the Crown, you know...."

If my heart had not been beating so quickly, I should have liked to study their faces at leisure. The history of the last two days was written with tolerable clearness. Nigel had told Arthur—and possibly his own father—the story of his visit to Adelphi Terrace; he had hinted sufficient to incite one or both to take the matter up officially. Then Philip had intervened and depicted himself as bound in honour to take no step until the expiration of the armistice. Their faces told a pretty tale of "pull devil, pull baker," with Nigel at the head, Philip at the feet, and Arthur twisting and struggling between them.

I had no need to ask why the flat had not yet been searched, but I repeated my question.

"And when *are* you going to search it?" I added.

Arthur attempted a compromise.

"If you will give me your word...." he began.

"Not a bit of it!" I said. "Are you bound or are you not? Sylvia's in the room to settle any doubts on the subject."

He yielded after a struggle.

"I will take no steps to search the flat until after midday on Monday, provided Mavis is restored by then."

I made another attempt to rise, but Arthur waved me back into my seat.

"I have not finished yet. As you point out, Sylvia is in the room. I wish to know how she got here, and I wish still more to know how she was ever spirited away in the first instance."

"I know nothing about the getting away. She may be able to throw light on that. Hasn't she told you how we found her?"

"She has given me your version."

"Then I don't suppose I can add anything to it."

"You might substitute a story that would hold a little more water."

"I am afraid I am not naturally inventive."

"Since when?"

His tone told me that I had definitely lost Arthur as a friend— which was regrettable, but if I could play the part of whetstone to his repartee I was content to see him draw profit from the *débris* of our friendship.

"It is only fair to say that you and Aintree are regarded with a good deal of suspicion," he went on. "Apart from the question of the flat...."

"Not again!" I begged.

"I have not mentioned the report of the officers who watched Miss Davenant's house in...."

"Nigel has," I interrupted. "*Ad nauseam.* My interview was apparently very different from their report. Suppose we have them in?"

"They are not in the house."

"Then hadn't we better leave them out of the discussion? What else are we suspected of?"

Arthur traced a pattern on the blotting-pad, and then looked up very sternly.

"Complicity with the whole New Militant campaign."

I turned to the Seraph.

"This is devilish serious," I said. "Incitement to crime, three abductions, more in contemplation. I shouldn't have thought it to look at you. Naughty boy!"

Arthur was really angry at that. I knew it by his old habit of growing red behind the ears.

"You appear to think this is a fit subject for jesting," he burst out.

"I laugh that I may not weep," I said. "A charge like this is rather upsetting. Have you bothered about any evidence?"

"You will find there is perhaps more evidence than you relish. Apart from your intimacy with Miss Davenant...."

"She's a very pretty woman," I interrupted.

"...you have successfully kept one foot in either camp. You were present when Rawnsley told me of the abduction of Mavis, and added that the matter was being kept secret. Miss Davenant at once published an article entitled 'Where is Miss Rawnsley?'"

"If she really abducted the girl, she'd naturally notice it was being kept quiet," I objected.

"On the day after Private Members' time had been appropriated, Jefferson's boy disappeared; Miss Davenant must have been warned in time to have her plans laid. She referred to my midland campaign, and had an accomplice lying in wait for my daughter with a car, the same day that Rawnsley made his announcement that there would be no autumn session."

"You will find all this on the famous Time Table," I reminded him.

"She got her information from some one who knew the arrangements of the Government."

"I'm surprised you continued to know me," I said, and turned to the Seraph. "It's devilish serious, as I said before, but it seems to be my funeral."

Arthur soon undeceived me.

"You are both equally incriminated. Aintree, is it not the case that on one occasion in Oxford and another in London, you warned my daughter that trouble was in store for her?"

The Seraph had been sitting silent and with closed eyes since his single intervention. He now opened his eyes and bowed without speaking.

"I suggest that you knew an attempt would be made to abduct her?"

"No."

"You are quite certain?"

"Quite."

"Then why the warning?"

"I knew trouble was coming; I didn't know she would be abducted."

"What form of trouble did you anticipate?"

"No form in particular."

"Why trouble at all?"

"I knew it was coming."

"But how?"

He hesitated, and then closed his eyes wearily.

"I don't know."

Arthur balanced a quill pen between the first fingers of both hands.

"On Wednesday last your rooms were visited, and the question of a search-warrant raised. You obtained a promise that the warrant would not be applied for if my daughter and Miss Rawnsley were restored within five days. Did you know at that time where they were?"

"No."

"When did you find out?"

"I don't know where Miss Rawnsley is. I didn't know where your daughter was till we came to the house."

"We none of us know our hats are in the hall till we look to make certain," Nigel interrupted; "but you found her?"

"Yes."

"No one told you where she was?" Arthur went on.

"No."

"Then how did you find her?"

"I believe she has told you."

"She has given me Merivale's version. I want yours."

"I don't know."

"How did you start?"

"She's told you. I walked out of the house, and went on till I found her."

"How did you know where to look?"

"I didn't."

"It was pure coincidence that you should walk some thirty miles, passing thousands of houses, and walk straight to the right house—a house you didn't know, a house standing away from any main road? This was pure coincidence?"

"I knew she was there."

"I think you said you didn't know till you got there. Which do you mean?"

"I felt sure she *was* there."

"You felt that when you left London?"

"I knew she was in that direction. That's how I found the way."

"No one had told you where to look?"

"No."

"Of the scores of roads out of London, you took just the right one. Of the millions of houses to the west of London you chose the right one. You ask me to believe that you walked thirty miles, straight to the right house, because you knew, because you 'felt' she was there?"

"I ask you to believe nothing."

"You make that task quite easy. I suggest that when you were given five days' grace you went to some person who knew of my daughter's whereabouts, and got the necessary information?"

"No."

Arthur retired from the examination with a smile of self-congratulation, and Nigel took up the running.

"Do you know where my sister is?"

"No."

"Can you—er—*feel* where she is?"

"No."

"Can you walk from this house and find her?"

"No."

"How soon will you be able to do so?"

With eyes still closed, the Seraph shook his head.

"Never, unless some one tells me where she is."

"Is any one likely to, before Monday at noon?"

"No."

"Then how do you propose to find her?"

"I don't."

"You know the consequences?"

"Yes."

Nigel proceeded to model himself on his leader with praise-worthy fidelity.

"I suggest that the person who told you where to look for Miss Roden is no longer available to tell you where to look for my sister?"

"No one told me where to look for Miss Roden."

"But you found her, and you can't find my sister?"

"That is so."

"You suggest no reason for the difference?"

For an instant the Seraph opened his eyes and looked across to Sylvia. Had she wished, she could have saved him, and his eyes said as much. I, too, looked across and found her watching him with the same expression that had come over her face when he suggested the possibility of a woman being hidden in his rooms the previous Wednesday morning.

"I suggest no reason," he said at last.

Nigel's examination closed, and I thought it prudent to ask for a window to be opened and water brought for the Seraph. Sylvia's eyes melted in momentary compassion. I walked over and sat beside her at a discreet distance from her mother.

"Not worth saving, Sylvia?" I asked.

A sceptical chin raised itself in the air, but the eyes still believed in him.

"How did they get hold of me?" she asked, "and how did he find me? How *could* he, if he didn't know all along?"

"Remember Brandon Court," I said.

"Why didn't he mention it?"

I pointed to the Bench.

"My dear child, look at them! Why not talk higher mathematics to a boa-constrictor?"

"If he can't make them believe it, why should I?"

"Because you *know*."

"What?"

"Everything. You know he's in love with you, and you're in love with him."

"I'm not!"

Her voice quivered with passion; there was nothing for it but a bold stroke. And one risk more or less hardly mattered.

"Can you keep a secret, Sylvia?"

"It depends."

"No. Absolutely?"

"All right."

I lowered my voice to a whisper.

"There *was* a woman in his rooms last Wednesday, and she is the woman I am engaged to marry."

Her look of scorn was caused less by concern for my morals than by pity for my simplicity in thinking she would believe such a story.

"I don't believe it."

"You must. It's your last chance. If you let him go now, you'll lose him for ever, and I'm not going to let you blight your life and his, if I can stop it. You must make up your mind now. Do you believe me?"

Her expression of scorn had vanished and given place to one of painful perplexity.

"I'm not...."

"Do you believe me, Sylvia?"

She hesitated in an agony of indecision, until the moment was lost. The water had arrived, and Arthur was dismissing me from the Presence.

"You're not going to arrest us, then?" I said.

"I reserve perfect freedom of action," he answered, in the Front Bench manner.

"Quite right," I said. "I only wish you'd reserved the inquisition till this boy was in a better state to receive it. Would it interfere with your liberty of action if I asked you to say a word of thanks either to Aintree, myself, or both? I believe it is usual when a man loses his daughter and has her restored to him."

A few minutes more would have tried my temper. Arthur sat down again at his table, opened a drawer, and took out a cheque-book.

"According to your story it was Aintree who was chiefly instrumental in making the discovery?"

"That was the lie we agreed on," I said.

Arthur wrote a cheque for two thousand pounds, and handed it to the Seraph with the words—

"That, I think, clears all obligations between us."

"Except that of manners," I exclaimed. "The House of Commons—"

But he had rung the bell, and was tidying his papers into neat, superfluous bundles.

Philip had the courage to shake me by the hand and say he hoped to see me again soon. I am not sufficiently cynical to say it was prompted by the reflection that Gladys was my niece, because he was every whit as cordial to the Seraph.

I shook hands with Sylvia, and found her watching the Seraph fold and pocket the two thousand pound cheque.

"He's taking it!" she said.

"Your father should have been ashamed to make the offer. It serves him right if his offer's accepted. Don't blame the Seraph. If Nigel and your father proceed on the lines they've gone on this afternoon, one or both of us will have to cut the country. The Seraph's not made of money; he'll want all he can lay hands on. Now then, Sylvia, it's two lives you're playing with."

She had not yet made up her mind, and indecision chilled the warmth of her eyes and the smile on her lips. I watched the effort, and wondered if it would suffice for the Seraph. Then question and answer told their tale.

"When shall we see you again?" I heard her ask as I walked to the door.

"I can hardly say," came the low reply. "I'm leaving England shortly. I shall go across India, and spend some time in Japan— and then visit the Islands of the South Seas. It's a thing I've always wanted to do. After that? I don't know...."

CHAPTER XIV
THROUGH A GLASS DARKLY

"The instant he entered the room it was plain that all was lost....

"'I cannot find it,' said he, 'and I must have it. Where is it?... Where is my bench?... Time presses; and I must finish those shoes.'

"They looked at one another, and their hearts died within them.

"'Come, come!' said he, in a whimpering miserable way: 'let me get to work. Give me my work.'

"...Carton was the first to speak:

"'The last chance is gone: it was not much....'"

—Charles Dickens
A Tale of Two Cities.

As I helped the Seraph out of the house and into a taxi, I was trying to string together a few words of sympathy and encouragement. Then I looked at his face, and decided to save my breath. Physically and mentally he was too hard hit to profit by any consolation I could offer. As a clumsy symbol of good intention I held out my hand, and had it gripped and retained till we reached Adelphi Terrace.

"Never mind me," he said, in a slow, sing-song voice, hesitating like a man speaking an unfamiliar language. "It's you and Joyce we've got to consider."

"Don't worry your head, Seraph," I said. "We'll find a way out. You've got to be quiet and get well."

"But what are you going to do?"

"I've no idea," I answered blankly.

The Seraph sighed and lifted his feet wearily on to the seat opposite.

"You played that last hand well, Toby. I'm afraid you'll have to go on playing without any support from me. I'm dummy, I'm only good for two possible tricks."

I waited to see the hand exposed.

"I can't find Mavis," he went on. "You see that?"

"I do."

"You must ask Joyce to tell you. She spoke a few words this morning, and she's getting stronger. If she refuses ... but she won't if you ask her."

"If she does?"

"You must go on bluffing Nigel. He doesn't know who's in the flat, and old Roden doesn't know either. They'd have searched three days ago, they'd have arrested us to-day on suspicion if they hadn't been afraid of making fools of themselves. Keep bluffing, Toby. The keener you are to get the search over and done with, the more they'll be afraid of a mare's nest." The words trailed off in a sigh. "If there's anything I can do I'll do it, but I'm afraid you'll find me pretty useless."

"You're going quietly to bed for forty-eight hours," I told him.

He raised no protest, and I heard him murmur, "Saturday night. Sunday night. Monday night. It'll be all over then, one way or the other."

On reaching the flat I carried him upstairs, ordered some soup, and smoked a cigarette in the hall. Maybury-Reynardson was completing his evening inspection, and when he came out I asked for the bulletin.

"It's in the right direction," he told me, "but very, very slow. The mind's working back to normal whenever she wakes, and she's been talking a little. I'm afraid you must go on being patient."

"Could she answer a question?"

"You mustn't ask any."

"I'm afraid it's absolutely necessary."

"What d'you want to know?"

"The police will search this flat on Monday if we don't find out before then where Miss Rawnsley was taken to when she disappeared."

Maybury-Reynardson shook his head.

"You mustn't think of bothering her with questions of that kind. If you did, I don't suppose she could help you."

"But you said the mind was normal?"

"Working back to normal. Everything's there, but she can't put it in order. The memory larder is full, but her hands are too weak to lift things down from the shelves."

"It's a matter of life and death," I urged.

"If it was a matter of eternal salvation I doubt if she could help you. Do you dream? Well, could you piece together the fragments of all you dreamt last night? You might have done so a moment after waking, little pieces may come back to you when some one suggests the right train of thought. That's Miss Davenant's condition. To change the parallel, her eyes can see, but they see 'through a glass darkly.'"

I thought the matter over while he was examining and prescribing for the Seraph.

"We're in a tight corner, Seraph," I said when he had gone. "I don't see any other way out, I'm going to take the responsibility of disobeying him."

He offered no suggestion, and I walked to the door of Joyce's room and put my fingers to the handle. Then I came back and made him open his eyes and listen to me.

"I'll take the blame," I said; "but will you see if you can make her understand? She's known you longer."

It was not the true reason. When I reached the door I was smitten with the fear that she would not recognise me, and my nerve failed.

We explained our intentions to a reluctant nurse; I fidgeted outside in the hall and heard the Seraph walk up to the bedside and ask Joyce how she was.

"I'm better, thanks," she answered. "Let me see, do I know

you?" There was a weak laugh. "I should like to be friends with you, you've got such nice eyes."

The Seraph took her hand and asked if she knew any one named Mavis Rawnsley.

"Oh, yes, I know her. Her father's the Prime Minister. Mavis, yes, I know her."

"Do you know where she is?"

"Mavis Rawnsley? She was at the theatre last night. What theatre was it? She was in the stalls, and I was in a box. Who else was there? Were you? She was with her mother. Where is she now? Yes, I know Miss Rawnsley well."

"Do you know where she is now?"

"I expect she's at the theatre."

She closed her eyes, and the Seraph came back to the door, shaking his head. I tiptoed into the room, looked round the screen and watched Joyce smiling in her sleep. As I looked, her eyes opened and met mine.

"Why, I know you!" she exclaimed. "You're my husband. You took me to the theatre last night, when we saw Mavis Rawnsley. We were in a box, and she was in the stalls. Some one wanted to know where Mavis was. Tell them we saw her at the theatre, will you?"

She held out her hand to me; I bent down, kissed her forehead, and crept out of the room. The Seraph was lying on the bed we had made up for him in my room. I helped him to undress, and retired to the library with a cigar—to forget Joyce and plan the bluffing of Nigel.

My first act was to get into communication with Paddy Culling on the telephone.

"Will you do me another favour?" I began. "Well, it's this. I want you to get hold of Nigel and take him to lunch or dine to-morrow—Sunday—at the Club. Let me know which, and the time. When you've finished eating, lead him away to a quiet corner—the North Smoking Room or the Strangers' Card

Room. Hold him in conversation till I come. I shall drop in accidentally, and start pulling his leg. You can help, but do it in moderation; we mustn't make him savage—only uncomfortable. You understand? Right."

Then I went to bed.

On Sunday morning I started out in the direction of Chester Square, and made two discoveries on the way. The first was that our house was being unceasingly watched by a tall Yorkshireman in plain clothes and regulation boots; the second, that the Yorkshireman was in his turn being intermittently watched by Nigel Rawnsley. His opinion of the Criminal Investigation Department must have been as low—if not as kindly—as my own. On two more occasions that day I found him engaged on a flying visit of inspection—to keep Scotland Yard up to the Rawnsley mark and answer the eternal question that Juvenal propounded and Michael Roden amended for his own benefit and mine at Henley.

Elsie received me with anxious enquiries after her sister. I gave a full report, propounded my plan of campaign, and was rewarded by being shown the extensive and beautiful contents of her wardrobe. I should never have believed one woman could accumulate so many clothes; there seemed a dress for every day and evening of the year, and she could have worn a fresh hat each hour without repeating herself. My own rule is to have one suit I can wear in a bad light, and four that I cannot. With hats the practice is even simpler; I flaunt a new one until it is stolen, and then wear the changeling until a substitute of even greater seediness has been supplied. My instincts are conservative, and my hats more symbolical than decorative; for me they typify the great, sad law that every change is a change for the worse.

My only complaint against Elsie was that her wardrobe contained too much of what university authorities would call the "subfuse" element. The most conspicuous garments I could find were a white coat and skirt, white stockings and shoes, black hat and veil, and heliotrope dust coat. I am no judge whether they looked well in combination, but I challenge the purblind to say they were inconspicuous. To my eyes the *tout ensemble* was so striking that I laid them on a chair and gazed in wondering admiration until it was time to call up Gartside and warn him that I stood in need of luncheon.

Carlton House Terrace had a depressing, derelict appearance that foreboded the departure of its lord. All the favourite pictures and ornaments seemed to have been stowed away in preparation for India, neat piles of books were distributed about the library floor, and every scrap of paper seemed to have been tidied into a drawer. We sat down a pleasant party of three, and I made the acquaintance of Gartside's cousin and aide-de-camp, Lord Raymond Sturling. An agreeable fellow he seemed, who put himself and his services entirely at my disposal in the event of my deciding to come for a part or all of the way. I could only avail myself of his offer to the extent of sending him to see if Mountjoy's villa at Rimini was still in the market, and if so what his figure was for giving me immediate possession.

Gartside himself was as hospitable as ever in offering me every available inch on the yacht for the accommodation of myself and any friends I might care to bring with me. I ran through the list and found myself wondering if Maybury-Reynardson could be persuaded to come. I had hardly known him long enough to call him a friend, but he had gone out of his way to oblige me in coming to attend Joyce, and on general principles I think most big London practitioners are the better for a few days at sea at the close of the London season.

I called round in Cavendish Square for a cup of tea, and told him he was pulled down and in need of a change.

"Look at the good it did my brother," I said. "Just to Marseilles and back. Or if you'll come to Genoa and overland to Rimini, I shall be very glad to put you up for as long as you can stay. It's Gartside's own yacht, and I'm authorised by him to invite whom

I please. He's a capital host, and you'll be done to a turn. The only fault I have to find with his arrangements is that he carries no doctor, and I'm sufficiently middle-aged to be fussy on a point like that. Anybody taken ill, you know, anybody coming on board ill, and it would be devilish awkward. I shall insist on a doctor. He'll be Gartside's guest, but I shall pay his fees, of course, and he can name his own figure. What do you think of the idea? We shall be to all intents and purposes a bachelor party."

When Maybury-Reynardson's name was first mentioned to me on the evening of Joyce's flight, the Seraph had justly described him as a "sportsman." Under the grave official mask I could see a twinkling eye and a flickering smile.

"It depends on one case of nervous breakdown that I've got on hand at present," he said. "If my patient's well enough...."

"She's got to be," I said.

"When do you sail?"

"Friday."

"You can't make it later?"

"Absolutely impossible."

"This is Sunday. I'll tell you when we're a little nearer the day."

"She must be moved on Thursday afternoon."

"Must? Must?" he repeated with a smile. "Whose patient is she?"

"Whose wife's she going to be?" I asked in my turn.

"I suppose it'll be pretty hot," he said. "First week in August. I must get some thin clothes."

"Include them in the fee," I suggested.

"Damn the fee!" he answered, as we walked to the door.

Paddy Culling had arranged to give Nigel his dinner at eight. I had comfortable time to dress and dine at Adelphi Terrace, and nine-thirty found me wandering round the Club in search of company.

"Praise heaven for the sight of a friendly face!" I exclaimed as I stumbled across Paddy and Nigel in the North Smoking Room.

"Where was ut ye dined?" asked Paddy, as I pulled up a chair and rang for cigars. To a practised ear his brogue was an eloquent war signal.

"In the sick-house," I told him, "Adelphi Terrace."

"Is ut catching?" he inquired. "It's not for my own self I'm asking, but Nigel here. I owe ut to empire and postherity to see he runs no risks."

I reassured him on the score of posterity.

"He's just knocked up and over-tired," I said, "and I'm keeping him in bed till Wednesday or Thursday."

"Then he'll not be walking ye into the Lake District to find Miss Mavis for the present," Paddy observed with an eye on Nigel.

"He'll be walking nowhere till Wednesday at earliest," I said with great determination.

Paddy cut a cigar, and assumed an air of dissatisfaction.

"I'd have ye remember the days of grace," he grumbled.

I shrugged my shoulders without answering.

"Where's me pound of flesh?" he demanded. "Manin' no disrispec' to Miss Mavis," he added apologetically to Nigel.

"I'm afraid I can't help you to find her," I said.

"Can the Seraph?"

"I don't suppose so. In any case he can do nothing for the present."

Paddy returned to his cigar and we smoked in silence till Nigel picked up the threads where they had been dropped.

"You say Aintree's ill," he began cautiously. "If I were disposed to regard the time of illness as so many *dies non*, would he be in a position to find my sister by the end of the week?"

"Frankly, I see no likelihood."

"It's an extra five days."

"What good can they do? Or five weeks for that matter?"

"You should know best."

"I have no more idea where your sister is than you have, and no better means of finding out."

"And Aintree?"

"In speaking for myself, I spoke for him. If he knew or had any means of finding out he'd tell me."

Paddy flicked the ash off his cigar and entered the firing line.

"When the days of grace have expired, ye'll have yer contract unfulfilled?"

"And we shall be prepared to face the consequences."

"Och, yer be damned! Is the Seraph?"

"He can't help himself." I had sowed sufficient good seed and saw no profit in staying longer. "I shall see you both to-morrow at noon?"

"Not me," said Paddy. "I've searched the place once."

"You, Nigel?"

"If I think fit," he answered loftily.

"I only ask, because you mustn't worry the Seraph. You can search his rooms, but you mustn't try to cross-question him. He's not equal to it."

"I think you'd be wise to accept the extension of time."

"My dear man, what's the good? If we can't find your sister, we can't. Saturday's no better than Monday. As Monday was the original time, you'd better stick to it and get your search over."

"If Aintree's ill...."

"Humbug! Nigel," I said. "If you believe we're harbouring a criminal, it's your duty to verify your belief. If you think you can teach Scotland Yard its business, bring your detectives and prove your superior wisdom. Bring 'em to-morrow; bring 'em to-night if you like, and as many as you can get. The more there are," I said, turning at the door to fire a last shot, "the more voices will be raised in thanksgiving for Nigel Rawnsley."

The following morning I just mentioned to the Seraph that

we need expect no search-party that day, and then went on to complete certain other arrangements. Raymond Sturling called in on the Tuesday morning to report his success in the negotiations for Mountjoy's villa at Rimini. I rang up my solicitor and told him to conclude all formalities, and on the Wednesday afternoon dropped in at Carlton House Terrace, and mentioned that Maybury-Reynardson had cleared up odds and ends of work and felt justified in accepting my vicarious invitation to accompany the Governor of Bombay as far as Genoa. On Thursday I called at Chester Square.

Elsie's car was standing at the door when I arrived, and she had paid me the compliment of putting on all the clothes I had most admired on the previous Sunday. Very slim and pretty she looked in the white coat and skirt, and when she smiled I could almost have said it was Joyce. The face was older, of course, but that difference was masked when she dropped the black veil; the slight figure and fine golden hair might have belonged to either sister.

I complimented her on her appearance, and suggested driving round to Adelphi Terrace. The Seraph was still rather weak and in need of attention, and though I had two nurses in the flat to look after Joyce, they would not be there for ever. As we crossed Trafalgar Square into the Strand I recommended Elsie to raise her veil.

"Just as I thought," I murmured as we entered Adelphi Terrace. My plain-clothes Yorkshireman was watching the house from the opposite side of the road; Nigel was watching my plain-clothes Yorkshireman from the corner of the Terrace.

"Bow to him," I said to Elsie. "He may not deign to recognise you, but he can't help seeing you. Quite good! Now then, remember that sprained ankle!"

With a footman on one side and myself on the other, she was half carried out of the car, across the pavement and into the house. The ankle grew miraculously better when she forgot herself, and started to run upstairs; I date its recovery from the moment when we passed out of my Yorkshire friend's field of vision.

I said good-bye to the Seraph while Elsie was in Joyce's room. I never waste vain tears over the past, but when I saw him for the last time, weak, suffering and heart-broken—two large blue eyes gazing at me out of a white immobile face—I half regretted we had ever met, and heartily wished our parting had been different. Ill as he was, I could have taken him; but it would have been an added risk, and above all, he refused to come. As at our first meeting in Morocco, he was setting out solitary and unfriended—to forget....

Despite our dress-rehearsal the previous day, an hour had passed before Joyce appeared in the white coat and skirt, black hat and heliotrope dust-coat. She greeted me with a weak, pathetic little smile, bent over the Seraph's bed and kissed him, and then suffered me to carry her downstairs. As in bringing Elsie into the house, the footman and I took each an arm, across the pavement into the car. My Yorkshire friend watched us with interest, and I could not find it in my heart to grudge him the pleasure. He must have found little enough padding to fill out the spaces in his daily report. And all that his present scrutiny told him was that a woman's veil was up when she entered a house, and down when she left it.

We drove north-west out of London, to the rendezvous fixed by Raymond Sturling on the outskirts of Hendon. Maybury-Reynardson awaited us, and directed operations while we shifted Joyce into a car with a couch already prepared. Her luggage had been brought from Chester Square in the morning and was piled on the roof and at the back.

"A *mariage de convenance*," Sturling remarked with a smile, as he saw me inspecting the labels.

"Lady Raymond Sturling. S.Y. *Ariel*, Southampton," was the name and destination I found written.

"It may save trouble," he added apologetically. "I thought you wouldn't mind."

His foresight was justified. We drove slowly down to Southampton and arrived an hour before sunset, Joyce in one car with Maybury-Reynardson, Sturling with me in the other. I had anticipated that all ports and railway termini would be watched for a woman of Joyce's age and figure, and we were not allowed to board the tender without a challenge.

"My wife," Sturling explained brusquely. "Yes, be as quick as you can, please. I want to get her on board as soon as possible. Sturling—aide-de-camp to Lord Gartside, to Bombay by his own yacht. There she is, the *Ariel*, sailing to-morrow. These gentlemen? Mr. Merivale and Dr. Maybury-Reynardson. Friends of Lord Gartside. That all?"

"All in order, my lord."

"Right away."

As the tender steamed out I turned to mark the graceful lines of the *Ariel*. She was a clean, pretty boat at all times, and when I thought of the service she was doing two of her passengers, I could have kissed every plank of her white decks. Her mainmast flew the burgee of the R.Y.S., and the White Ensign fluttered at her stern; I remember the official reports had announced that the new governor would proceed direct to Bombay, calling only at Suez to coal. The Turkish flag flying at the foremast showed that Gartside was taking no steps to correct a popular delusion.

"Lady Raymond Sturling's" nurses arrived by an early train on Friday morning, followed at noon by Gartside in a special. We sailed at three. Paddy Culling sent wireless messages at four, four-thirty and five: "Sursum corda" was the first; "Keep your tails up" the second; and "Haste to the Wedding" completed the series.

I was not comfortable until we had passed out of territorial waters. Any one nurse may leave her patient and walk abroad in search of air and exercise: the second must not quit the house till the first has returned. I remembered that too late, when our two friends were already on board; and until I heard the anchor weighed, I was wondering if the same thought had stirred the sluggish imagination of the plain-clothes Yorkshireman. Whatever his suspicions, it appears that he did not succeed in making them real to Nigel. If he had there would have been no undignified raid on Adelphi Terrace next morning, and the feelings of one rising young statesman need not have been ruffled.

While Maybury-Reynardson was paying Joyce his nightly visit, I paced the deck with Gartside, silently and in grateful enjoyment of a cigar. As the light at the Needles dwindled and vanished, we became as reflective as befitted one man who was leaving England for several years, and another who had left her for ever. It was not till we had tramped a dozen times up and down that he broke his long silence.

"How did you find Sylvia?" he asked in a tone that showed how his thoughts had been occupied.

I told him the story as she herself had heard it, adding as much of the earlier history as was necessary to convince him.

"Perhaps I'm not leaving so much behind after all," was his comment. "Good luck to the Seraph! He's a nice boy."

"He'll need all the luck he can get," I answered. "You'll get oil and water to mingle quicker than you'll bring those two together. Tell me how it's to be done, Gartside, and you'll put the coping-stone on all your labours."

In the darkness I heard him sigh.

"I can't help you. I'm not a diplomatist, I'm just a lumpy, good-tempered ox. Sylvia saw that, bless her! Poor Paddy!" he added softly. "He's as fond of her as we any of us were."

I mentioned the trinity of wireless messages.

"That's like Paddy," he said with a laugh. "Well, he's right. You're the only one that's come out on top, and good wishes to you for the future!"

We shook hands and strolled in the direction of our cabins.

"You don't want thanks," I said, "but if you do you know where to come for them."

"Oh well!" I heard him laugh, but there was no laughter in his eyes when the light of the chart-room lamp fell on his face. "If I can't get what I want, there's some satisfaction in helping a friend to get what *he* wants."

"I'll have that copied out and hung on my shaving-glass," I said. "I shall want that text during the next few months."

"What are you going to do?"

"I'm going to bring Sylvia and the Seraph together," I answered in the same tone I had told Joyce I was going to break the Militant Suffrage movement.

"And how are you going to do that?"

"God knows!" I replied with a woeful shake of the head.

CHAPTER XV
THE RAID

"I can see you flying before the laughter like ... tremulous leaves before the wind, and the laughter will pursue you to Paris, where they'll make little songs about you on the boulevards, and the Riviera, where they'll sell your photographs on picture postcards. I can see you fleeing across the Atlantic to ... the immensity of America, and there the Yellow Press, pea-green with frenzy, will pile column of ridicule upon column of invective. Oh, ... do you think it isn't worth while to endure six months' hard labour to amuse the world so profoundly?"

—W.S. Maugham
"Jack Straw."

The appropriate milieu for Individualism is a desert island inhabited by the Individualist.

Another or others may have expressed the same sentiment in earlier and better language: I have become attached to my own form by use and habit. The words rise automatically to my lips whenever I think of the Davenant women; of Elsie and her obstinate, ill-advised marriage, her efforts to regain freedom, the desperate stroke that gave her divorce in exchange for reputation, her gallant unyielding attempt to win that reputation back.... Or maybe I find myself thinking of Joyce and her loyal long devotion to a cause that lost her friends and money, gained her hatred and contempt, and threatened her ultimately with illness, imprisonment and—well, I prefer not to dwell on the risks she was calling down on her foolish young head.

It was a courageous, forlorn-hope individualism—the kind that sets your blood tingling and perhaps raises an obstinate lump in your throat—but it was wasteful, sadly wasteful. I remember the night Elsie joined us at Rimini. I met her at the station, escorted her to the Villa Monreale, led her to Joyce's bedroom, watched them meet and kiss.... "Gods of my fathers," I murmured, "what have you won, the pair of you, for all your courage and endurance?"

The individualism showed its most impracticable angularity when you tried to force it into a cooperative, well-disciplined scheme like our escape from England. Sometimes I marvel that we ever got away at all; You could count on Gartside and Sturling, Maybury-Reynardson and the nurses, Culling and the Seraph; they were not individualists. It was no small achievement to make Joyce and Elsie answer to the word of command. Do I libel poor Joyce in saying she would have proved more troublesome had her head ached less savagely and her whole body been less weak? I think not. Elsie certainly showed me that the moment my grip slackened she was bound by her very nature to take the bit between her teeth and bolt to the cliff-edge of disaster.

I blame her no more than I blame a dipsomaniac; I bear her no ill-will for causing the one miscarriage in my plans. I am not piqued or chagrined—only sorrowful. Had she obeyed orders, we might have seen her spared the final humiliation, the last stultification of her campaign to win a reputation.

When I called Gartside to witness my intention of moving heaven and earth to bring Sylvia and the Seraph into communication, I did not mention that I had already taken the first step. We sailed on Friday at three, and at three-thirty Culling was to post a letter I had written to Sylvia. I have no natural eloquence or powers of persuasion, but I did go down on my knees, so to say, and implore her again not to let two lives be ruined if she had it in her power to avert catastrophe. Only a little sacrifice of pride was demanded, but she must unbend further than at their last meeting if she was to overcome the Seraph's curious bent of self-depreciation.

Then I frankly worked on her feelings and described the

Seraph's condition when we left Adelphi Terrace. His nerves had broken down during the anxious days before her disappearance; and the strain of finding her, the disappointment of her reception after the event, and the day by day worry of having Joyce in the house and never knowing when to expect a search-warrant or an arrest, had proved far too great a burden for his overwrought, sensitive, highly-strung nature.

I said it was no more than common humanity for her to see how he was getting on, and made no bones of telling her how bad I thought him. Elsie was due to slip out of Adelphi Terrace on the Friday evening, catch the nine o'clock boat train to Calais, run direct to the villa at Rimini and make all ready for our arrival. I make no secret of the fact that when I wrote to Sylvia I was not at all relishing the idea of the Seraph lying there with no one but the housekeeper and her husband to look after him.

Perhaps Elsie too did not care for that prospect, perhaps she speaks no more than the truth in saying he grew gradually worse after our departure, perhaps her pent-up individualism was seeking a riotous, undisciplined outlet. Nine o'clock came and went without bringing her a step nearer the Continental boat train. At ten she was still sitting by his bedside, at twelve she had to watch and listen as he began to grow light-headed. Not until eight on the Saturday morning did she steal away to her sister's deserted room and lie down for a few hours' sleep. By that time she had called in her own doctor, veronal had been administered, and the Seraph had sunk into a heavy trance-like slumber.

He was still sleeping at noon when Sylvia arrived in obedience to my letter. Her coming was characteristic. As soon as she had decided to swallow her own pride, she summoned witnesses to be spectators of what she was doing. Sylvia could never be furtive or other than frank and courageous; she told her mother that she was going immediately to Adelphi Terrace and going alone.

Opposition was inevitable, but she disregarded it. Lady Roden forbade her going, reminding her—I have no doubt—of Rutlandshire Morningtons, common respectability, and the Seraph's entire unworthiness. I can picture Sylvia standing with one foot impatiently tapping the floor, otherwise unmoved, unangered, calm and intensely resolute. The homily ended—as is the way of most sermons—when her mother had marshalled all arguments, reviewed, dismissed, assembled and reinspected them a second and third time. Then Sylvia put on her hat, called at a florist's on the way, and presented herself at Adelphi Terrace.

The Seraph's man opened the bedroom door and came back to report that the patient was still sleeping.

"I've brought him some flowers," she said. "I suppose it's no good waiting? You can't say how soon he's likely to wake up?"

Something in her tone suggested that she would like to wait, and the man showed her into the library, provided her with papers, and withdrew to answer a second ring at the front door bell.

Sylvia was still wandering round the room, glancing at the pictures and reading the titles of the books, when her attention was attracted by the sound of men's voices raised in altercation. Some one appeared to be forcing an entry which the butler was loyally trying to oppose.

"Here's the warrant," said a voice, "properly signed, all in order. If you interfere with these officers in the discharge of their duty, you do so at your own risk."

Sylvia listened with astonishment that changed quickly to alarm. The voice was that of Nigel Rawnsley, speaking as one having authority.

"One of you stay here," he went on, "and see that nobody leaves the flat. The other come with me. Take the library first."

The door opened, and for an amazed moment Nigel stood staring at the library's sole occupant.

"Sylvia!" he exclaimed. "What on earth brings you here?"

His tone so resembled her mother's that all Sylvia's latent opposition and obstinacy were called into play.

"Have you any objection to my being here?" she asked.

He shrugged his shoulders.

"It was rather a surprise."

"As I don't always warn you beforehand, I'm afraid a good many things I do must come as a surprise to you."

"And to yourself?"

"You must explain that."

"Surely no explanation is needed?"

"No explanation is wanted. We can start level, and I needn't bother to explain my presence here."

Nigel hastened to welcome a seeming ally.

"I imagine Aintree could supply that," he said.

She drew herself suddenly erect in a pose that demanded his right to use such words. The vindictiveness of his tone and the jealousy of his expression warned her that the Seraph lay in formidable peril.

"I want to find what Aintree and his friends have done to my sister, and I suppose you have a little account to settle with him in respect of an uncomfortable few days you lately spent at Maidenhead."

"Do you imagine he had any hand in that?" she asked contemptuously.

"He knew where to look for you," was the significant answer, "and he found that out from the woman he's been hiding in these rooms. As it's too much trouble for him to find out where my sister is, I've called to gain that information from the lady herself."

"What are you going to do?"

"Search the flat."

"And if she isn't here?"

"She *was*."

"Are you sure?"

"Oh, I admit I didn't see her. It may have been any one. But there's a very strong probability, and I'm going on that."

"And if there's no one here now?"

"She must have got away."

"Yes, I think I could have worked that out for myself."

"What d'you mean?"

"What are you going to do if you find no one?"

"If there's no woman now, the woman who got away was Miss Davenant. If Aintree has been harbouring Miss Davenant...." He paused delicately.

"Well?"

"I'm afraid he'll have some difficulty in persuading a judge not to sentence him to a considerable term of imprisonment."

"You'll have him arrested?"

"That is one of the regrettable but necessary preliminaries. *I* shan't do anything."

"Except rub your hands?" she taunted.

"Not even that," he answered with supercilious patience. Then, seeing no profit in pursuing his conversation with Sylvia, he raised his voice to summon the detectives into the library. "We'll take this room first," he told her, "and then leave you undisturbed."

The detectives did not answer his summons immediately and he turned to fetch them from the hall. As he did so Sylvia saw him start with surprise. Two paces behind them, an unseen auditor of their conversation, stood Elsie Wylton. With a slight bow to Sylvia she entered the library and in the Seraph's interests requested Nigel to carry out his search as quickly and silently as possible.

"He's sleeping now," she said, "but he's been awake most of the night, so please don't disturb him. If you'll search the other rooms, I'll stay here and talk to Miss Roden."

Nigel retired with a nicely blended expression of amazement, humiliation and menace. As the ring of his footsteps grew gradually fainter, Elsie turned to Sylvia with outstretched hands.

"I'm so glad you've come," she began. "I was afraid...."

"How long has he been ill?" interrupted Sylvia in a voice of stern authority.

"It's some time now...."

"And how long have you been here?"

There was an unmistakable challenge in her tone. Elsie's thoughts had been so much concerned with the Seraph, her mind was so braced in readiness to meet Nigel's attack, that for the moment her own share in the quarrel with Sylvia was forgotten. The library door stood open; outside in the hall the amateur detective was directing operations.

"Some time," she answered with studied vagueness.

The simmering suspicions of eight ambiguous weeks were brought to boiling point in Sylvia's mind.

"How long?" she repeated.

Elsie leaned forward, a finger to her lips; before she could speak, the hall was filled with the creak of heavy boots and Nigel appeared in the doorway.

"She's not here," he announced.

"Who were you looking for?" Elsie inquired, masking her impatience at his untimely return.

"Your sister."

"Oh, I could have told you that."

"She *was* here."

"Was she? What a pity you didn't come sooner! Why, Mr. Merivale invited you on Sunday, he told me. When he met you at your Club. I'm afraid you and the—er—gentleman outside have had your journey in vain."

Nigel's face flushed at the taunt and a certain uncomfortable prospect of polite criticism from the Criminal Investigation Department he had undertaken to educate.

"Not altogether," he said.

"No?"

"We've found Aintree."

"Ah; yes. I wanted to get him away to the sea, but he's not fit to move yet."

"He may have to."

"Not yet."

"A warrant for his arrest won't wait for him to get well—and away."

Nigel had never learned to disguise his feelings, and the threatening tone of his voice left no doubt in Elsie's mind that he was rapidly becoming desperate and would double his stakes to retrieve his earlier losings.

"So you're arresting him?" she said.

"He has obligingly piled up so much evidence against himself," he answered with a lift of the eyebrows.

"The same kind of evidence that led you to search these rooms for my sister?"

Nigel stood rigidly on his dignity.

"That will be forthcoming at the proper time and place."

"Unlike my sister," she rejoined in a mischievous undertone.

"Possibly she may be forthcoming when Aintree has been arrested."

A provoking smile came to disturb the last remnants of gravity on Elsie's face, lending dimples to her cheeks and laughter to her eyes.

"Possibly he won't be arrested," she remarked.

"You will prevent it?"

"I leave that to you."

"It's a matter for the police. I have no part or lot in it."

Elsie laughed unrestrainedly at his stiff dignity.

"You'll move heaven and earth to spare yourself a second humiliation like the present," she told him with a wise shake of the head. "It's ridiculous enough to search a man's rooms for a woman who isn't there, but you can't—you really can't arrest a man for harbouring a woman when there's no shred of evidence to show she was ever under the same roof."

Her mockery deepened the flush on Nigel's thin skin to an angry spot of red on either cheek.

"You forget that several of us visited this place the day after Miss Roden disappeared," he answered.

Elsie looked him steadily in the eyes.

"I have every reason to remember it."

"Your sister was here then."

"You saw her?"

"I heard her."

"You heard *a* woman."

"It was your sister or yourself."

"Or one of a million others."

Nigel thumped out his points on the top of a revolving book-case.

"I had the house watched. No woman entered or left till yesterday. Barring two nurses, and they're accounted for. You or your sister must have left here yesterday."

"And not come back?"

"No."

"Well, that makes it much easier, doesn't it? If one went out and never came back, and you find the other here the following day, it looks ... I mean to say, a perfectly impartial outsider might think, that it was my sister who got away and I who remained behind."

"Exactly. And it's on the same simple reasoning that Aintree will be arrested."

Nigel crooked his umbrella over his arm and slowly drew on his gloves. It was a moment of exquisite, manifest triumph. Elsie stood disarmed and helpless; Sylvia was too proud to ask terms of such a conqueror.

"All the same, what a pity you didn't come before the bird was flown!" Elsie suggested with the sole idea of gaining time.

"It's something to have found Aintree at home," Nigel returned.

"And you're going to arrest him for harbouring my sister?" Elsie walked into the hall and stood with her fingers on the handle of the door. Her heart was beating so fast that she felt sure she must be betraying emotion in her face. There was only one way of saving the Seraph, and she had resolved to take it. That it involved the immediate and irrevocable sacrifice of her reputation did not disturb her: she was filled with pity and doubt—pity for Sylvia, and doubt whether Nigel would accept her sacrifice. "I suppose—you're quite certain—he wasn't harbouring—*me*?"

Nigel's unimaginative mind hardly weighed the possibility.

"There's no warrant against you."

"Fortunately not."

"Then why should he harbour you?"

Elsie waited till her lips and voice were under control. Then she turned away from Sylvia and faced him with the steadiness of desperation.

"It's a very wicked world, Mr. Rawnsley."

There was a moment's silence: then Sylvia leapt to her feet with cheeks aflame.

"D'you mean you were here the whole time?"

"Some one was. Ask Mr. Rawnsley."

"Were you?"

"D'you think it likely?"

"How should I know?"

Elsie hardened her heart to play the unwelcome rôle to its bitter end.

"You know my character, you've not had time to forget my divorce or the way I thrust myself under the noses of respectable people. Have I got much more bloom to lose?"

"It's not true! The Seraph ... he *wouldn't*!"

"You used to see us about together."

"There's nothing in that!"

"Enough to make you cut him at Henley." Each fresh word fell like a lash across Sylvia's cheeks, but as long as Nigel dawdled irresolutely at the door it was impossible to end the torture.

"*Will* you say whether you were here the whole time?" she demanded of Elsie.

"'Course she wasn't," Nigel struck in. "There are convenances even in this kind of life. Merivale was here the whole time."

"*Was* he?" Elsie asked. Every new question seemed to suck her deeper down.

"I have his word and the evidence of my own eyes."

"You know he was actually living here? Not merely dropping in from time to time? It's important, my reputation seems to hang on it. If I was the woman Lord Gartside found, and Mr. Merivale didn't happen to be living here to chaperon us, the Seraph couldn't have been harbouring my sister, but it's good-bye to the remains of my good name. And if Mr. Merivale *was* here, I couldn't have been living here too, and the Seraph may have harboured one criminal or fifty. Which was it? I don't like to guess. Mr. Rawnsley, just tell me confidentially what you believe yourself."

Nigel bowed stiffly and prepared to leave the room.

"As the conduct of the case is not in my hands," he answered loftily, "my opinion is of no moment."

Elsie held the door open for him, shaking her head and smiling mischievously to herself.

"So there's nothing for it but a general arrest? Well, *che sera sera*: I suppose it'll be all over in a week or two, and then we shall be let out in time to see the fun. It'll be worth it. I wish women were admitted to your Club, it 'ud be so amusing to hear your friends chaffing you about your great mare's nest. 'Well, Rawnsley, what's this I hear about your giving up politics and going to Scotland Yard?' Men are such cats, aren't they? Every one would start teasing you at the House, the thing 'ud get into the papers, they'd hear of it in your constituency. Can you picture yourself addressing a big meeting and being heckled? A woman getting up and asking how you crushed the great militant movement and brought all the ringleaders to book? One or two people would laugh gently, and the laughter would spread and grow louder as every one joined in. They'd laugh at you in private houses and clubs, and the House of Commons. They'd laugh at you in the streets. Funny men with red noses and comic little hats would come on at the music halls and imitate you. They'd laugh and laugh till their sides ached and the tears streamed down their cheeks, and you'd try to live it down and find you couldn't, and in the end you'd have to leave England and live abroad, until they'd found something else to laugh at. You're going? Not arresting us now? Oh, of course, you haven't got the proper warrant. Well, I expect we shall be here when you come back. Good-bye, and good luck to you in your new career!"

The door closed heavily behind his indignant back, and Elsie turned a little wearily to Sylvia, bracing herself for an explanation that would be as hard as her recent battle. The mockery had died out of her voice and the laughter out of her eyes.

"Shall I go and see if the Seraph's awake yet?" she temporised, "or would you prefer to leave a message?"

Sylvia tried to speak, but no words would come—only a dry, choking sob of utter misery and disillusionment. With hasty steps she crossed to the door and fumbled blindly for the handle.

"Miss Roden! Sylvia!"

"*Don't* call me that!"

"I'm sorry. Miss Roden, I've got something to say to you!"

"I don't want to hear it, I only want to get away!"

"You must listen, your whole life's at stake—and the Seraph's, too."

The mention of his name brought her to a momentary standstill.

"What is it?" she demanded.

"You must shut that door."

"I won't."

Elsie wrung her hands in desperation. Outside on the landing, three paces from where they were standing, Nigel Rawnsley had paused to light a cigarette.

"It's about—the woman who was here," she whispered as he began to descend the stairs.

"Was it you?"

Elsie shook her head.

"No, say it! say it! Yes or no."

The sound of Nigel's descending footsteps had abruptly ceased at the angle of the stairs.

"For God's sake come back inside here a minute!" Elsie implored her.

"I won't, it's no good; I shouldn't believe you whatever you said. If you weren't here, why did you say you were? And if you were— Oh, let me go, let me go!"

With a smothered sob she broke away from Elsie's restraining hand and rushed precipitously down the stairs. Nigel tried to walk level with her, but she passed him and hurried out into the street. Elsie closed the door and walked with a heavy heart into the library. On a table by the window reposed the bouquet of flowers that Sylvia had brought—lilies, late roses and carnations, all white as the Seraph loved them. Taking them in her hand, she tiptoed out of the room and across the hall to the Seraph's door. He was still sleeping, but awoke in the early afternoon and inquired whether any one had called.

"The search-party," Elsie told him, forcing a smile.

"Who was there?"

"Young Mr. Rawnsley and two detectives."

"Was that all?"

The pathetic eagerness of his tone cut her to the quick.

"Wasn't it enough?" she asked indifferently.

The Seraph shielded his eyes from the light with one hand.

"I don't know. Sometimes I used to think I knew when other people—some people—were near me. I fancied—when I was asleep—I suppose it must have been a dream—I don't know—I fancied there was some one else quite close."

He turned restlessly on the bed and caught Elsie's fingers in a bloodless, wasted hand.

"How did you keep the search-party out?" he inquired.

"I didn't. They came in, and looked into every room. For some unaccountable reason," she added ironically, "Joyce was nowhere to be found."

"Were they surprised to see you here?"

"A little. I told them you were seedy and I'd called to inquire."

The Seraph lay silent till he had gathered sufficient strength to go on talking.

"I suppose they really thought you'd been here the whole time?"

"Oh no!"

"But how else...."

"I don't know," Elsie interrupted quickly. "You must ask *them* who the woman was Mr. Rawnsley heard the first time he was here. They couldn't say it was me without suggesting that you and I were both compromised."

She sprinkled some scent on a handkerchief and bathed his forehead.

"Do you think you can get some more sleep, Seraph? I want to get you well as soon as possible, and then I must take you abroad. London in August isn't good for little boys."

"Where shall we go?"

"I must join Toby and Joyce at Rimini."

The Seraph sighed and closed his eyes.

"I can't go there yet. They'll be—frightfully happy—wrapped up in each other—all that sort of thing. I don't want to see them yet."

Elsie dropped no hint of the time that must elapse before Joyce was strong again or "frightfully happy."

"Where shall it be then?" she asked.

The Seraph pressed her fingers to his lips.

"You go there, Elsie. I must travel alone. I shall go to the East. I shan't come back for some time. If ever."

The effort of talking and the trend of the conversation had made him restless. Elsie smoothed his pillow, and rose to leave the room.

As he watched her walk to the door, his eyes fell for the first time on the bouquet of roses and lilies.

"Who brought those?" he inquired.

"I found them in the library," she answered.

"Is there no name?"

For a moment she pretended to look for a card, then shook her head without speaking. As she saw him lying in bed, she wondered if he would ever know the price at which his freedom from arrest had been purchased. Of her own sacrifice she thought little; it was but generous payment of a long outstanding debt. All her imagination was concentrated on Sylvia—her sanguine, happy arrival, the morning's long agony, her hopeless, agonised departure.

"And no message?" the Seraph persisted with a mixture of eagerness and disappointment.

"No."

"I wonder who they can be from."

"One of your numerous admirers, I suppose," Elsie answered carelessly. Then she opened the door, walked wearily to her own room, and tried—unsuccessfully—to cry.

CHAPTER XVI

RIMINI

"We left our country for our country's good."
—George Barrington
Prologue.

We arrived in Rimini at the end of the first week in August—
Joyce, her two nurses, Maybury-Reynardson and I. Elsie joined
us as soon as we were comfortably settled in the villa, and has
stayed on week after week, month after month, tending her
poor sister with a devotion that touched my selfish, hardened
old heart. Dick came for a few days before the beginning of the
law term; otherwise we have been a party of three, as the doctor
and nurses returned to England as soon as Joyce appeared to be
out of danger.

Rimini turns cold at the beginning of November, and we have
had to make arrangements for going into winter quarters. Cairo
and the Riviera are a little public for two escaped criminals, but
I hear there is a tolerable hotel at Taormina; and as Joyce has
never been in Sicily before, we might spend at least the beginning of our honeymoon there. For myself, I do not mind where
we go so long as we can escape from Rimini. I want no unnecessary reminders of the last three months, the weary waiting,
the frequent false dawns of convalescence, the regular relapses.
They have been bad months for Joyce, but I venture to think
they were worse for Elsie and myself. In my own case there
definitely came an early day when my nervous system showed
signs of striking work; it was then that I embarked on my first
and last venture in prose composition.

When she is well enough to be bothered with such vain
trivialities, I shall present my manuscript to Joyce. I hope she
will read it, for I have intended it for her eyes alone; and if she

rejects the task, I shall feel guilty of having wasted an incredible amount of good sermon paper. And when she has read it, she must light a little fire and burn every sheet of it; not even Elsie must see it, though she has been instrumental in giving me information over the last chapters that I should not otherwise have obtained.

I think my decision is wise and necessary. In part the book is too intimate an account of Sylvia's character and the Seraph's feelings for me to be justified in making it public: in part, the pair of us have already done sufficient injury to Rodens and Rawnsleys without giving the world our candid opinion of either family: in part, we have to remember that during the last eight months, wherever we found the law of England obtruding itself on our gaze, we broke it with a light heart and untroubled conscience. There is not the least good in taking the world into our confidence in the matter of these little transgressions.

In a week's time there will be a quiet wedding at the British Consulate; it will take place in the presence of a Consul who has treated me with such uniform kindness that I have sometimes wondered if he has ever heard of such things as extradition orders. Our marriage will be the last chapter of one phase in my life. It opened on a day when I walked up the steps of the Club, and paused for a moment to gaze at the altered face of Pall Mall and read on a contents-bill that the old militants had broken every window on the east side of Bond Street, interrupted a meeting, and burnt down an Elizabethan house in Hertfordshire. "Shocking," I remember thinking, "and quite unimpressive." Before I was twelve hours older, Fate had introduced me to a young woman whose machinations may or may not have been infinitely more shocking; they were certainly not unimpressive.

The closing scenes of the Militant campaign are soon given. Elsie left London and joined us here as soon as the Seraph was fit to travel. That was three days after Nigel's second raid. They must have been anxious days, as our rising young statesman seems to have been torn between a quite bloodthirsty lust for revenge and a morbid horror of another fiasco as humiliating as his search-party. Elsie went round by Marseilles, saw the Seraph on board a P. and O. mailboat bound for Bombay and came overland to Rimini. When I met her and heard the details of her flight, I could tell her that all danger was over, and—if Justice had not been done—the stolen goods had at least been restored.

The news reached us as we came out of the Bay. Gartside and I were on deck, watching the sun strike golden splinters out of the hock-bottle towers of the royal palace at Cintra. The wireless operator came down with a tapped message that Mrs. Millington had revealed the whereabouts of Mavis Rawnsley and young Paul Jefferson. He added that the police had so far discovered no trace of that hardened criminal—Miss Joyce Davenant.

When Elsie joined us and told me the story of the Rawnsley raid, I could not help thinking once again, *"Plus ça change, plus c'est la même chose."* The gallant fight she had made for freedom and reputation ended in disaster, and she left England branded with the stigma that the Divorce Court had striven to impose and we had fought tooth and nail to remove. Joyce's struggle for the suffrage ended, as she now knows, in putting the suffrage further from the forefront of practical politics than it has been for a generation. When the recording angel allots to each one of us our share of responsibility in moulding the face of history, what effective change will be credited to the united or separate efforts of Rawnsleys and Rodens, Seraphs, Davenants and Merivales?

Two results stand out. The first is a marriage that will be celebrated at the Consulate in a week's time, the second is a listless letter penned in exile, signed by the Seraph and dated from Yokohama. Joyce knows I am tolerably fond of her, and will acquit me of speaking rhetorically if I say that I would wipe the last eight months—and all they mean to us both—from the pages of Time, if I could spare the Seraph what he has been through since I dined with him that first evening at the Ritz. Here is the letter, and no one will be surprised to learn that I spent a melancholy day after reading it.

"I send you the last chapters of Volume III. As you've waded through the earlier stuff, you may care to see the record brought up to date. I call it 'The End' because there's nothing more to write, and if there were, I shouldn't write it. Some day I suppose I may have to write again, when my present money (Roden's money) is exhausted. Not till then.

"India was one disappointment, and Japan another, though the fault, I imagine, lay in my lack of appreciation. The South Seas will be a third. '*Caelum non animum mutant qui trans mare currunt.*' I don't want to move on, but I can't stand Yokohama any longer.

"When I get to San Francisco I shall probably cross the States, arriving in New York at the end of December. Then I suppose one has to see this Panama Canal. After that, God knows.

"Before I left England I was looking for the MS. of the earlier chapters of Vol. III. I couldn't find them. Did you by any chance get them mixed up in your luggage? If so, please destroy them at once, with the new chapters, as soon as you have read them. Don't let anybody see them, even Joyce. In this I depend on your friendship and honour.

"I hope Joyce is all right again now. Give my love to her and Elsie, and take my best wishes for yourself. You—I suppose—are a fixture at Rimini, or at any rate out of England. I can't answer for myself, but I don't expect we shall meet again. You must have found me a depressing host in London. I'm sorry. Good-bye."

He said that even Joyce was not to see the third volume—put me on my honour, in fact—and see it she shall not. There is another reason. I read those last chapters and then went through the whole volume from beginning to end. Without exaggeration the effect was overwhelming—his style is so artless, his pathos so unpremeditated. I felt as if I had been re-reading Hardy's most poignant novels—"Tess" and "Jude" and "A Pair of Blue Eyes." It was horrible. I went up to my room, lit the fire and prepared for the holocaust.

Then I was tempted. Yes, he puts me on my honour, depends on my friendship, all that sort of thing.... But I did not burn a sheet. It was a chilly evening, I lit a cigar, and waited for the pyre to burst into destructive flame. As I watched and meditated, Sylvia's little face seemed to look at me out of the fire, the black coals crowning her forehead as I used to see it crowned with her own lustrous hair. I thought of our last meeting when she struggled with her devils of pride and unbelief; and of her meeting with Elsie when she came in hope and left in humiliation. I confess I love Sylvia very dearly—love her as all men love her—for her beauty, her queenliness and clean, passionate pride; love her because I know something of her loneliness, her passion for service, and the repeated rejections of her sacrifices. And I love her a little more on my own account, because she talked to me as if I had been her own sister, and I perhaps know—better than any one—what she must have been through during those sad, mad months in England.

Well, I broke faith with the Seraph and wrote her a line of overture. I was perhaps a fool to do it, as I had already had evidence in plenty of my incompetence to play the *rôle* of Providence. "I am sending you the MS. of a book," I told her. "It is the third volume of Gordon Tremayne's 'Child of Misery'. I know you have read the first two volumes, for we have discussed and admired them together a dozen times. Did you ever suspect who the author was?

"In telling you it was the Seraph, I am breaking my word to him and running the risk of being branded and disowned.

I must tell you, though, to explain the existence of the third volume. I watched it being written, day by day. That evening on the Cher, when he anticipated some words you were going to say, the words had already been written down as part of the current chapter. I saw him brought up short when you were spirited away and the connection was broken. Most wonderful of all, I was present when the connection was re-established and he jumped up like one possessed, exclaiming, 'Sylvia wants me!'

"When you have read these pages, you will not be in a position to doubt any longer. He loves you as no woman was ever loved before, and in him you have found the half that completes and interprets your '*âme incomprise*.' Get him back, Sylvia. I don't know how it's to be done, but you must use your woman's wit to find a way. I'm asking for his sake and yours, not for mine—though I would give much to see 'The Child of Misery' growing to happier manhood.

"I am afraid you will say I am hardly the man to ask anything of you or yours. The Rodens and Merivales have hardly made a success of their recent relationship. But I should like to be forgiven. What is my crime? That I helped to keep justice from touching a woman who had done you and your family a great wrong. Well, Sylvia, you'd have done the same thing and told the same lies, had you been in my place and had you wanted Joyce as badly as I wanted her. So will you forgive me and be friends? And if you forgive me, will you forgive the woman who's going to be my wife in a few days' time? I must reconcile myself to the idea of being estranged from the rest of your family, but (between ourselves) I'll let 'em all go if you'll write and say Joyce and I are not quite such monsters of iniquity as you may have thought us.

"One thing more. When you've read the third volume, you will no longer doubt that Mrs. Wylton's presence in Adelphi Terrace was due to charitable impulse towards Joyce and the

Seraph. And you ought to think well of any one who played the Good Samaritan to the Seraph. Don't try to rehabilitate her character in public; it can only be done at a risk to the Seraph's personal safety. And in any case you won't convince a man like Nigel or the men he's already told the story to.

"Return me the MS. when you've read it, will you? I was entrusted with its destruction, and put on honour not to let another soul read it. You see how I keep my trust. The worst thing you can say of me is what I've already said of myself—that most damning of all judgments—that I meant well."

I sent that letter to Sylvia nine days ago, and received her reply this morning. She returned me the MS., and I burnt it—with the knowledge that I was destroying one of the greatest literary treasures of this generation.... Well, they had to do the same with some of Ruskin's letters.

"I wish you had not told me to send you back the book," she began. "I should have liked to keep it. Or rather—I don't know—I half wish you hadn't sent it at all. The time that has passed since the beginning of August has been rather hard to bear, and the book has only turned misgiving into certainty.

"Of course I forgive you! As if there were anything to forgive! And Miss Davenant too. I hope she is better now. Will you ask her to accept my love and best wishes for the future? And of course I include you. We were good friends, weren't we? As I said we should be the first time we met. Only I said then that you would find me worth having as a friend, and I'm afraid I did everything I could to disprove it. You stood me awfully well. I think you knew most of the dark corners in my mean little soul—and if you did, perhaps you see that I didn't do much beyond showing my true nature.

"This isn't a pose—I'm really—well, I was going to say 'broken'—but I hope I'm a little more tolerant. You'd hardly recognise me if you saw me, there's little enough of the 'Queen Elizabeth' about me now. It's a horrid, flat world, and I wish I could find something in it to interest me. May I ask for just one good mark? You wrote to me when you left England, telling me to swallow my pride and go to see the Seraph. Well, it was a struggle, but I did go—as you know. When I got there, I seemed to find more than I could bear, and so of course everything went wrong. But I did try, and you will give me my one little good mark, won't you? I want it.

"Mother says I'm run down and in need of a change, so Phil's taking me over to the United States at the beginning of December. There's a sort of Parliamentary Polytechnic Tour to Panama, every one who can get away is going to see the Canal. I don't in the least want to go, but I suppose the States can hardly be duller than England, and as long as mother thinks I must have a change, change I must have. If it isn't Panama it will be somewhere worse.

"We shall spend Christmas in New York. Will you send me a letter of good wishes to the Fifth Avenue Hotel? And tell me where you are going to settle permanently and whether you will let me come and see you. If your wife will not mind, I should like to see you both again—well and happy, I hope. Somebody must be happy in this world, or it wouldn't go on. I don't want to lose you as a friend; I'm feeling lonely enough as it is.

"I am hardly likely to see the Seraph again, but if you meet him, I should like you to give him a message. Say it is from a woman who did him a great wrong: say she now knows the wrong she did him and has been punished for it. Tell him you know how much she hates ever apologising or admitting she was wrong, but that she wants him to know of her apology before she finally passes out of his memory. Will you tell him that? It won't do any good, but it will make me more comfortable in my mind."

At the bottom of the page six words had been scratched out. I did not mean to read them, but the obliteration was incomplete, and the firelight shining up through the paper enabled me to decipher: "Oh, my God, I am miserable." Then followed the signature: "Affectionately yours (may I sign myself 'affectionately'?) Sylvia."

After reading her letter I concentrated my thoughts on the question how to blot out time, annihilate space, bridge two continents, and bring two proud, sore, sensitive spirits into communion. My method of attaining concentration of mind is to think of something different and wait for inspiration to solve my original problem. Joyce may remember the day when I stumped into her room and talked at large of honeymoons and winter resorts. That was the time when my mind was concentrated on the problem of Sylvia and the Seraph. She will further recollect assenting to my suggestion of a villa at Taormina.

On leaving her room I strolled round to the bank to see if they had agents in Sicily or could give me any information on the subject of a suitable villa. They were kind but helpless, and eventually I thought it the safer course to write for rooms at an hotel and look for a villa at our leisure. Ambling out of the bank, I wandered in the direction of the telegraph office.

Inspiration came in the interval between wiring for rooms and engaging berths on the Wagon-Lits—I knew it would. As soon as our places were booked I walked back to the telegraph office and cabled to the Seraph at Yokohama. "Letter and enclosures received with thanks," I wired. "All nonsense about not meeting again. Will you lunch Christmas Day, one-thirty? Fifth Avenue Hotel, New York.—TOBY."

Then I came back to the Villa Monreale.

Joyce's first words were to tell me I had been away a very long time. Flattering as this was, I had to justify myself and account for every moment of my absence. She wanted to know what I had wired to the Seraph, and as husbands and wives *in posse* should have no secrets from each other, I showed her the draft of my cable. Her face was a study.

"My dear!" she exclaimed, "we can't go all the way to New

York even to see the Seraph. You suggested Taormina when you left here...."

"Quite so," I assented.

"Did you order rooms?"

"Yes."

"Then we can't go to New York."

"I never proposed to."

"Why did you invite the Seraph to lunch with us there?"

"I didn't."

"Toby!"

She was not satisfied till I spelt out the draft of the cable word by word; and then she rather resented my remarks about the incurable sloppiness of the female mind. As a matter of fact, I cannot claim originality for the phrase; I believe a Liberal Prime Minister coined it as a terse description of his opponents' mental shortcomings. I only borrowed it for the nonce.

"Will—you—lunch—Christmas Day—" I pointed out. "It doesn't say we shall be there to receive him."

"I don't understand it," she said rather wearily. I have since honourably resolved not to be guilty of facetiousness when we are married, but at the moment I was rather pleased with my little stratagem.

"I'm arranging for some one to be there to meet him," I said.

"Who?" she asked.

"A young woman named Sylvia Roden," I answered.

And even then her appreciation of my diplomacy was grudging.

EPILOGUE

TRISTRAM.
"Raise the light, my page! that I may see her—
     Thou art come at last, then, haughty Queen?
Long I've waited, long I've fought my fever;
     Late thou comest, cruel hast thou been."
ISEULT.
"Blame me not, poor sufferer! that I tarried;
     Bound I was, I could not break the band.
Chide not with the past, but feel the present!
     I am here—we meet—I hold thy hand."
                    —Matthew Arnold
                    "Tristram and Iseult."

I had intended to write no more, but as we left the Consulate to-day after our wedding, a cable was handed me by my smiling Italian valet.

"Paddy Culling for a bob!" I said, as I opened it and prepared for some whimsical message of congratulation.

I was wrong. The cable was my reply from Yokohama.

"No offence intended," it ran. "Delighted lunch as suggested.—Seraph."

www.ingramcontent.com/pod-product-compliance
Lightning Source LLC
Chambersburg PA
CBHW020613260626
47157CB00003B/994